SWEET AND SOUR

SWEET AND SOUR

MONIQUE TURNER

Chicken House

2 Palmer Street, Frome, Somerset BA11 1DS
www.chickenhousebooks.com

First published in the UK in 2026
Chicken House
2 Palmer Street
Frome, Somerset BA11 1DS
United Kingdom
www.chickenhousebooks.com

Chicken House/Scholastic Ireland, 89E Lagan Road, Dublin Industrial Estate, Glasnevin, Dublin D11 HP5F, Republic of Ireland

Text © Monique Turner 2026
Illustration © Ali Al Amine 2026

The moral rights of the author and illustrator have been asserted.

All rights reserved.
No part of this publication may be reproduced, transmitted, downloaded, decompiled, reverse engineered, used to train any artificial intelligence technologies, or stored in or introduced into any information storage and retrieval system, in any form or by any means, whether electronic or mechanical, now known or hereafter invented, without the express written permission of the publisher. Subject to EU law the publisher expressly reserves this work from the text and data mining exception.

This book is a work of fiction. Names, characters, businesses, organizations, places, events and incidents are either the product of the author's imagination or used in a fictitious manner. Any resemblance to actual persons, living or dead, events or locales is purely coincidental.

For safety or quality concerns:
UK: www.chickenhousebooks.com/productinformation
EU: www.scholastic.ie/productinformation

Cover design by Ali Al Amine
Interior design by Ali Al Amine
Typeset by Dorchester Typesetting Group Ltd
Printed in the UK by Clays, Elcograf S.p.A

1 3 5 7 9 10 8 6 4 2

A CIP catalogue record for this book is available from the British Library.

PB ISBN 978-1-917171-28-1
eISBN 978-1-917171-63-2

Let's be honest, I wrote this book for myself.

It was a great excuse to order takeout and call it 'research' at my publisher's expense.

Sorry if I've left greasy fingerprints on some pages.

Just ignore the pizza crust crumbs in the spine, you'll be fine.

Also by Monique Turner

Island of Influencers

CHAPTER 1

Machines were built to help artists, but slowly they've claimed art for themselves.

Those are the words swimming around my head as Dad falls into the chair at the kitchen table, his face buried in his hands as he sobs away the most recent bout of bad news.

The creative industry isn't for people any more; art isn't the product of human emotion. One by one, artists like my dad have been pushed out.

Dad takes in a deep, rattling breath as he steadies himself. Me and Mum have our hands on his shoulders, comforting him as his body shakes in shock. I sniff back my own tears and clock Mum's desperate bid to keep a stoic expression. We knew this day was coming; we'd seen the same news arrive on the doorsteps of many others in the industry. But I guess, like the people from the late Middle Ages, we hoped the plague might skip our house.

It hasn't.

'I'm fine.' Dad sniffs, his cheeks red and wet from his tears. 'I'm OK. It'll be OK. I knew it was coming.'

'They've officially let you go?' I ask.

Dad nods. Mum dispenses some cold water from the fridge into a glass and hands it to him. He gulps it down in one, wincing from the instant brain freeze it must give him. I imagine the pain helps a little, takes his mind off what's just happened for a moment at least. 'It's not their fault; they're up against it too.'

For as long as I can remember, Dad has been an artist. Every day after school, before Mum got back from her job as a receptionist at the local hospital, Dad would keep my brother and me occupied in his studio. We'd watch him paint and even help him make slow-motion animations from playdough.

When we got older, Dad tried his hand at digital art and found that he was better than all right at it. I helped him promote his stuff on Photorah when that social platform first came about, and his followers skyrocketed. I was pretty jealous about it at the time, considering my only followers consisted of family and the very few friends I have at school, but it made him happy and landed him an agent too.

'My agent couldn't have been sorrier,' Dad sighs. 'It's not what any of us want, but I understand that it's the way things are going. Such a shame. So much talent lost from the books . . . my old mates. And everything looks the same nowadays, there's just no life in art any more. It's all so . . . so . . .'

I squeeze his shoulder in solidarity. After years of work as a cover designer and illustrator for some of the most popular fiction authors, and now through the recent months of trepidation and speculation, Dad's agent decided to end their professional relationship. There's no need to hire real creatives now; they take too long to create the work and cost too much to commission. Art these days is produced by artificial intelligence.

Dad forces a smile, trying to pretend he's not absolutely devastated. I furrow my brow, willing things to be different. He might truly be one of the last of his kind.

'So, what now?' Mum asks, her voice gentle and low.

'I-I guess I find another job,' Dad says, almost in a whisper. 'I think they might take me back at that old sausage factory I used to work at, eh? I was pretty good at packing those crates into the back of the lorries. There wasn't a single worker there quicker than me.' He fakes a laugh.

'Things have probably changed since you last worked there,' Mum says. 'It was twenty-odd years ago. Doubt the same guy owns it any more.'

'Well, I'll get in touch, you never know. Listen, Mikah, don't tell your brother, OK? Not yet. I don't want him worrying. Let me get my feet on the ground again before we start making this public knowledge.' Dad nods at me curtly, and stands from the table, straightening his shirt.

I nod back. Instructions understood. My little brother, Rohan, is only ten. I'm sixteen. *Almost an adult*, Dad would say. Though I'm not sure I'm equipped to handle the information that my dad has just lost his job to an AI program any more than a ten-year-old is.

'A-And I know we've spoken about it before,' Dad says, his voice crackling and unsure, 'but I want you to have a think about the college course you've picked, son. Performing arts is fun but ... you've seen the struggle I've been through in this industry. It might be worth ... you know ...' It pains him to say it and I hold my breath, waiting to bear the weight of his words. 'Doing a course that'll get you somewhere in life.'

The blood in my veins runs cold and I don't realize Dad's left the kitchen until Mum puts her hand on my shoulder.

Her warm, blue eyes lock with mine. 'Don't think on it too much,' she says softly. 'Zach should be here any minute and you two are going to have a great night, like always. OK? Everything will work out in the end. It always does.'

I flash her a smile as fake as Dad's and make for the stairs, bypassing Dad on the sofa as he chats on the phone to someone I assume used to own the sausage factory. Before I can even make it to the top of the stairs, the doorbell rings and Zach lets himself in without invitation.

That's how it's always been. My family have known Zach's family since we both turned up to nursery sporting the same backpack and formed an instant bond. Some of the tension falls from my shoulders as he catapults up the stairs and barges past me on his way to my bedroom, his backpack rattling with snacks.

He'll understand my family's recent peril. His mum

owns an indie gaming company and is up against the recent surge of AI too. Is any creative industry safe?

As I round my bedroom door, Zach's already firing up my computer and loading the livestream for the Global Influencer Awards. It's an annual event where all the best social media stars are celebrated for their contribution to worldwide entertainment. We love it. Watch it every year. I'd always hoped to be on there one day, but my faceless Tubeify channel currently sits at a meagre two thousand subscribers.

'Dad got dropped today,' I say, closing the door behind me.

Zach snaps his head around, pausing his desperate bid to get the evening started as he flashes me a look to match my inner devastation.

'Mate,' he offers. He doesn't really need to say anything else; we both know what this means. Art is dead. AI killed it and buried it in an unmarked grave. 'How's he taken it?'

I shrug. 'Not well. He's hiding it, trying to save face in front of me and Mum. Doesn't want us to tell Rohan. How's your mum?'

Zach huffs and throws his backpack on to my bed. 'She doesn't tell me much, but I know things are getting harder for her. She's working longer hours, barely sleeping, lost like five kilos. Just two years ago she was being celebrated as the leading woman within the industry, a pioneer of gaming entertainment. She built VaderVerse while still in college, her first game an instant hit – like, it was actually groundbreaking at the time.'

'Oh, man, *Faerie Pools* was the best game ever!'

Zach chuckles, his eyes filling with pride. 'Yeah, but it's like people have forgotten that. Everyone got bored waiting for the next one. When she announced the sequel, the gaming world went into a frenzy – but that was three years ago and they're still in the early stages of development. The fans got impatient and some rando made a replica of it with AI and now no one's interested in the real thing because the copy is good enough. Mum's gutted. She's spent a fortune on this remake – almost tanked the business doing it.'

We fall into silence.

Zach runs his fingers through his black hair. His parents are Japanese, but he was born and raised in the south of England. He's been my best mate basically my entire life, though no one really knows why. We're like chalk and cheese to the outside world. He was blessed by the gods with his looks: muscular, handsome and everything is in proportion to his height. His eyes are wide and deep brown, his hair thick and shaggy, his jawline could cut glass, and his lips are full and rose-tinted. Not to mention his fashion sense is on point. Today, he's wearing a pressed black shirt with his top three buttons open, the sleeves rolled up, and smart baggy black trousers and a belt with silver detail to match his rings and chain. All the girls love him. And he loves them. Which makes him the most eligible bachelor in school.

Then there's me: painfully skinny and so tall that

people ask me to give them a heads-up if it starts raining, with acne-scarred skin and a nose I hate. People at our school call me 'Ratatouille', because apparently I look like the chef from that old cult animation film. I hate it. I hate how I look compared to Zach.

On my computer, a host wearing a glittering gold dress beams her shiny veneers at us from the red carpet. 'Welcome! Welcome to the fifth annual Global Influencer Awards ceremony. We have an excellent line-up. Some incredible talent to celebrate in some interesting categories. But first let's have a quick chat with some of the influencers up for awards tonight.'

The camera slowly pans around, showcasing a massive live audience behind barriers, screaming and yelling at the famous faces parading down the red carpet. I squint to get a better look.

I don't follow a single creator. I don't even know if I should call them that – they're creators from the new social giant iGENect, and they're all humanoids. Robots created to be perfect idols and product promoters. An exasperated huff leaves my lips, and Zach mutters under his breath.

Machines were built to help artists, but slowly they've claimed art for themselves.

The words flood my mind again. I've heard them repeatedly, in old videos by Tubeify influencers booted from social media by iGENect celebrity humanoids. The first digitally created human was simply something fun on the internet, nothing more. Then some genius made a robot in the likeness of a human that was meant to ease the everyday burdens of existence, like laundry and lawn mowing, so that people could spend more time engrossed in books, laughter and music. But something happened between then and now. Bigger experiments. Boundaries pushed. Lines crossed.

And now we're watching an awards show celebrating art and content creation while trying to spot the elusive human among an army of artificial intelligence.

I blame that online challenge hosted last year by the now infamous content creator Sgt Hound. He hosted an online gameshow called *Island of Influencers*, where the most recognizable influencers from the golden days of Tubeify competed against one another to be crowned the ultimate influencer. Only the arena turned out to be a giant laboratory that stole their identities in order to make the army of AI humanoids that have since taken over the creator world.

I shake my head and start to vent my frustrations to Zach when my bedroom door flies open, and a blurry figure rushes into my bedroom.

CHAPTER 2

Isobel plonks down on the corner of my bed, her phone in her hand. She has a massive grin spread across her face and her shimmering, wavy brunette hair cascades over her shoulders.

I clear my throat, and she flashes her amber eyes at me. My heart flutters and I can feel my cheeks turning red. I still can't believe she's my girlfriend.

Her family moved down the road from mine when we were both twelve, and I'd see her gliding along the pavement on her rollerblades every day after school. Come rain or shine, she was always there, and I'd be at the kitchen window waiting to catch a glimpse of her.

Should have known then that I was crushing on her, but it wasn't until we shared classes together that things really took off. For some reason, she didn't mind chatting with me in science. It was one of my favourite subjects and she didn't have a clue what she was doing. I liked helping her and she seemed to like my bad jokes.

Isobel beckons me in for a kiss and I oblige, warranting a gagging sound from Zach. It makes me chuckle.

I only managed to garner the courage to ask her out a couple of months ago. Luckily, she said yes, despite my stuttering voice, acne-riddled face and awkward demeanour. An involuntary smile creeps over me as I realize just how good she's been for my self-confidence.

'I've had the best news. You know the social media marketing course I'm taking in September? Well, they've just announced a new module for this academic year. We're going to be studying artificial intelligence and how we can use it to be more efficient. It means down the line we get things done quicker for clients and I can charge more for efficiency. Isn't that cool?'

My heart sinks.

Zach flashes a look of concern but keeps his opinions to himself as he begins unloading his bag of snacks on to my desk beneath a poster of my favourite band, Doze Emblem.

'I-I don't know what to say,' I admit. 'Didn't you say just last week that AI was ruining the creative industry for everyone?'

'Yeah, but—' she starts, but I cut her off.

'And guess what? Dad's agent let him go because no one is hiring him for work any more. AI took his job. He's gutted.'

Isobel drops her gaze to the floor. 'I'm so sorry to hear that, Mikah. I am.' I can hear in her voice just how sorry she is, but it doesn't lessen the sting. 'Look, AI isn't going anywhere, so I just think we need to learn how to work alongside it. If we approach it as a tool, rather than thinking about it replacing actual jobs—'

'It *is* replacing actual jobs, Iz!'

She grimaces like I'm a parent scolding her for bad grades. 'I agree people are taking things a little too far right now, but it could just be teething problems. After a few years, when it becomes something that's an everyday part of our lives, we'll have a better understanding of what can be automated for ease of living and what still needs human hands.'

'The only people automation is helping are the people at the top of the food chain,' Zach adds. 'It's killing normal people like our parents; putting us all out of jobs.'

Isobel shrugs. 'I don't believe that. My course is teaching me how to blend life with AI. If AI can help ease some of my workload, then I don't see why that's a bad thing. You know how busy I am with helping Mum around the house now that Dad's gone, and on top of my studies – it's a lot. Incorporating AI into my life will free up some of my time. What if it can help me?'

It's like the air has been sucked from my bedroom.

We're silent.

'A-Are you mad at me?' she asks, her voice quiet and unsure.

'No!' I grab her hand and squeeze. 'I'm not mad ... I-I think it just came at a bad time is all.'

I try to see reason. She's right; AI can help in situations like hers, where she's already overloaded with too much responsibility. I can see why it'd be handy for her.

But for people like my dad, who've spent their whole life learning a skill only to have a robot do it quicker and cheaper, it's a disaster.

She flashes me a weak smile and guilt floods me. I know this course is something she's been looking forward to all year, and now that the summer holidays have arrived, I can only imagine how eager she is to get started, come September. For me, it's a different story. I'm going to college to study performing arts. That's another industry with AI creeping over its doorstep. Who needs to employ real actors and have them on set for months at a time when the directors can just use their digital image to create CGI replicas of them on-screen?

Isobel's phone buzzes, and she groans as she clocks the caller ID. 'Mum. I told her I'd babysit Evie so she can go out with her mates tonight.'

'But you just got here,' Zach says.

I frown. 'That shouldn't be your responsibility, Iz. The awards are about to start. Stay and watch a bit at least.'

'My mum hasn't put this on me, babe,' she says. 'I offered to help. Since Dad left, she's been really struggling. She's a parent to three kids and has two full-time jobs; she deserves a break. It's all good, I can study while Evie sleeps. Enjoy your night.'

She gets to her feet and plants a soft kiss on my lips, barely catching my eye. Her jovial manner has been replaced by the grown-before-her-time persona she puts on whenever too much is expected of her. She goes and I fall on to my bed in defeat as the host for the Global

Influencer Awards gushes about the 'talent', while all the iGENect influencers make their way down the red carpet and stop for a brief interview.

Zach throws me a tube of ScorchaSnaps with a wink and I can't stop the grin spreading over my face. I love these! The packaging is black with bright orange flames and font, and they're as deadly as one might expect. 'Thought those might make you feel a bit better,' he says. 'Wanna talk about it?'

A huff escapes me. 'What's there to say? I can hardly change her mind if she genuinely believes AI is here to help us, can I? She's looking to get into an industry that can benefit from it. I'm not.'

My annoyance is quelled somewhat by the scent of spice as I pop the lid of the tube of crisps. ScorchaSnaps have only been in the shops for less than a week but trying to get your hands on a tube of them is like trying to find real gold in your back garden.

'Can you believe these were created by someone who was just bored one day in her kitchen?' I say, shaking my head as I slam a crisp into my mouth. I roll my eyes to the back of my head, and this warrants a laugh from Zach.

The thick crisp gives a satisfying *snap* as I chow down on it, and I wince as the lethal concoction of spices, sugars and preservatives seeps on to my tongue and burns the already delicate corners of my lips.

'See, *that's* what influencing used to be about,' Zach agrees. 'Just a woman in her kitchen making food.'

It's true. The creator put ScorchaSnaps on the menu

in her family's restaurant and travel influencer Where-WaldaWanders happened to pop in for a quick bite. One viral video and the big food companies were tearing each other apart to have ScorchaSnaps on their books.

'You don't hear stories like that any more, do you? Not since all the big "influencer brands" were replaced with products made by already massive corporations with fakefluencer faces plastered on them. Everything's fake, manufactured.'

That woman and her crisps were discovered over two years ago. Things don't work like that any more, not since iGENect and their robot influencers took over the internet. *Dead Internet Theory* – a conspiracy that social media is slowly being turned into a platform purely for consumption, driven by automatically generated content – isn't just a theory I used to watch videos about any more. Half of the comments online are automated messages from bots. They don't even make sense most of the time.

Zach grabs the tube from me and gasps. 'What the hell, mate! How have you—'

I lick the orange dust from my fingertips and shrug. I've inhaled that whole tube.

Zach sniggers as he chucks the tube aside and goes for some salted caramel pretzels. 'Lucky for you, I have more of a sweet tooth. I can't even get through a handful of ScorchaSnaps before they start burning. Don't know how you handle it.'

'Iron stomach, mate,' I joke, winking and making for a

share bag of BBQ Bacon Bitz crisps and a can of fizzy Coconut Candyfloss Spritz.

'Bottomless stomach more like, and it'll be your downfall one day.'

We continue to stuff our faces with the insane bounty of snacks Zach brought as the army of humanoid celebrities heads along the red carpet, venting our frustrations at the screen as if the host and guests can hear us.

Kottage Kay – the very first iGENect humanoid prototype, and the winner of the *Island of Influencers* show – saunters along the red carpet, waving at the crowd gathered on either side, contained behind barriers. From the outside, she looks like the perfect human; *the* beauty standard we're all trying to achieve with facial filters and plastic surgery, but her truth can't hide from the paparazzi's glare. Cameras flash, momentarily exposing the lenses behind her glass eyeballs. A shiver runs down my spine.

Zach and I can barely believe the stream of humanoids we're seeing parading around, smiling and waving as the crowd cheers and shouts their callsigns.

'Kay! Look over here, Kay! One more picture, please, Kay!'

'George, can you sign my arm, please?'

'Anna, oh my god, it's Anna!'

Each 'influencer' stops by the host and answers a series of questions about their channels and niches, always ending their interviews with the same rhetoric: 'I'm just here to celebrate creativity and to help bring entertainment to the masses,' with a beaming smile, like it's programmed into them. I scoff. Well, it is programmed into them.

'Jeez,' Zach says, throwing down his packet of jelly spiders. 'I've seen more life in a graveyard.'

I can't help snorting at this.

AI celebrities were designed to feed the insatiable hunger of the audience looking to be endlessly entertained, while simultaneously keeping the big brands and companies happy by ensuring their walking, talking product promoters remain controversy free. But is endless content really entertaining when it's devoid of anything that feels human, that builds connection? I don't think so.

My head feels wobbly, and my legs numb, but that might be from eating so much salt and sitting cross-legged on the floor for an hour. Social media isn't the same any more. I want it back to how it used to be, not this advertisement-friendly, big-corporation-run empire. I want real, gritty vlogs from people my age going through the same stuff I am; I want unpolished and badly edited; I want communities of loyal channel watchers again.

We move through our bounty of snacks like we never again expect another meal, eyes glued to the computer screen as the award show moves into the presentation section of the evening.

'And the award,' says the host, 'for Largest Audience in a Small Niche goes to –' there's a drumroll – 'Locksmith!'

The audience of well-mannered humanoids clap in unnerving sync, all flashing the same soulless grin into the camera as it pans their faces. Zach slams his fist into his array of sugary sweets and salty snacks. 'Ha! Like the robot didn't steal every single content idea from Grandrew George, the guy who rates locks and latches on his Photorah page. This is boring – there's not a single content creator I actually watch here.'

I can't disagree. For the first time since the Global Influencer Awards became a thing, I'm finding myself completely disinterested – and furious.

After Locksmith gives his empty thanks, the host returns to the stage with a new award. This one made of glass and in the shape of a diamond.

'Three incredible influencers have been put forward for Most Unique Talent,' she says. 'But there can only be one winner ... AnnaConda!'

The camera pans to a petite girl with huge, round eyes, flawless skin and blushed lips. She looks like a child's doll, straight out of the box, another artificial influencer, and her content is whatever her audience wants it to be. This isn't even fun to mock any more; it's just sad.

Buzz.

Zach, who looks as if he's on the verge of punching a hole right through my computer as AnnaConda glides up the stage to accept her award, whips his phone from his pocket and finds the newest notification on his screen.

'Oh my goodness,' Anna coos into the microphone,

her large eyes scanning the room with an empty gaze. 'It's been a dream of mine for so long to be standing here in front of you, accepting an award for my contribution to the entertainment industry.'

I snort coconut fizz through my nostrils and choke. She can't be serious.

'It takes a lot of hard work and energy to produce the work I have on my iGENect page, but I endeavour to bring content to my audience whenever they wish for it – that's the beauty of me and my platform.'

I can't help rolling my eyes. 'As if AnnaConda is actually using her speech to say how hard content creation is when she's a literal *robot* and doesn't have to do anything people don't program into her.'

Zach doesn't reply. He's looking at his phone, staring at a message. He turns the screen towards me.

> Message from: Mum
> Sent: 19:52
> I wanted you to hear this from me before you see it on the news tomorrow. VaderVerse is going into liquidation. Your dad and I have tried to get round it, but we don't have any money left in our personal accounts to keep bailing the business out. We're potentially looking at filing for personal bankruptcy too because it'll help lessen the financial blowback from worker salaries. I didn't want you to be blindsided when they run the story in the morning. I'll be home tomorrow evening, and we can discuss then. Love you x

My blood runs cold. Zach's eyes shine with tears as I lay my hand on his shoulder.

A plague on both our houses.

I steady my gaze on the screen as AnnaConda raises her award to the glinting stage lights, catching a beam within her hollow glass eyes, granting me a glimpse of the technological marvel beneath her perfectly curated silicone structure. Her smile is dazzling and it cuts through what little patience I have left for this award show and the state of the arts industry.

'We have to end this takeover,' I say.

CHAPTER 3

The corners of Zach's eyebrows knit together, causing a deep crevasse to form between them. He blinks away tears, his cheeks pink and blotchy. He's trying to hold back his anguish, and that makes my blood boil.

'I mean it,' I say. 'I'm so tired of living in a world where we're set up to fail. Like, at least our parents got a taste of the creative life first, right? We'll never get that chance, Zach!'

'Maybe it's better to never have the chance to live the life of your dreams than to lose it once you've finally achieved it,' he says. 'What are our parents going to do now? Your dad struggled through the worst day jobs ever to finally achieve his artistic dream, and my mum doesn't know anything other than VaderVerse . . . How're they going to cope?'

I swallow the lump in my throat. God, he's right. 'We have to do something.'

Zach keeps his eyes low, still processing the news of the demise of his mother's business. I open my mouth, ready to spew more harsh truths about the creative industry and how AI is ruining it, but something about his expression stops me in my tracks. I don't want to add to his pain.

Ping.

That's a Tubeify notification if I ever heard one.

I grab my phone from beside the computer screen still showing a slew of humanoids winning awards in categories such as Most Innovative Creator, and activate face recognition. I click the notification and am instantly sucked on to the profile of Tubeify's most prolific investigation channel. TheHarperHerald. One of the contestants in the infamous *Island of Influencers* challenge, the girl who blew the lid on the whole identity-theft situation and tried to stop AI influencers taking over. She's live on her channel and I join the stream. She's in the back of a taxi alongside her famous cousin, Belle Deveraux. Both girls look pained and panicked.

'So, we finally got into the Global Influencer Awards ceremony,' Harper begins. 'Only to be kicked right back out again the moment we started asking questions about why no human creators have been nominated this year.'

'This is serious, you guys,' Belle chimes in. 'They're trying to silence anyone who speaks out against iGENect and their army of humanoid celebrities.'

Harper speaks again: 'Real people, like you – consumers, viewers – you're screaming out for real content, but the big companies aren't listening. Tubeify can't pay human creators any more, so all we're left with is AI content over on iGENect. None of us are happy watching soulless voids of product promotion. This isn't art; it isn't entertainment. But the people behind iGENect are trying to silence us; they don't want real people making a living from content creation or art any more.'

'We're the only ones who still have a voice in this matter,' Belle says. Her white-blonde hair with baby-blue roots cascades over her shoulders – messy, like she's just been jostled around. 'But we don't know how long we have left to spread the word before they do find a way to keep us quiet. If you think this doesn't affect you, think again. How much of your daily life revolves around your phone? When was the last time you spoke to an actual human being instead of a bot while trying to return a cute blouse that doesn't fit right, or went to an in-person stylist to find your colour instead of using an app that mistakes you for a light winter when you're actually a dark autumn?'

'Everyone's losing their livelihoods to this plague of robots.' I shift uncomfortably as tears well in the on-screen Harper's eyes. 'It's not just content creators and artists suffering – no one is safe.'

All the day's anger surges through me and a guttural growl escapes my lips. I exit the livestream, overwhelmed with defeat, and glance at Zach. I expect to see resignation plastered on his face too. But his lips have formed a thin line that mirrors the one returning between his brows.

'How do we stop it?' he asks, the words forced through clenched teeth.

I'm almost taken aback. I know I *said* I was serious about doing something to end the takeover of AI in the creative sphere, but *am I serious?* How the hell could someone like me do anything impactful enough to create change? I shake my head. 'I-I don't actually know,' I admit.

'You're right about doing something; we can't stand back and watch all our dreams come crashing down around us. Iz might be stoked about AI helping with her marketing course, but VaderVerse was my family's legacy, my parents worked themselves to the bone for it. I always dreamt of taking over when Mum finally decided to retire. That's what I've been planning for my whole life. I-I don't know anything else. I haven't planned for anything else. What do I do? I'll have to spend the summer replanning my entire life!'

Those words hit me like a freight train. I march to my computer and click out of the Global Influencer Awards. 'We start by taking back our support of *anything* to do with AI content.'

Zach chuckles. 'What's one livestream switched off going to do, mate? Millions of people across the world are feeding into this. There're, like, five actual human creators left on Tubeify and most of their stuff is behind subscriptions in order to make any actual money from their content. It's not possible to boycott AI content any more.' With a scoff, he picks up a can of Mocha Chino Latte from our hoard of snacks and holds it up. 'Besides, what does it matter if we're avoiding award shows if we're still supporting the brands by buying their merchandise?'

I grab the can from his hands and slam it back on to my desk. Damn it, he's right. But it's near impossible not to buy anything from these fakefluencers when the shops are filled with them. They've taken over everything.

'We have to get the audience back to Tubeify,' Zach says. 'Brands follow the consumers, right? So, if we get people watching humans making content again, surely the money will follow and social media will go back to how it used to be, with AI just as, like, this side character that helps but isn't the main attraction?'

I knit my own brows and think on it, pacing until I swear I can see the threads of the carpet begin to fray. 'There's no human on this earth that can outperform a robot – they don't have to sleep, they don't get burnout from coming up with ideas, because they're trained to scrape the internet for content so that they can rehash things already done by others. The whole reason AI content has popped off is because the audience always wants more, but what your mum created with the original *Faerie Pools* was insane, bro. That's the kind of art and entertainment we need again. Years of love and labour went into that game and it's still a cult favourite even twenty years on.'

Zach focuses on my blank computer screen. 'Yeah, that's the kind of stuff that lives for ever. If we want people to come back to human creations, then whatever we're creating *must* be worth waiting for. It has to be so good, so tantalizing, so irresistible, that between uploads, people are entertaining themselves with chatter about us, theorizing about what we'll put out next, filled with constant anticipation. Like when Doze Emblem's new album came out a couple of years ago and they dropped cryptic teasers all over the place, in their social posts and on stickers on random lamp posts around the world.'

My eyes widen and fire floods my veins. 'Yeah . . . yeah! Oh, man, that was peak! Literally couldn't think about anything else the entire build-up and even for like a month after the album drop, because it was just so good. I still remember all those old Viper chats that popped up out of nowhere to speculate about the lore and solve the puzzles.'

I start laughing, my mind trailing back to the best summer of my life, two years ago. Then a wave of sadness hits, and a lump forms in my throat. I haven't felt that level of excitement, or been involved in a community of like-minded people like that since.

'We gotta do something that AI can't replicate,' I offer.

Zach raises an eyebrow. 'AI can steal and imitate everything created online, mate, so how do we do something it *can't* do?'

I flash him a knowing smile. 'What did I just say AI *doesn't* need to do and therefore that puts human creators at a disadvantage?'

He wracks his brain for any slither of valuable information handed out in the last half hour of our dismay. 'S-Sleep?'

He's unsure but bang on.

'Sleep,' I say, nodding. 'A very human thing, wouldn't you say?'

'So . . . you want us to make content about . . . sleep? Like ASMR for sleeping or like literally video us sleeping at night?'

'No, not exactly. But think of other things that only humans can do that robots will *never* be able to replicate. What can a human do that a machine can't?'

His brow furrows. I'm pretty sure he's given himself a headache by the time he says: 'Feel?'

'Feel! Eat! Bleed! Suffer! All that human stuff they think is a weakness. Do you remember that video Harper and Belle made right after *Island of Influencers* finished, exposing everything that happened after the cameras had been shut off? Someone had to prove they were human by pricking their finger and making themselves bleed.'

Zach grabs a cinnamon and nutmeg ChokaBloka bar from Kottage Kay's Kitchenary brand on my desk. 'And Kottage Kay never ate a single thing during the livestream. How many times did they show her cooking but never eating? We thought it was weird at the time – maybe just some bad editing – but it made total sense when Harper and Belle finally told us what Kay really is.'

'If we want to build an audience, we need connection. Connection happens when people feel seen and understood. Well, robots can't understand the silly plights of us humans, can they? So, maybe we need to focus on those human traits of ours instead of seeing them as a weakness like the businesses behind the AI influencers do. We can rebrand my old channel; it already has a couple of thousand subscribers.'

The corner of Zach's lips twists into a mischievous smile. 'I'm in.'

CHAPTER 4

'If we want to prove to the world that it's far more interesting watching real humans online than it is watching these perfect, brand-appealing humanoids, then our channel needs to focus on a very human element and evoke that in our viewers too – the ability to feel,' Zach says, pacing my room.

I nod, adrenaline pumping through my veins. 'I suppose we genuinely could run a livestream of one of us sleeping. Pretty sure some Japanese guy did that like a decade ago to pay for his tuition fees or something.'

'Sure,' says Zach. 'Are you volunteering? Because I sure as hell don't want to wake up to a load of messages from strangers telling me that I fart worse than a lactose-intolerant person who's just eaten five kilos of cheese.'

I knit my eyebrows. Good point.

'OK, maybe we eliminate that off the list entirely. Sleeping is a human necessity, but not necessarily interesting enough. Let's revisit the fact that robots can't bleed ...'

We sit in silence, letting the cogs turn in our heads. I

think back to all the old videos and creators I used to watch on Tubeify before it became a dead platform.

A tiny lightbulb beams alight in my head.

'Stunts?' I blurt out.

'Stunts!' Zach repeats, eyes wide. 'Cool stunts, stupid stunts, stunts that make you gasp in awe and cover your eyes through fear of someone getting hurt. Brilliant! We'd need to think of some stunts that haven't been done yet, though. Our generation watched parkour across skyrises, people scaling the world's tallest buildings with no ropes or harnesses, and explorers delving deep into catacombs and through abandoned radioactive cities.'

'Sounds dangerous,' I say, anxiety creeping through my chest. 'But I guess that's the point. It has to be dangerous if we want to grab the audience's attention, right? Make them *feel* something for us. These AI celebs can upload content five, six, ten times a day. We'll be lucky if we can get one video out a week, so it *has* to be worth waiting for.'

'I'll volunteer,' Zach adds, his pacing coming to an end. 'I've got my BMX and I can start pushing myself to do bigger things. I've done plenty of parkour, and gymnastics and skiing too – and considering my rugby background, I think I can handle a lot of the rough and tumble.'

I glance over his body, muscular and robust without being too overpowering for his average height. That familiar sting rips through my chest. He's travelled all over the world with his parents, as his dad's always been big on 'living in the moment', and his mum's company ensured they could afford adventure holidays and racing experiences. His Photorah posts during summer break would make any wannabe travel influencer jealous.

'You should focus on another aspect of humanness,' he adds. 'Something a little less dangerous and more ... fun?'

That sting intensifies and I rub my chest as the envy consumes me. It's a feeling I've grown used to over the years whenever I'm in Zach's presence, but it never hurts any less. He's going to look all macho and daredevil while I'm – what? – the channel's clown? I frown.

Zach notices and his face drops slightly. 'We'll think of something super-cool for you too. It's me and you, remember? Dream team.'

I flash a half-smile and nod. But I can't help feeling a pang of regret when I consider letting Zach become a part of my existing Tubeify channel. That's mine – my one space where I'm not overshadowed by my best mate's good looks or mysterious personality that keeps all the girls coming back for more and all the guys desperate to be affiliated with him.

'What kind of things interest you, mate?' Zach asks, his voice tender, as it always is when he knows I'm stuck inside my own head.

My eyes land on the display of party food discarded on my bedroom floor. 'I think I could make a pretty cool eating channel? I can eat a lot, as you know – you ever heard of mukbang?'

Zach ponders this. 'Kinda.'

'It started in Korea. People livestream themselves eating. Viewers eat their meals at the same time so that they don't feel lonely. It's a pretty cool concept; I've watched a few videos. I know it got quite big with Tubeifyers before all this iGENect computer-generated influencer stuff. Maybe I can bring it back?'

'Nice! I like that idea. I'll be giving the audience what they think they want: entertainment. You'll be giving them what they need: connection. Sounds like a wicked team, if you ask me.'

A grin spreads over my face and I slam my open palm into his, shaking his hand like we've just made a blood-brothers pact.

'Let's film your first mukbang now.' Zach claps his hands and before I know it, he's throwing random snacks at me. There isn't much left, just the dregs of each item, barely enough to satisfy my taste for them, let alone film an entire mukbang. I know what Zach's doing. He's gone into damage-control mode, attempting to prove that he isn't meaning to cast his huge shadow over me, but it's overwhelming.

Before I can even tell him this or acknowledge how pitiful our food offerings are for the mukbang, his phone camera is in my face and he's counting down from three on his fingers.

My eyes widen as I stare into the lens and my head goes fuzzy. I feel the blood pumping through my veins and my vision begins to blur. I open my mouth to speak, grab the almost-empty packet of BBQ Bacon Bitz with a shaky hand, and gawp at the camera.

Zach's face falls and he searches my expression with worried eyes before pulling the camera away and replacing his phone in his pocket. 'You good, mate?'

My tongue is dry and instead of words exiting my mouth, I cluck and choke. Truthfully, I hadn't thought about the impact of having a camera shoved right in my face. Sure, I've made Tubeify content for two years now, but it's all been faceless. Just gameplay with silly commentary over the top as I explain what my action plan is. I never wanted to be in front of the camera as myself; that's an entirely different beast from playing a character in acting class. Who'd want to watch *me* being *me* anyway? Everything about me is cringe.

As if he's been party to my inner turmoil, Zach says: 'You can hardly make mukbang content if you're not comfortable on camera. Like, your mouth is literally the star of the show . . .'

I let out an exasperated laugh. 'I know . . . it all just seems a bit sudden. I haven't had a chance to consider what type of mukbanger I want to be yet.'

He frowns and quickly steers in another direction. 'Just out of curiosity, which one of us is going to be doing the editing of these videos? Because I still have cricket and rugby over the summer. I can't be a stuntman, sportsman *and* a creative genius – a guy's gotta have some downtime, you know?'

I raise my eyebrows. Again, another good point. 'Iz edits all my current Tubeify videos. I know these would require more effort, but I could ask her?'

Zach pulls a face, but he makes no suggestion that he wouldn't particularly like her to be involved. So, I grab my phone again and hit video call. When Isobel answers, my bedroom is filled with the cries of her little sister, Evie.

'Studying's going well, then?' I joke.

Isobel just groans and rubs Evie's back while rocking her gently.

After filling her in on my and Zach's plan to bring back the golden days of social media, Iz goes quiet.

'You want to prove that human-made content is better entertainment than anything created by AI, and therefore it's worth waiting for, investing in, and championing?' she says at last.

'Exactly,' I say, pride washing over me.

She nods, still cradling Evie in her arms as the toddler falls into a peaceful slumber. 'Interesting idea. Cheki messaged earlier to say her dad's holiday cottage down by Durdle Door is free and asked if I wanted to stay there with her to house-sit. Mum said I could, so long as I come back and help out occasionally. I could ask if you guys can tag along?'

This time, I'm the one nodding enthusiastically into the screen. 'We could be like a content house or something!' I glance over at Zach. He's quiet.

'I'll ask her,' Iz says before hanging up.

My bedroom falls silent once more. Zach's staring out of my window.

'You good?' I ask.

'Yeah,' Zach replies. 'Just thinking.' He gathers his thoughts before he turns to me and says: 'This is still *our* thing, right?'

'Of course,' I say. 'We started it, it's *ours*. We're the founding members.'

He grins at me and slaps his palm against mine.

CHAPTER 5

Two days later, Mum and Dad drop me off at Cheki's dad's holiday home in Chaldon Herring – a quaint village near the Dorset coast with narrow lanes, where the cottages have thatched roofs and ivy growing up the stone, and all the villagers know each other by name. It's early evening. Luckily, Cheki was more than happy for me and Zach to join in with her house-sitting duties. 'The more the merrier,' she'd said, and my parents sounded almost grateful to have me out of the house for the holidays.

Cheki waits by the front door – rounded at the top and made of dark oak, with wisteria framing the small windows – beckoning us inside. She's Isobel's friend from her fine arts class, but I've grown fond of her over the last couple of months too.

With a look of pure disbelief, Mum hands me my stash of rubbish from the back seat of her car – wrappers and packets of sherbet dip, toffee yumyums and a chocolate-orange muffin. I flash her a smile, feigning innocence, and wave my parents off as their Volvo disappears around the country lanes out of sight. I haul my bags to the front door, catching Zach as he drags his entire wardrobe and haircare kit along the gravel drive.

Isobel's already made her way inside and deposited her belongings by the front door.

'I'm starving,' I mutter as Zach and I lug our suitcases and bags inside the four-bedroom cottage.

'You can't be serious,' Isobel scoffs. 'What's all that in your hands?'

I try to hide the empty wrappers and packaging behind my back but Zach peels them from my fingers, laughing at the sight. 'Empty calories,' I say, shrugging.

'Bottomless pit,' Isobel offers instead.

'I don't know where you put it all, Mikah,' says Cheki. 'There's nothing to you. You could eat a whole horse and still look like you live off nothing but air.'

I laugh at this. Mum and Dad always say I must have an iron stomach due to my never-ending hunger and never-changing weight. Good metabolism, I guess.

Cheki is like a little ray of sunshine in human form. She's what my parents refer to as a 'trustafarian' because her family is stinking rich, but she dresses like she lives off the land and has no need for worldly possessions (despite her hoard of expensive worldly possessions). Her hair is cropped to her chin, and she wears a long feather in one side and beads in the other.

She makes me laugh. It's like we're polar opposites. I've never met anyone so sure of themselves and comfortable in their own skin, while I'd do anything to become someone else.

'Obviously I'm taking the master suite,' Cheki says. 'But the others are a free-for-all. Help yourse—'

Before she can even finish her sentence, Zach and I are wrestling on the stairs, desperate to snag the best bedroom. I want a room with a window overlooking the sweeping fields and swimming pool in the garden. Zach jabs his finger between my ribs, making me squeal and lose my footing on the steps. With a hearty chuckle, he advances towards the room, but I'm not so easily defeated. I lunge at him, taking him down with a headbutt to the back of the knees.

He squawks like a seagull and we both lose it completely.

As we grapple on the top landing, moving closer to the room only by millimetres, a shadow falls over us.

'Tut, tut, tut, when will you boys ever learn?'

Isobel takes one giant step over our mangled bodies on the floor and skips towards the bedroom, throwing her backpack on the double bed, claiming it.

'Ha! We get the best room,' I say smugly, jumping to my feet and folding my arms. 'Tough luck, pal.'

'We?' asks Isobel, appearing in the corridor again. 'What do you mean, this is *my* room. It's a four-bedroom house, we get a room each.'

Zach sniggers and jabs me in the ribs as my face falls. 'W-we're not sharing?'

'Not with the way you snore, I need my beauty sleep,

babe. You can come in for cuddles before bed, but that's it.'

My heart sinks into my stomach – this was our chance to act like a proper couple for the summer – but I know there's no arguing with her. Reluctantly I claim the remaining bedroom upstairs and Zach takes the downstairs room.

As we gather in the largest sitting room, I can't help smirking at the attire Cheki dons: baggy pants made of discarded rags that are three sizes too big for her and held up with a bungie cord around her waist, and an oversized tee with an old punk band logo print on the front.

'With all the money your parents give you,' I say, taking a seat on a grey sofa, 'you choose to dress like that!'

Cheki scoffs. 'This top is vintage, thank you very much. And these pants are designer.'

'You wouldn't believe how much it costs to dress like you've found all your clothes in the bin,' Isobel chortles. 'Cheki is a proper fashionista.'

Flashing me a side-eye, Cheki takes a seat on the sofa closest to the window overlooking the driveway. Zach crouches on the floor beside me, nonchalantly playing with the rings on his fingers.

'If we do all the heavy work tonight, then these next five weeks should be a breeze,' Isobel says. 'I've already caught Cheki up with the message behind the channel. Humans over AI. We need to research the types of videos that used to pop off before AI took over, and jot down how you can recreate those videos, but better – with that human twist.'

'Cool,' I say. 'Maybe we should order the takeout first?'

Isobel rolls her eyes but flashes me a smile. My stomach does a somersault.

She whips her phone out and changes location on her MealzOnWheels app, and the room is instantly filled with vocalized fast-food requests: cheeseburger with large chilli cheese fries; twelve-inch BBQ chicken pizza with extra olives and green peppers; large cod with extra-large chips and gravy, and an extra pot of gravy on the side; mozzarella sticks with a tangy tomato dip; chocolate-filled doughnut balls with caramel drizzle; duck rolls, spring rolls, prawn toast, sweet and sour chicken, egg fried rice, banana and pineapple fritters ...

My parents have never been strict with our family diet, but even I know they'd be turning pale at the foods I plan on eating during our five weeks of summer freedom. I don't care. When will I ever get this opportunity again?

Isobel struggles to keep track. 'Jeez, Mikah, are you really going to eat all of this? Don't forget we're living off the generosity of our parents while we're here. At least until we can start making our own money from the channel.'

'I'm so hungry.' I rub my belly. 'All I had in the car was snacks.'

'Fine, but you'd better put all this food to good use. We can film your first mukbang video tonight.'

My stomach drops. Tonight? Oh god, I'm still not ready. I spent the past two days confessing to Isobel my phobia of being on camera as myself. She listened and comforted me, but I'd hoped she'd come up with a solution. Seems like she hasn't. I'm suddenly not hungry any more. Unusual for me. I love food.

Ever since Zach and I chose our niches, I've been watching mukbang videos non-stop and found I like it much more than I care to admit. Old Tubeifyer Noboki-Eats used to chat to the camera in between delicate bites of food, sharing her day with the fans on the other side of the camera, making jokes and interacting with the comment section. Her channel was less about the food and more about making people feel connected.

In contrast, an American girl called Chomping-Qweenie was all about the food ASMR. She'd ramp up the sounds of her eating, slurping and chewing.

'Stop panicking,' Zach whispers from the floor by my feet. He gives my knee a nudge. 'You'll be great, just do what comes naturally to you. No one gets it right the first time, 'K?'

''K,' I say, shooting him a grateful nod.

Food challenges were popular back in the day too, with Tubeifyers taking on huge amounts of food, or the spiciest peppers, or even just seeing how much they could eat in twenty minutes.

'Mikah,' Isobel starts. 'I've been thinking about what you said the other night, about how you're scared to show your face online. I-I think I might've found a solution.'

From a kitchen counter behind the door, she produces a large carrier bag and begins unravelling the plastic from the contents inside. I notice her hands are shaking a little. We all move closer. She pulls four strangely shaped lumps of plastic free and holds one up. A mask.

Black, and shaped like a human skull with slits cut out to enable the wearer to see.

'Do you remember a few years ago when it was cool to wear masks online and stuff?' she asks. 'Maskify really took off, loads of people were creating content wearing masks to hide their identity. Girls in the book community *loved* it, for some reason. The anonymity kinda gave old content a fresh spin because the mystery of the person behind the mask got people talking and speculating. So, these masks could be a great way to create intrigue and get an initial interest in the channel, while also helping you combat your insecurities, Mikah.'

I raise both my eyebrows. 'O-OK,' I stutter. 'I like that idea but . . . isn't the whole point of doing this to show that *humans* are better than AI at creating content? If we hide ourselves, we could be anyone or anything.'

'Exactly! We could be anyone behind these masks. You've never particularly wanted to be a social media influencer, have you? You just like making content. The anonymity would allow the audience to see themselves in us, while putting the focus on the human stuff we're doing. Eating, bleeding, suffering, feeling . . .'

'But how will I—' I begin.

Isobel pulls a second mask from the stack. This one has the mouthpiece cut out, enabling me to consume food without revealing my face. My heart thuds and I jump to my feet, pulling her in for the biggest hug I can muster.

The doorbell rings and snaps us back into reality. Food is here.

'Well,' Isobel says through her laughs, 'it's your time to shine, babe. Best switch your phone to record and set the stage for your mukbang debut.'

CHAPTER 6

A mountain of food almost obstructs my view of the camera. Mozzarella sticks, a twelve-inch BBQ meat feast pizza with cheese-stuffed crust, honey-mustard chicken wings, crispy battered onion rings and an array of dips and sauces (BBQ, sweet and sour, sour cream and chive, ranch, honey mustard). My mouth salivates as I place my mask over my face. I wriggle my nose into place but it's squished against the plastic, making it difficult to breathe.

'Let me just get the angle right,' Isobel mutters as she readjusts the camera for the umpteenth time.

'Come on, I'm so hungry,' I say, reaching for a slice of pizza.

Zach slaps my hand away and wags a thick finger at me. 'She needs to get a good thumbnail of you with the food before you start eating. That food mountain is what's going to draw people in, otherwise no one will click the video to watch it in the first place.'

I know he's right. A great thumbnail and title will persuade people to click. What's more interesting than the prospect of some scrawny guy putting away the equivalent of a family-sized meal in one sitting?

'OK, done,' she says. 'Start whenever you're ready.'

I nod, and reach my shaking hand across the food display for a mozzarella stick. Slowly, awkwardly, I shove it in my mouth and chow down. My eyes flick from the coffee table to the camera lens on the phone. 'Mmm,' I say, going for another one.

Laughter fills my ears, and I snap my head towards the sofa by the window. Zach is on his knees, his face buried in his hands as he snorts and splutters into them, Cheki has tears in her eyes, and Isobel can't even look at me.

'What the hell was that?' Zach gasps through each chuckle. 'Mmm,' he mocks, laughing even harder.

My cheeks get hot underneath my mask and my stomach twists and knots. 'I–I'm nervous!' My voice cracks and this warrants even more laughter from Cheki.

'I've never heard anyone sound less enthusiastic about food in my life,' Isobel adds. 'You can't put that on the internet, people will have a field day. Imagine everyone from school seeing that.'

'You try being up here, eating with a camera pointed at your face and your mates judging you from the sidelines.'

'We're just trying to make sure you don't make an absolute wally of yourself,' Zach says. 'And *that*, mate, was cringe.'

Isobel regains control of herself. 'I really thought the mask would help with your nerves. What is it that's bothering you?'

Without even thinking, my eyes flutter to Zach, who's wiping a tear from his eye. His forearms are massive, owing to his time spent on the field and in the gym.

My own arms are pale and noodle-like. My face is hidden, but the rest of me isn't.

A lump forms in my throat.

It's as if Zach has heard my thoughts. 'No one's going to be looking at you, mate,' he says gently. 'There's a mountain of food in front of you – all the greasy, fat, calorific foods that people would *love* to be able to eat without repercussions. Watching you eat it is like second best. Besides, the contrast between this gross amount of food and your skin and bones will make the video super-enticing, along with the mystery of the mask.'

I nod, though I'm not sure I agree. What I could really do with is a brown paper bag to hyperventilate into, but I reckon that might come off as a bit dramatic.

'The best thing is to just eat the food as quickly as you can, as messily as you can,' Isobel suggests. 'That way, you're not worrying about what you have to say or look like, or even sound like.'

'OK.' I take a deep breath and tell Isobel to start recording again. When she gives me the thumbs up, I crack my neck and begin feasting. The food is cold and all I can taste is oil and salt, but it's so moreish. I slam my mozzarella sticks into the array of dips, dripping cheese and buffalo sauce on to the coffee table (which warrants a grimace from Cheki), barely chewing before I swallow.

The pizza is harder to get through, considering I've

never eaten one so quickly before, but with some ranch dipping sauce, I manage it without so much as a hiccup. After the chicken wings, I'm on a roll, laughing between each crumb landing on my lap, slurping the excess sauce from every bite I take. And then, as soon as it's begun, it's all over.

I wipe the coffee table clean of the concoction of sauces with my last chunk of crispy onion ring and relish it, before finishing off with a burp and a rub of my gut.

'Until next time, friends,' I say to the camera, my words muffled by the food still half-chewed on my tongue. 'Peace.' I throw up a sticky, sauce-coated peace sign and collapse on to the sofa.

'Nice!' Zach rushes to me and slaps me on the back, making me burp for a second time. He cackles and waves his hand in front of his nose. 'Oh, mate, go and brush your teeth, will you? Those onion rings are *nasty*.'

I blow a kiss in his direction, hoping the scent gets right up there in his nostrils. Zach gags and playfully punches me in the shoulder.

'Zach, come and help me get the cleaning stuff out!' Cheki calls from the kitchen and he rushes off.

'That was so good, babe.' Isobel flashes me a smile so beautiful it rivals sunrise on a frosty winter's morning. 'Gross as hell, but the sheer amount of food you just scoffed down in one sitting is impressive and bound to grab the audience's attention.' She sits beside me and wipes BBQ sauce from the corner of my lip. 'Proud of you.' My cheeks turn red.

'I had a thought while I was almost choking on the last chicken wing – we should give ourselves a name. Like, what's our content house called? What do we go by? If we're rebranding my current channel with new content, then we can't keep using my current username.'

'True,' says Zach, coming back in with a bucket of cleaning bottles. 'Captain_SeaCraft might work for a gaming channel but sounds too much like a one-man show for a content house.'

Isobel raises an eyebrow. 'Good point. And, if we're going down the anonymous route, we don't want to be using our real names either. If any of these videos land in the algorithms of people we know, they'll recognize us instantly and then the whole point of the masks is . . . well, pointless.'

'What if we use the military alphabet?' asks Cheki, as she delicately scrubs hazard-yellow cheese sauce from the grains in the coffee table, a deep frown etched on her face. 'We can use the corresponding word to our first initial. Right, next time you do a mukbang, put a cloth down. This coffee table is like one hundred years old, passed down from my great-grandparents. My dad will go crazy.'

I mouth *Sorry* to her as she glares at me.

'I like that idea,' Isobel interjects. 'Zach would be Zulu, and Mikah would become Mike.'

'Mike?' I can't stop my face contorting into disgust. 'Too close to home – how about Echo? I can be Echo. Fitting, since I'm the only one with a mask that allows me to talk.'

'And me?' asks Cheki.

I raise an eyebrow. 'You want to get involved?'

She cocks her head as if I've just spoken another language. 'Obviously. I'm not letting you guys crash here for free out of the goodness of my own heart. I want in.'

Zach lets out a little chuckle and nods his approval.

'All right, then,' Isobel says. 'I guess Cheki's name would be Charlie, unless you wanted to use Foxtrot for Francheska instead? I don't need an alias, since I'll be behind the camera.'

'Oh! I like Foxtrot, it's cute.'

'Cool,' Isobel says. 'What about a house name?'

'Hmm, something like Extreme Elites,' Cheki offers.

Isobel's eyes light up. 'That's good! Let's be Extreme Elites.'

'Oh, no – that was just an example. That's already an established content house on iGENect. I was just saying we should have something *like* it.'

I frown. 'iGENect has a content house? All their creators are humanoids. What do they need a content house for?'

Cheki loads the channel on her top-of-the-range Tanaki Foundation NexiFlex phone. I can't help frowning at the irony of her using a Tanaki Foundation product when that's the exact empire we're trying to burn down.

My eyes scan the Extreme Elites channel. Three artificial intelligence humanoid influencers pose for a group photo, fronted by the award-winning AnnaConda, with her long, shimmering black hair and vomit-inducing red bow. Each of the fakefluencers looks flawless: smooth, blemish-free skin; perfectly straight, white teeth; button noses; bright, wide eyes; full, soft lips; not a hair out of place. I roll my eyes. Another erasure of humanity: individualism.

Next, I read their tagline: **A bunch of friends going to the extremes to bring you entertainment daily.**

Friends? Robots can't form friendships. Friendship requires *feelings*. Cheki scrolls through the channel, and as she does, I pick up on various video titles:

> **We Scaled the Empire State Building!**
> **Playing Hide and Seek with a Lion and her Cubs**
> **Watch Us Out-Ski an Avalanche!**

They're uploaded a day apart, as if this perfect trio have travelled halfway around the world in a week, doing various activities. Zach leans over my shoulder and groans. 'Well, there goes my stunt idea,' he says. 'They've already done it. Better than I can. Easier than I can.'

Fury surges through my chest and I gesture for Cheki to close the iGENect app. 'All right, so they've beaten us to it. Robots have their own content house and are doing all the cool stuff we want to do. So what? Let's compete with AnnaConda and her gang of humanoids. Let's do what they do, but better. We'll be more entertaining because the content will be raw and *real*. Do you want to see someone flawlessly backflip on the slopes or do you want to see someone butcher the landing and end up in a tree upside down?'

This warrants a couple of giggles.

'Extreme Elites are the perfectly curated soulless voids we're trying to overcome. And us . . .' I start pacing, my hands behind my back like a supervillain. 'We're the opposite. The anarchists of the algorithm . . . *Digital Demons*, if you will, here to watch the current world burn and rebuild it better than before.'

CHAPTER 7

The sun has barely broken the horizon when Isobel calls us down for breakfast the next day. I roll out of bed, yawning and groaning at the early wake-up call, and seeing how grim I look in the mirror, I'm quite glad Iz decided we should sleep separately.

It must have been gone three in the morning when we finally dragged our weary bodies up to bed. 'You'll be grateful we got the hard stuff done and out of the way upfront,' Isobel had said as we crafted our new online identities, mind-mapped a month's worth of content per niche, and rejigged my old Tubeify channel under the new brand, *Digital Demons*.

After completing the nine-step skincare routine Isobel made for me, I head downstairs.

'I thought we were having a lie-in?' I ask mid-yawn as I join Zach at the breakfast bar.

The cottage kitchen is almost as big as my parents' living room, and every cupboard is stocked to the brim with canned food, ingredients and top-of-the-range equipment.

'What part of "we only have five weeks to blow this channel up before we start college" did you not understand last night?' Isobel huffs, throwing glasses of orange juice in front of us.

'These five weeks are going to fly by! It's nice having the company,' Cheki admits. 'When Dad asked me to house-sit, I was sure this was going to be the dullest summer of my life.'

'My parents love that I'll be out of the house for so long,' I say. 'They're going to use my bedroom for storage while they redecorate the living room.'

'Lucky you,' Isobel says. 'My mum hasn't stopped texting since I got here, asking when I'll be back. You have no idea how hard I had to beg her to let me stay here for the holiday. My granny is practically moving in for the summer to help with Evie while I'm away.'

Zach leans over the breakfast bar, a smug smile on his face. 'My parents have gone to Japan to visit family, have a break after all the mess of their company. They offered to pay for me too, but . . . it's nice to get away from the talk of bankruptcy for a bit, you know? I might still head out there when we're done with this.'

I nod, but the thought of Zach leaving has anxiety flooding me. 'I guess we'd better get started as soon as breakfast is done, then.'

'Good job Cheki's dad had a food delivery before we arrived,' Isobel says. 'Fridge is full! It'll save us a fortune if Mikah doesn't eat it all in a day.'

I chuckle, then frown as she navigates the kitchen like

she's lived here her whole life, grabbing tins of beans from the cupboard and bacon and sausages from the fridge.

'I'll do that,' I say, taking the packet of bacon from her hands.

'It's fine, Mikah, I've got it.' She tenses her hand over the packet, unable to relinquish the responsibility.

'You don't need to look after us,' I whisper to her. 'You're on holiday, relax.' I pry her fingers from around the bacon packet and set it down. Reluctantly she listens and takes a seat at the breakfast bar. 'Zach, give us a hand, will you?'

Zach groans and drags himself to the oven. 'And here was me thinking you were going to make me a nice romantic breakfast.'

'You wish.' I grin.

We slap up a decent full English breakfast complete with fried eggs, grilled tomatoes and hot buttered toast. The scent of home-cooked food coaxes Cheki awake and I can't help but feel proud as Isobel devours every morsel on her plate without complaint.

Zach drops his fork to his own clean plate and belches so loudly I swear the windows rattle in their frames.

'Disgusting!' Cheki bellows, jutting away from the breakfast bar so quickly that her chair makes a noise not too dissimilar to a fart. 'Who raised you, a pig?'

'Pigs are highly intelligent creatures, actually,' Zach claps back. 'Anyway, you'd better get washing up so we can start filming.'

'Me? I'm not your servant.'

'No, but we cooked, so you need to do the dishes,' I say, backing Zach up, picking bacon out of my teeth. 'S'only fair.'

'What about Iz? She didn't cook!'

'I'm busy organizing the day's filming schedule,' Isobel says, having already pulled out her laptop.

With a frown and some choice words muttered under her breath, Cheki collects our plates. Zach nudges me in the ribs, failing to suppress his laugh as we watch her try and decipher which product under the sink she should use.

'It's like watching an alien navigating Earth for the first time,' I say.

'Like a fish out of water,' Zach replies.

While we wait for Isobel to finish putting together a detailed filming schedule for our second video – this time, focusing on Zach and showcasing human agility – I grab the masks from the kitchen counter and examine them more closely. I didn't get a chance to last night, considering the focus was on me and my mukbang.

Each mask is in the shape of a human skull, complete with hollowed-out cheekbones and 3D teeth. The mask covers the entire face but has large slits as eyeholes, allowing us to show the emotion we know AI can never replicate.

Mine's a little different, considering there's a large gap where the teeth should be so that I can consume food for the audience. Each mask looks intricately designed, like they've been sketched by hand first. But the mask itself feels flimsy, like it's been mass-produced from an endless sheet of cheap plastic.

'Where'd you get these?'

'Huh?' Isobel glances over the top of her laptop. 'Oh, the masks? From a website that specializes in mask making.'

'I recognize the design type.'

'Yo, me too,' says Zach, grabbing his own mask. 'Didn't get a proper look last night but I knew there was something familiar about them. Maybe there's a . . . aha!' He points to a tiny logo printed at the edge of the mask near the chin. 'That's the Delirium Designs logo. Knew I recognized the style – her masks and headdresses are sick!'

'Ah! No way you got these from her,' I add, flipping the mask over. 'She's good. Surprised you got them so quickly; she's usually got a waiting list of months.'

Isobel lets out a weird little laugh and averts her gaze to her laptop.

I turn the mask over in my hands again, studying it, and frown. 'Her stuff always looks so much sturdier in her pictures on Photorah. Could have sworn her masks were better made than this. It just feels so . . . fragile.'

Isobel slams her laptop closed and jumps to her feet. 'We need to start filming. Mikah's mukbang was uploaded late last night and had barely any views – we need to keep the content cart rolling if we're to get picked up by the algorithm. Consistent uploads at consistent times.'

With that, she flicks the laptop under her armpit and

marches out of the kitchen, beckoning us to follow. Zach throws me a hand gesture: *What the hell is up with her?* And I shrug back. I trust her. She knows the most about this stuff.

We head into the garden and Isobel gathers us on the bench under the wisteria growing over the cottage. She's planned the backdrop to be aesthetically pleasing for social media, but the image makes me laugh considering the video we're about to film.

Cheki, Zach and I position ourselves on the bench, trying to keep a relaxed vibe. Isobel positions the camera in front of us, making slight alterations to centre the image. We're all wearing black and donning our new masks. I wiggle my nose, trying to manoeuvre it into a more comfortable position. I'd have thought an experienced mask-maker like Delirium Designs would've wanted our measurements before putting these together. The nose hole is much too small for my hooter and Cheki's mask doesn't compensate for her round face, meaning her cheeks are awkwardly poking from the sides. Zach flexes his biceps in his black vest, trying to find the perfect balance between a relaxed state and looking effortlessly jacked. I yank my long-sleeved top over my hands and shimmy further into my mates, hoping they'll hide how scrawny I am compared to Zach.

'Looking good,' Isobel says. 'Mikah, can you shuffle forward, please? No point in being all the way behind Cheki when you're the mouthpiece for the group. You ready? Know what you're going to say?'

I swallow, hard, but my throat is dry. We decided we'd make this explainer video for the channel on our way to bed last night and that I'd be the speaker.

Zach nudges me again. 'You got this, bro,' he says, his words muffled by his own mask. He shifts uncomfortably beside me, flexing his bicep again and repositioning himself so that his body is in focus of the camera. I imagine it's difficult for him too. The mask hiding who I really am is giving me confidence I've never had before, but for Zach, it's taking away the looks he's always used to get by in life.

'Everyone ready?' Isobel asks. When we all mumble 'Yeah,' in unison, she gestures a countdown with her fingers.

Three, two, one ...

'Welcome, friends,' I say, in the deepest, most confident voice I can muster. 'We come to you as mortal instruments, embodying all that it means to be human, encapsulating the very things that artificial intelligence cannot replicate, no matter how many upgrades or downloads it receives. You do not need to know our identities, for we represent all of you. We represent what it means to *be* human. We are Digital Demons, a collective of individuals hell-bent on returning the internet and the world to its former glory, to when humans reigned, and humanoids were merely an idea scribbled in the notebook of a science-fiction writer.

'We are here to reclaim art from the grip of technology, to bring content creation back into the hands of real people, to say no to the giant corporations like iGENect and the Tanaki Foundation, who want to replace humans with AI. Join us as we embark on our quest to put humans back at the top of the food chain.'

'You *will* be entertained,' Cheki, Zach and I chant together. Our new house slogan.

Isobel holds her hand in the air, and we stay frozen in our spots on the bench. She counts her fingers down and, on zero, makes a cut-throat action to signal that the recording has been stopped. 'Nicely done!' she grins. 'Very dramatic, absolutely eye-catching. Hopefully it'll get people talking and watching the channel. Now – content! Zach, you're up. Let's see how far we can push the human body until it breaks.'

CHAPTER 8

We disperse from the bench and start grabbing our equipment, which is basically just our phones on selfie sticks. Cheki's dad owns an impressive collection of cameras and lenses, but our channel needs the 'home-made' look that iGENect content is lacking.

Zach heads towards the manicured lawn beside the pool area.

I grimace at what he's about to do, but he gives me a reassuring wink. Sure, Zach was always known in school for being a daredevil, but that was just to impress whichever girl he fancied. Now, with the possibility of an endless audience watching, my chest tightens at the thought of how far he'll take this.

'Ready?' Isobel asks, phone on a 360 selfie stick.

Cheki has her phone attached to a stationary tripod, catching a wide angle of the action, while I'm to follow Zach with my handheld.

I'm doing the intro, so I walk in shot as Zach replaces his mask, psyching himself up for his performance. I pull my own mask over my face again as Isobel counts me down.

'Hey, guys, Echo from Digital Demons. Today, Zulu is going to attempt parkour around our content house. You may have seen the recent Extreme Elites video, where AnnaConda, Khristoff and Noruwai effortlessly skywalk up famous landmarks. Beautiful, but they were never in any danger. And that's boring. This might not be as aesthetically pleasing as scaling the Eiffel Tower, but if Zulu falls, he *will* be injured. Stage is all yours, Zulu...'

I step out of shot. Zach nods, takes a deep breath, and launches himself towards the hip-height chain-link fence surrounding the pool area, landing perfectly on the thin metal bar at the top. He effortlessly walks the fence, throwing a somersault and landing clean on the rail again. I gasp in awe. Despite Zach swapping gymnastics for rugby a couple of years ago, he can still perform as well as he always could. Jealousy bubbles in me and I swallow it down. I've never even been close to his level of fitness.

Isobel is grinning behind her phone as she and Cheki capture every angle of his stunt. Zach attempts a backflip and lands on the fence again, but this time, he jolts his shoulders and ribcage as if he's just been shot, flailing his arms in sync to the movements of his torso. Then, he falls backwards on to the grass beneath, his body folding in half, like he's made of playdough.

I freeze as he remains motionless on the ground, my heart pounding in my chest.

Zach uncurls himself and jumps to his feet, a muffled laugh escaping the edges of his mask. I laugh too, relieved, and the girls give him a cheer.

But Zach doesn't stop there. He legs it across the garden, jumping from one wall to the next, flipping over benches and dive-bombing through a tree swing, perfectly balancing his content between cool stunts and goofy 'death falls'. Soon, I'm completely entranced, running behind him, giggling like a little kid in the school playground.

I catch his eyeline and it's like he's inviting me in. He runs at me, and I make for him too; we both jump at the same time, colliding mid-air, falling to the ground as stiff as boards, eyes wide and silent. We hold our positions on the floor for a few seconds and then burst into unbridled laughter. Zach gently kicks my shin, and I return it with a noogie.

For his final act, Zach makes for the trampoline, dragging it all the way from the lawn to the side of the house.

He mumbles something from behind his mask, which would be completely incoherent to anyone who wasn't standing directly beside him like I am. I turn to the camera in Cheki's hand and repeat his words: 'Zulu is about to attempt a stunt he's never done before; he's going to scale the building and jump from the roof on to the trampoline.'

Cheki's hands shake as she watches Zach scale the drainpipe up the side of the cottage. The pipe wobbles and creaks, threatening to snap. I grimace at the thought. Cheki's dad would probably throw us out at the slightest hint of damage to his multi-million-pound holiday home and my own parents would ground me for life.

When Zach reaches the roof, he stands on the edge and turns so his back is facing us. Again, my heart is racing, not least because he could potentially miss the trampoline altogether and seriously injure himself. I want to call out and check that he's sure about this, but I don't want to stop him in his stride.

Without warning, Zach falls backwards, plummeting towards the ground. But everything happens so quickly that he's in the air again before I can even gasp, bouncing back up to the roof, walking up the side of the cottage, twisting and turning and somersaulting. With one of his bounces, he turns to us and gestures for me to join him. I launch myself on the trampoline, timing it perfectly with his elevation. When he lands, he sends me shooting into the air.

Wind rushes into the gaps at the side of my mask and cools my sweaty forehead. All my organs swish and slide inside me, making me clutch my stomach and giggle relentlessly at the feeling. When I land, I stop myself from rising again, so that I can return the favour to Zach by double-bouncing him. He launches into the sky, far beyond the roof of the cottage. I laugh – until I realize just how big the drop is for him now.

As he falls back down towards me, fear rushes through my chest. He tumbles on to the trampoline and is launched sideways, his head aiming for the metal frame. I launch myself towards him and slide beneath his body just in time, throwing my hands beneath his head and taking the impact.

I groan as his skull crushes my hands into the metal and gasps fill my ears as the others rush forward.

'Oh my god! Are you OK?' Isobel asks, her worried eyes searching the pair of us still tangled on the trampoline. Her phone is lowered by her side.

Cheki's stopped filming too.

'We're good,' Zach mumbles.

I awkwardly laugh as he lifts his head and releases my hand, sending a shooting pain up my arm.

'Sh-Shall we film an outro?' Cheki asks hesitantly, raising her phone again.

'No,' I say, a little more sternly than I mean to, trying to sound calm as I cradle my throbbing hand. 'I think that's a good ending. It's a cliffhanger. Might get people posting comments asking what happened and whether we're OK. Us falling and you guys rushing to help with shaky camera work is a brilliant hook for the next video.'

'You're hurt,' Isobel says, reaching for me.

'Just bruised, I think.'

'We need to get some ice on it.'

She leads me to the kitchen, leaving the others in the garden to speculate on how well they think that video will do in the algorithm.

Isobel directs me to hold my hand under the cold running water and I flinch as the icy blast meets throbbing pain. 'How's your mum?' I ask through clenched teeth, trying to take my mind off the pain.

Isobel sighs. 'She's trying her best. She's just not the same since Dad left. Evie cries constantly, my brother refuses to do anything around the house and Mum's reached her limit, what with her two jobs. I'm doing what I can but it's never enough.'

With my uninjured hand, I hold hers and squeeze. She squeezes back and then releases me to get some ice from the freezer. I dry off and head to the breakfast bar.

'I told her I'd go back in a couple of days, maybe spend a weekend at home and get the house together again for her. I feel so guilty being here . . .'

'You shouldn't, Iz. You're only sixteen. You're not the primary carer for your family. Your dad's a . . . well, you know what I think of your dad. It's the summer holidays and you need to enjoy your youth before the big bad world turns us into adults and sucks all the joy from our lives.'

She scoffs. 'I don't consider you getting hurt to be fun, but who knew Zach would be so agile, considering his size?'

I laugh, then I catch sight of my scrawny arms and a wave of panic washes over me. How will I look beside him in the video? Muscular Zach and lanky me? 'D-Do you think . . .' I begin, but I think better of it.

'No, go on,' she urges, nudging me.

The words tumble from my tongue clumsily. 'Do you think I need to go to the gym and bulk up a bit? Like Zach, I mean?'

She frowns. 'No. Why would you think that?' After some awkward silence, she moves her stool closer to mine and grabs my face in her hands. Her warm, amber eyes meet mine. 'If I didn't like you for exactly who you are and what you look like, I wouldn't be with you. Stop listening to those little gremlins inside your head. To me, you're perfect.'

I swallow my embarrassment and we fall into silence again, both staring at my bright red hand that's seriously swelling. She wraps the ice-filled towel around it and I sniff back my tears. Well, this is what we've got ourselves into.

CHAPTER 9

I take my place at the coffee table while Isobel and Cheki lay out food in front of me, trying to get the right angles so that everything I'm about to devour can be seen by the online audience.

I don't see the point in going to so much effort. My first mukbang has gained sixty views from my already established subscribers and only two comments, one of which is a guy questioning why my content has changed from POV gaming to eating videos, and saying he doesn't want to see me stuff my face.

Half of me feels ridiculous for even attempting to film another one, but this is how content creation goes. It takes time for the algorithm to decipher what niche you're in and push it out to the right people – and we're trying to do it in five weeks – and then there's the battle of getting engagement. Most people don't engage with content that doesn't already have a whole load of likes and comments, for fear of going against the crowd. *Then* there's the tiny problem of Tubeify having basically no users online any more, because all the content is being made by AI over on iGENect.

'How's that looking on the screen?' Isobel asks, as she tilts a bowl of baked beans slightly, shoving a folded piece of paper beneath to hold it in place. 'Oops!' A few beans roll out of the bowl and fall on to the coffee table, leaving a bright orange pool beneath.

'Thank god I put that tablecloth down,' Cheki says, rolling her eyes.

Zach watches, amused, from the sofa nearest the window. He's finalizing the description box of his first Tubeify video, mulling over the right key phrases to trigger the algorithm. 'Can't believe you're doing a mukbang with beans on toast,' he chortles.

I shrug, positioning my mask on top of my head in preparation. 'The internet loves nothing more than arguing about beans on toast.'

'We're ready for you, Mikah,' says Isobel.

They position themselves behind the camera. I slip on my mask and look at the phone on the tripod opposite me. Isobel counts me down from three.

'Hey, guys,' I say into the lens. 'Here to let you know that Zulu and I survived his parkour challenge. Only a bruised hand for me.' I flash my bandaged hand to the camera. 'Now for a super-fun one. At least for me! I know the world loves to drag us Brits for our funky dishes, but this is honestly a top-tier meal, and everyone should try it at least once in their lives! Beans on toast is my last meal of choice, for sure. The key is to get the right combination of flavours. Take your favourite brand of beans, nuke them on the hob and add a dash of brown sauce, get some thick tiger-loaf bread and smother it in lightly salted butter once toasted, then sprinkle mature cheddar on top before devouring every last crumb. Elite. I'm talking plate-lickingly good.'

The grins on both Isobel and Cheki's faces make me forget all about the camera and the lack of audience watching. I wave my arms over the display of beans and thick slabs of toast, both of which are quickly going cold.

'This right here, this is five tins of beans, a five-hundred-gram block of cheese and a whole loaf of bread. You guys think I can do it? To make this challenge even harder, I've set myself a time limit – twenty minutes, to get all of this down.'

Zach flashes me a knowing smile and shakes his head.

'Ohh, guys,' I say. 'Zulu is off camera and he's saying he doesn't think I can do it.'

'Not a—' he starts, but Isobel bulges her eyes at him and throws her finger up to her mouth. He frowns at her.

I knit my brows. He must have forgotten only I can talk. I take a deep breath and pull my phone towards me, clicking start on the timer already set up, then take my first slice of toast and scoop some cheesy beans from the bowl closest. Sauce drips through my fingers.

'Take a bite,' I say, holding the offering to the camera before slamming the British delicacy into my mouth.

I fit the entire slice in my mouth in one go, chewing furiously, and then slurp the last of the juice from the bowl, before moving on to the next. The cheese hits the spot left empty by a missed lunch. The timer counts down as I throw back as much as I can, scooping up the dropped beans from the table and furiously swallowing huge mouthfuls after barely chewing.

Isobel can barely meet my eye, and I know it's because I'm currently dripping bean juice from the corners of my mouth and chin like I've bathed in the tins. Cheki can't contain her grin as she watches me battle the timer.

I wipe the last of the spilt beans from the table into a bowl and slurp the contents into my mouth before slamming my slimy, orange finger on the stop button. I hold the phone to the camera, gasping for breath. 'Two minutes remaining – smashed it.' I let out the biggest belch I can muster and hold my sauce-coated hand to the camera. 'Just be grateful none of you at home have to share this house with me tonight.'

Isobel makes a cut-throat gesture and swipes her phone from the tripod. 'Nice. I'll get this uploaded tonight.'

'Tonight?' Zach frowns. 'I thought mine was going live tonight?'

'Oh, yeah . . . Well, I don't see any harm in uploading two videos. But, like, they need some time between. Maybe we can upload the mukbang around teatime and then yours later tonight?'

His frown intensifies. 'I thought the whole point of an upload schedule was to have content released at the same time every day, so the algorithm knows to expect us?'

'Well, the mukbang will stick to that schedule – I just

think a mealtime release will be better for that type of content. People will be hungry, looking for meal inspiration, maybe want something to watch while they eat their own meal. Five o'clock just seems like a good upload time for mukbang.'

'So, what time should my stunts be uploaded, then?'

I whip my mask off and make a mental note to wash all the bean juice from it. 'I-I guess your type of content is more of a weekend or evening watch,' I offer. 'I think Isobel is right in that food content uploaded around mealtimes makes sense.'

Zach glares at me and then averts his attention back to his screen. 'And why can't we all be in the mukbangs? Mikah is in my video, why can't I be in his?'

'Not exactly easy to eat without a hole cut through your mask,' Isobel says.

'Yeah, fine, whatever. But, like, you wouldn't even let me speak off-camera.'

It's Isobel's turn to frown. 'S-Sorry, I didn't realize that would bother you so much, Zach. We were in the middle of recording and I just think we shouldn't have so many people talking in one video, or it gets messy. And the masks are about anonymity, about how any of the audience members can be any one of us. Mikah is our mouthpiece, I think that's enough, otherwise it'll be too much.'

The room goes quiet. Eventually, Isobel breaks the stalemate by saying: 'I need to get this edited and uploaded,' before heading upstairs to her bedroom.

'This needs cleaning up,' Cheki says. 'It's so gross.'

I grab the bowls and plates and take them to the kitchen, running warm water to rid the crockery, my mask and me of the gooey sauce, and Cheki grabs a wet cloth from beside the sink. Neither of us says a thing.

By the time I head back into the living room, Zach has gone. I clock his silhouette through the window; he makes his way down the drive and disappears around the hedges, hands in his pockets and head hanging low.

I reset the cushions on the sofa and move the tripod from the middle of the room, before heading upstairs. The light is flickering from beneath Isobel's bedroom door, and I imagine she's hunched over her laptop, piecing together segments of my mukbang footage, tripling the speed of my eating and bringing it back to normal whenever I'm talking to the camera.

Part of me wants to go after Zach and make amends, but my stomach hurts from too much food. Project Digital Demons hasn't even been running for a week, and I'm already exhausted. Isobel wants us filming videos from dawn to dusk so that we have a catalogue of content on the channel for when we – hopefully – start pulling in the viewers.

After a quick shower, I climb into bed and grab my phone from my bedside table. A good hour of scrolling should help me wind down, or so I believe, until I spot an article on Photorah with a humanoid grinning back at me. AnnaConda with her pristine face is poised on the front cover.

My hand jitters over the screen, willing me to click and satisfy my morbid curiosity, but my brain is urging me to keep scrolling, to stop giving attention to the thing I'm trying to eradicate from the web.

Too late. My finger jitters violently and clicks the article.

The headline reads **REVOLUTIONIZING ENTERTAINMENT: How iGENect, backed by the unstoppable Tanaki Foundation, has changed the way we view and interact with content online.**

There are countless pictures of Mr Tanaki standing beside AnnaConda, showcasing her like he does with any of his new gadgets. In one picture, she sits on a white stool, with a white wall as the backdrop, and Mr Tanaki stands over her with a remote in one hand, smugly grinning. A modern-day Frankenstein story.

'What we've created with these humanoids,' Mr Tanaki is quoted as saying, 'is an immersive entertainment system. They can do anything, be anywhere, act any way the viewer wishes. For the past year, we've been replicating the content we've all come to know and love, but now we're turning the tide, taking entertainment in a new and better direction. Anna here is well versed in anything and everything. Want her to play chess? She can do that. Need to watch her drive a race car around a track? She can be programmed. There's no more having to seek out multiple creators to get a fix of your favourite thing – you can simply connect with one creator and have them perform for you, in whatever area of interest you desire.'

I scowl as I read on.

'Won't people get tired of watching humanoid creators like AnnaConda being absolutely perfect at everything?' asks the interviewer.

'That's the marvellous thing about the service we're offering at iGENect: the audience is always in control of the outcome. If they wish to see Anna fail at a specific task, they can choose to see that. If they want to see her flawlessly scale the Empire State Building, they can see that too. We aim to give the viewer an interactive experience with iGENect humanoid creators, putting them in charge, making them the puppet masters of their own entertainment.'

My heart sinks into my stomach. Humanoids at the will and whim of an audience starved of control in their own daily lives? I can't imagine any good will come of that.

CHAPTER 18

I don't even realize how dark it's got until there's a gentle knock on my bedroom door. I peel my eyes away from my screen and squint at the head popping through the door frame. Going off height and build alone, I know it's Zach.

I pull myself into a more suitable sitting position and my gaze follows him as he enters my room.

'Hey,' I say tentatively.

'Hey,' he repeats. 'Your beans-on-toast mukbang has gone live.'

I glance at the screen on my phone again and realize it's ten p.m. 'Nice. How's it doing?'

He shrugs, switching on a side light and eliminating my need to glare through the dimness. 'Could be better. You've got, like, twenty views so far. Iz is about to upload my first stunt.'

'Hopefully that will do better.'

We fall into an awkward silence.

'Look, mate,' we both say simultaneously and then laugh it off just the same.

'Let me go first,' I say, waving my hand. 'I'm sorry about what happened over the mukbang. I get where Isobel is coming from, not wanting to have too many people chatting in one video, keeping the focus on the task, but I honestly think that us interacting with each other is what will make us so appealing to the audience – like we could be any of the viewers' mates.'

'Yeah, yeah, that's what I was thinking.' He plonks down on the edge of my bed. 'Like, if we're all just masked and expressionless while undertaking all these *human* tasks, then we're no better than the robots we're trying to prove unworthy of the audience's time and attention, right?'

'Right!'

He laughs slightly, relief obviously flooding him, and I crack a smile too. I hate seeing him so down. It's not right, not Zach.

'I've been doomscrolling,' I say. 'Found loads of articles about people losing their jobs and that, reminded me of Dad. I know it might sound lame, but I want to do him justice – and your mum too.'

'Agreed.'

I find the relevant stuff on my phone and hand it to him.

'Jeez,' he says, eyes wide. 'Companies are actually using AI to monitor their employees at their desks now, tracking how many keys per minute they click and recording every millisecond they spend not working?'

I nod. 'Each time a worker leaves their desk, the

systems dock their pay. Every time they stop typing to take a sip of water, their pay gets cut, each conversation they have with a co-worker that isn't about work – monitored via facial expression, because if you're happy then you're not talking about work – incurs a penalty warning. Three warnings and you're out of the company.'

'Nah, that's whack. People can't even breathe! It's all about earning money for the company. No talking, laughing, eating or resting on company time. Just work non-stop from nine in the morning until five in the afternoon.'

'Not even the worst of it.' I grab my phone back and load a Photorah pic. 'Look at that masterpiece – this guy drew the entire skyline of Hollywood in pencil. Took him around five hundred hours, he reckons. Look at the detail! You can actually see people in their building windows making lunch or dancing with partners – how sick is that?'

Zach zooms in and flicks through the multiple pictures showcasing various details of the canvas that stretches almost two metres. 'Holy hell. That's incredible.'

'Look at the top comment,' I say, my voice a warning.

He scrolls and his face contorts in disgust.

The top comment says: **Nice! But you could have done that exact drawing in a couple of minutes with AI and saved yourself the time.**

Zach scrolls through even more comments and reads them aloud.

I did something similar with AI. Maybe not as detailed,

but the results are pretty sick!

Have you tried using the Sanka program? Can generate unbelievable images in a couple of minutes. I'm currently using it to make the cover of my new novel and it's been a lifesaver. It's like $20 a month. Compare that to paying someone like yourself to make the same artwork, and it's a no-brainer!

Another user has replied to this: Bit distasteful to say you prefer putting money in the pockets of super-rich Sanka CEOs instead of helping this artist make a living. 'Specially since in his last post he talked about no longer making enough from his art to get by.

Finally, there's a comment that brings me some hope: See? This is what AI can't give us. Real talent. Thanks for sharing! Sorry to hear that you're not selling paintings like you used to. That's a bummer. I'd buy one if I could afford it.

The artist and poster replied: Thanks for the comments! I want to inspire the next generation of art.

And to another comment, the artist has replied: Spent years teaching myself how to draw, doing minimum-wage jobs to pay the rent in the hopes of one day earning enough from my art to do that full-time. Got to enjoy living my dream for a couple of years, but now it looks like I'll have to get my janitor job back to pay the bills again. What a world we live in, eh? Automation – sold as making the world easier for everyone, really just making the rich richer and everyone else miserable and desperate.

His words make my stomach lurch. 'I wondered

whether we should weave their stories and these new ones into our videos to try and spread the word that automation isn't just affecting the arts any more, but every job sector.'

Zach nods. 'I saw your dad finally posted his news on his Photorah page this morning,' he says, his voice soft and understanding.

I take in a deep breath, having hoped to ignore the reality of my own family's situation. 'Funny thing is, none of his followers saw it due to the algorithm favouring AI content now. Social media's dead besides the bots. There isn't anything social about it any more. Dad announced his pain and artistic irrelevancy and there are no words of condolence, no uproar or sympathy. Just people watching from the sidelines, too afraid of acknowledging the problem in case it comes for them next.'

'Or too defeated to do anything about it,' Zach offers instead. 'That's how power works, right? You make people afraid. Condition them to believe it's better to just roll with what's happening than try and fight against it.'

'But we're not like that, Zach. I can't spend the rest of my life living like this. What's going to happen to the generations after us? To Evie, when she's our age? The world is screwed. We *have* to get our message out there. Our parents and grandparents might be willing to go along with this new normal, but we're not. Their time is over – our time depends on what we do right now.'

Zach nods, a steely expression on his face. 'Our videos aren't reaching who we need them to reach, right? Who even knows what the algorithm is any more on Tubeify. We need to draw attention to our channel. I wonder if there's anyone who would help.'

'TheHarperHerald?' I suggest. 'Or that news outlet that had to go incognito because people were spitting truths on there – damn, what's it called?'

'Vandalize. What if we shared our channel in sub-threads on there? What if we tagged outspoken influencers in our videos? I know it feels icky trying to capitalize off someone else's status, but we do need the reach, and no one can save the world on their own . . .'

'Anything is better than getting a measly fifty views on a video,' I say, checking the latest stats on my phone. 'Your parkour stunt has gone live, and it hasn't reached any viewers yet.'

He stares into the distance. 'Probably a good thing we have those masks. The only thing more embarrassing than putting yourself out there on the internet to be seen is not being seen by anyone at all.'

'All right. Let's research influencers actively speaking out against AI, then we need to bombard them with our stuff until they hopefully share it with their followers.'

I slam my hand into Zach's already open and waiting palm. We really are the dream team.

'We need to up our game too,' he says. 'Parkour, death falls, beans on toast – it's too tame. We need to showcase the perils of being human. We're not a choose-your-own-adventure character that can respawn after every pitfall; we're real people, facing the real possibility of injury and death to provide entertainment to the masses. I've already outlined my stunt for tomorrow. I'm nervous for it, but even if it fails, it'll be one hell of a watch, mate.'

CHAPTER 11

The next day, we gather around the pool the moment the sun has risen above the horizon to begin filming.

A warm hand wraps around my arm, and I turn to find Zach staring at me, dark circles around his eyes.

'You ready for this?' I ask, trying to keep my own nerves at bay.

He nods silently. 'Trust me. We're going to new heights.' He flicks the mask resting on top of my head. 'Come on, mouthpiece, we need you to spit some home truths and start riling people up.'

He gives me a playful noogie and saunters ahead. I laugh and pull the mask on to my face. It instantly crushes my nose, making breathing through it feel impossible. I take it off again and stare at it. How can a serious designer like Delirium Designs make products so uncomfortable for the wearer, yet tout how detailed her production is online? Weird.

At the poolside, everything is set up to film. There are two ring lights with Cheki's and Isobel's phones in the centre, cast into shadow by the luminescence of the stage lighting surrounding them. Zach whips off his T-shirt and attaches a waterproof camera to a body harness and straps it around his bare torso.

'I want every angle covered,' Isobel says, helping Zach secure his mask over his shaggy black hair. She stands on her tiptoes, reaching over his head as he attempts to smooth the hairs she's disturbing. Laughter escapes me, and then Zach flexes his pecs and Isobel laughs, rolling her eyes, and my own laughter catches in my throat. They look good together. All her mates say so too. I take a deep breath and shift my weight, peeling my eyes away before the sight tears my heart in two. She'd never cheat on me, and Zach's only doing what he normally does, but still envy washes over me.

'We want every video filmed in one take,' Isobel says, having finally wrestled the mask on to Zach's head. 'No redos, so every angle needs capturing. And no high-level editing afterwards. It'll give our channel the old Tubeify feel.'

Zach nods and mumbles something incomprehensible.

Isobel laughs and taps him three times on the shoulder as if to say, *Nice try*. 'See? That's why you're our mouthpiece,' she throws at me.

Despite not being able to see Zach's eyes through the mask, I know exactly what face he's pulling. Even though he himself called me the mouthpiece, he's bothered by my ability to speak while wearing the mask. Still, I'm certainly not going to take any spotlight away from him, especially not since he's about to carry out some dangerous trick with his muscles on display, and I'm going to spend lunchtime shovelling fast food in my mouth and dribbling grease down my chin.

'I'm just holding this other camera underwater next to him, yeah?' asks Cheki.

'Exactly,' Isobel says. 'Cover all angles. Right . . . we're ready. Masks back on, everyone. I'm stepping out of shot. Mikah, can you explain to the audience what Zach's going to do and how this proves his humanity, since no one can understand a word he says and all that?'

I nod sheepishly.

'Cameras recording? Nice! Everyone in position, action in three, two, one . . .'

Cheki stands by the poolside steps like a bodyguard, her arms folded in front of her, masked face tilted up as if she's looking down on the world and people below. The sight makes me laugh; I doubt she has even an ounce of malice in her. Zach shakes his arms and flexes his biceps, warming up for the challenge ahead. I freeze, ready to deliver my impromptu speech into the camera, but there's a problem. Which camera?

I glance at the five cameras currently rolling: Zach's bodycam, Cheki's handheld cam, the two phones within light rings and my own phone in-hand.

Just pick one, Isobel mouths to me, bulging her eyes. *That one!* She points to one of the ring lights that apparently captures all of us on a wide angle.

I move closer and shove my face into the centre of the shot. 'What you're about to witness is a stunt so dangerous that artificial intelligence could never replicate it. Zulu is going to undertake the Special Forces Ultimate Underwater Challenge. Recruits have been known to die during training due to the harshness of tasks like these. Death is something only the living can experience, and today Zulu is going to dance with death.'

I move aside, allowing the phone screen to once again capture the wide angle of the pool and give Zach his screentime as he prepares for his stunt. He slips off his shoes, stretches his neck, and throws a thumbs up to Cheki, who steps towards the pool with the handheld waterproof camera she borrowed from her dad's collection.

Beside the steps are two twenty-kilo ankle weights. I could barely lift them when Zach asked me to retrieve them from his bedroom, but he casually attaches them to his ankles like the weight is nothing. He struts to the stone steps and slowly descends into the crystal-clear water. Goosebumps immediately splatter his skin, and he can't hide the shiver rippling down his body. It might be the height of summer, but it's still England.

Cheki gets her camera ready by the water's edge, dangling it a few centimetres above on a pole long enough to reach the bottom of the pool.

Zach wades further into the water, until the top of his hair disappears beneath the surface. Then, he begins his laps, walking along the bottom of the pool, weighed down. Cheki follows along the edge.

The water distorts his position beneath the water, but his trail of air bubbles gives an indication of his general whereabouts. From above, the scene is pretty serene – boring, even. But below the rippling water, I know Zach is pushing himself to the limit.

My shoulders tense as the minutes tick on. He started strong but I can see he's slowing, the weights taking their toll. His legs must wobble as he drags them along the bottom, his lungs will be burning by now surely, and his throat muscles must be so tight as they will him to take a huge gulp of air.

That's enough, I think. *You've almost completed two laps. That's more than I could ever do, than most people could do.*

Isobel looks calm, but there's a faint crease between her brows. Cheki has come to a halt just over the halfway line of the pool, her camera still on Zach beneath the surface.

Instantly, I lunge forward, dropping to my knees at the poolside, trying to get a better glance at my best mate. He's standing there, not moving. At least, I don't think he is. The overhead rays of sunlight bouncing off the surface make the water mirror-like, and the ripples from his previous movements distort his body, giving the illusion of both movement and stagnation.

'He needs help,' I mutter, my body rocking on the pool edge, daring me to jump in as my mind warns me not to. He needs help but we're getting amazing footage.

But no. My best friend matters more. I slip my boots off and jump beneath the depths of the crystal water, causing a tornado of bubbles. I loose my breath slowly until my feet skim the bottom. My mask threatens to slip off my head from the pressure and I slam a hand against it, repositioning it as my eyes sting from the chlorine. Zach is like a statue, swaying gently forwards and backwards with the motion of the ripples around him. His hair waves around his mask, his head hangs, and his arms droop by his side. Through the small slits in his mask, I notice his eyes are closed, like he's snoozing.

I yank at the weights wrapped around his ankles, but I can't loosen the straps and my mask dislodges, blocking my vision. My chest contracts and fear rushes through me. I have to get to the surface. Now. Before I pass out too. I grab Zach underneath his left arm and begin to swim upwards, but the added weight around his ankles won't allow me to breach the surface. I yank him forward, walking along the bottom. Forward, upwards, it doesn't matter, so long as I get him out.

Despite his semi-conscious state, Zach's legs move with me. I urge him on as I try and suppress my own desperate need for oxygen. The water feels cold, and my legs are numb. Panic is taking over. But I drag myself on. *Right foot, left foot. Right foot, left foot.* I chant it over and over in my mind until my feet touch the steps.

Arms grab us from above, yanking Zach out of the water. When my head finally breaches the surface, I take such a deep breath that my lungs initially reject it, making me splutter and wretch. I lift my mask away from my face to let the water escape, trying to avoid the lenses of the static phone cameras.

'Is he breathing?' I manage through coughs, staring at

Zach's pale body.

I catch sight of Isobel. Her eyes are wide, face as pale as a creature that's never once seen the sun. She doesn't answer me. Instead, she begins chest compressions.

CHAPTER 12

It's gone four in the afternoon when the taxi pulls up outside the holiday cottage. Cheki and I sit quietly on the sofa, where we've remained since the ambulance drove Zach away, blue lights flashing, siren wailing.

Isobel climbs from the back seat of the taxi and meanders up the driveway, keeping her gaze low. Her fingers anxiously twist the ends of her brunette curls. I jump from my seat and make for the door, opening it wide to allow her entry. Her eyes are red and her skin pink and blotchy. I pull her in for a hug and she collapses into me.

'He's all right,' she mumbles into my chest. 'Like I said over text, they're keeping him in overnight for observations but he's fine. It's a blessing he's such a strong swimmer. I checked the footage, he was under there for a good five minutes.'

I suck in a deep breath, relief washing over me. 'He's insanely strong.' Then a wave of nausea floods my stomach at the thought of his brain being starved of oxygen for so long. He could have died. He nearly did!

Guiding Isobel to the sitting room, I push the thought from my mind. 'Did you manage to get through to his parents in the end?'

'Yeah, they'd just boarded a flight when I left,' Isobel says, dropping to the sofa. Cheki brings her a mug of camomile tea and she wraps her hands around it.

'I should probably let my parents know too,' I say almost to myself. 'They love Zach. Was he more alert when you left?'

A small chuckle escapes Isobel's lips. 'Alert? He was asking one of the nurses on a date. Although he was slurring his words and seemed tired, but he was cracking jokes, flirting, showing off his abs. Being Zach, really.'

I shake my head, but a massive grin spreads over my face. 'Love to hear it.'

'Did he say anything about the footage?' Cheki asks. 'I know it might seem a bit insensitive, given that he just almost died, but if we ditch it, doesn't that make his near-death experience pointless in a way?'

'Funnily enough,' Isobel says, swallowing her mouthful of tea, 'that's exactly what Zach said. He thinks the resuscitation and ambulance ride will make for great entertainment value and really proves the humanity we're trying to get at. In the editing process, he wants epic music and some comparison shots of artificial intelligence doing underwater stunts with ease. You know, to prove that it's not entertaining to watch if it comes easy. So much for the one-take wonders I envisioned, huh?'

'Are . . . are the iGENect robot influencers waterproof?'

Cheki asks, her eyebrow raised.

We all pause for a moment to think.

'Must be,' Isobel says. 'It rained inside the arena during *Island of Influencers*, right? And Kottage Kay coped with it. And she was their first ever prototype.'

'True. But is she waterproof or just like splashproof?' I ask. 'Like, is she swim-at-a-great-depth proof?'

'Good point. Maybe you guys can look it up and search for some footage while I begin editing?' Isobel takes one last sip of her tea before jumping to her feet and making for her bedroom.

I grab her wrist and move closer so that only she can hear. 'Are you all right?' I ask gently. 'It was a huge responsibility to go to the hospital with Zach.'

She flashes me a weak smile. 'Can I talk to you later?'

'Always,' I say. 'When you're ready.' I let her go and watch as she climbs the stairs.

'Haven't found any evidence of AI swimmers yet,' Cheki says, showing me the search of Tubeify on her phone. After a pause, she adds: 'Huh, this is interesting. Look at this recent upload.'

Among the many old Tubeify videos of real, human athlete swimmers taking part in competitions, there's an upload from TheHarperHerald, posted five hours ago. We haven't heard much from Harper or Belle Deveraux since they were booted out of the Global Influencer Awards.

The title of the video reads **ARTISTRY IS DEAD: CREATORS BECOME SLAVES TO AI.**

Cheki clicks the link and the video loads. Two people sit on a plush set, facing one another with a coffee table in between.

'Welcome to the channel,' the on-screen Harper says. 'You've been incredibly outspoken about the effect AI is having on the arts industry and today you've come in to tell my viewers what's happening on the publishing side.'

'Yeah, thanks for having me,' replies a second person, casually dressed in honey-mustard-yellow dungarees and black platformed boots. Her blonde hair sits in loose waves over her shoulders. Her face is stoic, but her eyes have that same defeated glint my dad's did when he'd just been let go by his agent.

I gesture for Cheki to turn the volume up on her phone as an information box pops up at the bottom of the screen reading: **TMT, author of the fantasy series** *Relics of Niskala*. I make a mental note to forward it to Dad later. See? It's not just book cover designers losing their jobs; it's the writers too.

The on-screen Harper stares into the camera as she delivers her next line: 'This interview will not be edited; it's just two people chatting about the current state of the entertainment industry. Some of the things discussed might be unsettling.' She turns her attention back to the author. 'There's been a dramatic increase in published books being written by artificial intelligence. What are your thoughts?'

The author laughs and shakes her head. 'It's killing the industry. There're publishing houses founded solely for the purpose of producing works fully created by AI. These super-bots are being fed work created by human hands, so that huge companies can churn out content at an impossible rate based off the hard work and ideas of real artists. Companies like the Tanaki Foundation and Sanka are stealing, plain and simple.'

'Did you ever consider that you might be one of the last human novelists to have their books on shelves?' Harper asks.

'Real artists are being pushed out of the industry by AI, but we will always write, even if creation of art becomes a rebellious act in our society. Humans need to create to feel alive.'

'And we all know that robots can't feel,' Harper agrees.

'Art is the product of a lived experience,' the author says, shrugging. 'How can AI write about a daring trek up a mountain if it hasn't felt the sensation of cold wind wrapping around exposed skin? Or paint a portrait of a forest if it hasn't heard the silence among the trees or smelt the carpet of moss covering trunks of long-dead yews? How can AI create a melody if it's never tasted the bitterness of unrequited love or held the rhythm of a broken heart? To create, one must live.'

'Only humans can do that,' I say at the exact same time as the on-screen author, tapping into her thought process.

'I just hope there's someone out there who can put a stop to this AI takeover before it's too late,' the author continues.

I swipe the Tubeify app closed on Cheki's phone as fury surges through my veins. 'Set the cameras up, I'm making a mukbang.'

'Right now?' Cheki asks.

'Right now,' I say. 'No editing. Just me eating live from start to finish – uploaded straight to Tubeify. We're the people to end this.'

I take the most random combination of foods from the cupboard: baked beans, cuppa-noodles, soup, crackers, a jar of gherkins, a four-pack of chocolate mousse and a bottle of hot sauce. I'm sure there are plenty of meals I could make, but something about that interview has sent me into a frenzy, like if I don't do something *right this second* the world might implode. Cheki watches me like I've gone insane. Maybe I have. I nuke the beans, soup and noodles in the microwave, then take everything into the sitting room and place it on the coffee table alongside a huge, empty, see-through bowl.

'That's such a weird meal,' Cheki says, setting her phone inside the ring light positioned directly in front of me.

I sit cross-legged on the floor with the food surrounding me and shove my Digital Demons mask on. 'Roll the camera,' I order.

As Cheki presses record and places herself out of shot, I begin:

'You're about to witness me eating the most rancid combination of food ever,' I say. Even I'm surprised by how confident I sound; that interview has me riled up.

'None of the products you see here have been created by or endorsed by AI influencers or brands. Let's see what happens to the human body when you combine all of this in one stomach at the speed of light.'

Without another word, I dive into the offerings, shovelling scalding beans, noodles and cold chocolate mousse into my mouth, swallowing it all down with a mouthful of hot sauce. I gag, but keep going, chomping down on the gherkins, slurping spoonfuls of cream of mushroom soup. I hate mushrooms.

Cheki hides behind her hands beyond the camera as I stuff my mouth until my cheeks stretch into the sides of my mask. My stomach gurgles and I reach for the bowl beside me.

CHAPTER
13

I raise my shaking hand above my head and just about manage to flash the weakest thumbs up known to man at the camera within the ring light. Then, I collapse behind the coffee table, groaning and clutching my stomach.

'Aaaaand CUT,' Cheki says, stopping the recording.

'Great,' I manage, yanking my mask off. Sweat drips down my brow and over my nose and another wave of nausea hits me.

'That was sick – no pun intended. Honestly, so gross and unnecessary. Definitely prime entertainment.'

I groan again.

'I'm not cleaning that up, though,' Cheki adds, gesturing her head towards the mess on the coffee table. Baked beans are mixed with spilt soup and one recently regurgitated gherkin lies, slimy, on the corner.

'Oh my god, what the hell happened?' Isobel's voice cuts through the sitting room. I didn't even hear her come downstairs. Her voice is half-jovial, half-concern.

'Content,' I stutter through dry heaves.

'A beautiful example of human limitations,' says

Cheki, a massive grin on her face. 'He managed to plough through the most horrendous mixture in just over five minutes. Commendable, actually. You wouldn't catch me mixing hot sauce and chocolate mousse.'

'Thought I was gonna spew at one point,' I say, a belch leaving my lips.

Isobel's face contorts in disgust, and she shakes her head at me. 'Well, this is exactly what we're trying to prove, right? AI can't eat or taste, so them trying to replicate this wouldn't be any fun at all. The entertainment value comes from your suffering, babe – sorry.' She gives a girlish giggle and a grin cracks over my face. 'Anyway, I've stitched together the foundations of Zach's underwater challenge. Still not sure we should post it, but I've just spoken to Zach on the phone and he's adamant it goes live by tomorrow.'

'Nice,' Cheki says. 'Glad he's OK, but what about the stunt he planned, considering he's injured? I'm happy to take it on, but if we want to cancel, we should probably call the zookeeper and—'

Isobel interjects: 'Should that still go ahead? Zach could have died today. We've already pushed the limits. We need to rein it in again.'

Cheki's face drops. 'But this is what Zach wants – he's already booked it.'

The familiar buzz of a phone pulls our attention. Isobel tuts and rummages in her jeans pocket for the device, bulging her eyes as she clocks the caller ID. She answers it and turns from us, heading back up the stairs.

'Hiya, yes, this is she,' she says as she wanders into the next room. 'Thanks for getting back to me. I'm actually calling on behalf of my clients, Digital Demons, a content house looking for a potential sponsor.'

I push myself to my feet, ignoring the disgusted noises and side-quips coming from Cheki, and whip my food-coated T-shirt over my head. It takes around thirty minutes and three thousand dry heaves to clear up the mess I've made. Eventually, though, I find myself climbing the stairs to Isobel's room, changed and somewhat presentable.

I knock gently on her door left ajar and push it open. She sits cross-legged on her bed, deeply entrenched in the editing of Zach's video on her laptop.

'Your eyes are red,' I say, closing the bedroom door behind me and taking a seat beside her. 'Did the sponsor say no?'

She laughs and wipes the tears away on the back of her hand. 'Yes, but that's not why I'm crying. I had a message from my brother saying Mum's not been coping since I left.'

My eyelids feel too heavy to keep open. 'I don't like it when you cry on your own.'

She closes the laptop and turns to face me. 'I've left a voice note with my dad, asking him to *please* go and help out with Evie.'

I roll my eyes. 'Fat chance of that. When was the last time you actually saw your dad?'

'Ages. That long ago I can't even remember.'

I move a strand of hair from her eyeline.

'God, I wish I had parents like yours,' she says. 'They've always been amazing to you and your brother. You can literally get away with anything. No worries, just free to be kids and discover who you are.'

'I think they'd love to have you as a daughter,' I say, shrugging. 'I reckon my mum secretly wanted us to be together since the day we met.' The memories make me laugh.

Isobel pushes the laptop away and lies down, resting her head on my lap. 'Do you think we'll still have time for each other once we start college?' she asks.

My heart twinges. 'Yeah, of course! I mean, I hope so. Why wouldn't we?' The reminder of college starting in just over a month's time makes my stomach drop. If we don't land a sponsor or start earning ad revenue from the channel soon, my dreams of reclaiming social media and saving the arts industry from bots will be over.

'I just worry that things might be harder once we've got different classes and timetables, you know? Like now, we get to spend all summer together and then it'll just change overnight.'

I find my fingers tangling in her long, chocolate curls, feeling the softness of each strand as it slips through my grasp. 'It won't be a problem if we don't make it a problem. As soon as we get our new timetables I can plan out moments to cross your path in the corridors, and schedule in bathroom breaks to blow you a kiss through the window of your classroom.'

She giggles and pink spreads across her cheeks. 'You'll get in trouble.'

I shrug. 'Don't care. Besides, who knows whether I'll go to college anyway. If the channel blows up, maybe I won't need to.'

She furrows her brow and lifts her head off my lap, pushing herself into a sitting position, her eyes locking on mine. 'What do you mean you might not go to college? I thought you were excited about your performing arts course?'

I take a long breath and pull my eyes away from her stare. 'I was – but after Dad lost his job and his agent let him go, I dunno, the arts industry just doesn't feel safe any more. At least with the channel, I feel like I'm doing something to combat the issue. If I stop this and take that course, I'll just be another wannabe performer who's hoping they "make it" before acting becomes a redundant profession. I can't explain it, Iz, but Digital Demons feels more important to me now. I have a mission, a reason for living. I don't just want to be an actor or a creator, I want to be known as the guy who saved the arts for everyone else.'

Her eyes soften as she fails to find the right words to comfort me.

Ding.

Both of our heads snap to the phones in our pockets instinctively. That's a Tubeify notification. Isobel sits up and retrieves her phone as I reach for mine.

'A new subscriber to the Digital Demons channel!' Isobel squeals.

Ding. Ding.

'Another like!'

'Which video is it?'

'Our explainer video,' I say in disbelief, eyes wide as I stare at the screen.

Isobel's eyes dart over her phone. 'Tubeify's put it on their homepage! It's driving traffic to the channel and the other videos too. How odd. Why now?'

'Hey! Have you guys checked out Tubeify?' Cheki yells from downstairs.

'I need to get this video of Zach's finished,' Isobel says, excitement flooding through her words. 'And if you're up for it, another mukbang tonight would be great! I don't know what's happening, but I reckon we have to capitalize on it *fast*.'

My stomach knots at the thought of more food. 'Yeah, OK,' I say, trying to sound enthusiastic about it. 'But I'm just doing a regular meal this time. Nice food. I'll order takeout.'

'Good shout, but don't forget that we need to keep an eye on our finances. We can't keep asking our parents for pizza money.'

The reminder of our dwindling pennies hits me right in the chest and I grimace at the thought of having to ask my parents for more holiday spend. Without another word or glance, Isobel throws herself into the video editing and I head downstairs to join Cheki, who's watching as the notifications roll in.

'Look how many people are finding us,' she says,

laughing. 'The explainer video is going crazy, and have a read of some of the comments on your last mukbang.'

I clock the viewer count is nearing five thousand. My eyes widen in shock. No way! I read the rapidly increasing stream of commentary by real, human people. Strangers. From all over the world. Watching me eat a repulsive concoction of food. I grimace at the thought.

> Nahhh, that was some nasty British food, says the username Mel_evalent.

> Never thought I'd see the day when a guy chowing down on beans and gherkins would entertain me, but here we are, comments GabriellaEllaElla.

> Squiddy has said: Interesting concept. Can't explain why, but the masks are doing something for me ...

The comments go on and on, some humorous, some genuinely curious, and others as foul as the video itself.

> Dunno what's happening, but I'm here for it.

> Is this the resurgence of Tubeify?!!?!

> Imagine if aliens came down and this video was all that remained of humanity lol

> Can't believe we're calling this 'entertainment', fellas. If I wanted to watch someone throw up a dodgy meal, I'd just go into town on a Friday night.

> Wtf is with the goofy-ass mask, my man?

A sudden wave of anxiety and euphoria courses through my veins. It's happening, it's actually happening! Our channel is taking off. How? I move in closer, mouthing over the words these strangers have written to me and about me.

'What about the explainer video?' I ask.

Cheki loads the other video. She scrolls to the comment section and my eyes widen at the most-liked comment sitting at the very top of the long thread of user engagement.

> This is what the internet needs! Wishing you all the luck in the world, guys. Hit me up if you need any guidance or assistance, I'd love to get involved.
> Thanks for tagging me. I'm sharing this right now! The sub-threads on Vandalize will eat this right up (lol)

The comment has been left by none other than TheHarperHerald herself. My fingertips tingle, and my chest bursts with pride. She knows who we are.

'That explains the sudden wave of views,' Cheki says, scrolling further into the comments. 'We can't stop now; we have to ride the wave while the tide's on our side.'

'I'm ordering takeout right now,' I say, whipping my phone from my pocket. 'I can easily get another mukbang filmed and uploaded tonight.'

A devilish smirk creeps over Cheki's face as she turns her head towards me. 'Don't forget what the zookeeper is bringing,' she says.

CHAPTER 14

A week passes by in a frenzy of mukbang content and planning. After a breakfast of waffles, streaky bacon and maple syrup, we're standing in the garden again, all masked up and ready to film.

'I think someone shared Zach's pool video last night, because there's been a wave of engagement,' Isobel says beside me, as she once again checks the angles of the phones set to record. She sucks in a deep breath and steadies herself. 'I'm happy but also ... it's so wrong that we're getting all these views on something that harmed him.'

'Don't,' I say. 'I can't stop thinking about him, lifeless in the pool. But I spoke to him last night and he said that's the point of the whole channel. And people seem to like the rebellious idea of us, that we're being the Digital Demons we promised to be.'

'I suppose,' she says, but her face gives away her trepidation. 'There were so many nicer comments on your latest mukbang too. Seems people really enjoy just watching people eat and chat.'

During my mukbang of chilli nachos and a burrito as large as my forearm, I told the audience the story about my dad and how he lost his designer job to AI. Must have hit a nerve with some people. Just from reading the comments, it's obvious that loads of others have been affected by it too. I spent all night thinking about it, taking on the pain of strangers.

'I think it's the combination of daredevil tricks and more personal content that keeps people coming back for more,' Isobel says. 'Sooo many people would love to be able to eat what you ate, and have your iron stomach. It's like they're living through you. Plus, your stories are real-life drama playing out before their eyes.'

'I still can't believe we're livestreaming this,' I say, glancing at the cameras ready to roll.

Isobel shrugs. 'Definitely wasn't my idea, but it's how Zach pictured it. Plus, lives get pushed by the algorithm, so it is a good strategy to get more viewers and subs . . . Ready when you are, Foxtrot.'

Cheki stands on the sandy-coloured paving slabs beside the pool Zach almost drowned in. She shakes her arms and jumps on the spot, then cracks her neck on both sides, readying herself for the task she's about to undertake.

I steady my own nerves. Rather her than me. God knows what went through Zach's head when he thought this up.

Still, as the reptile keeper steps into shot with his mystery box, I can't help wondering whether we're taking this proving-how-much-better-it-is-to-watch-humans-than-AI thing to the extreme. Maybe we've started too strong? We're only two weeks into the channel. If this is our baseline, how much more intense and thrilling will we have to make each video to keep our steadily growing audience entertained and watching? We're getting too rebellious, too quickly. We have three weeks left of the summer holidays before college begins, so we've been trying to record a bank of videos as well as keep to the upload schedule – it's Isobel's way of reassuring me that the channel will still go on, even if we don't manage to make it our full-time work before summer is over.

Now, however, I'm wondering whether some of these stunts are a good idea at all. Eating on camera until you feel physically sick is one thing, but pushing the boundaries of life and death is another thing altogether. My stomach feels queasy again, and not just from the mountains of burgers and cheesy chips I ate last night.

'Echo,' Isobel calls. 'We're waiting on you.'

I snap out of my stupor. She holds her thumb up, telling me that we're rolling and live.

There's no telling how many people will tune into the livestream, but I act like there's an audience anyway. I jump in front of the camera, adopting the confident strut and deeper voice that the anonymity of the mask has gifted me.

'Folks, what you're about to see is a highly dangerous stunt that should *not* be repeated at home, without the careful supervision of a professional,' I say, gesturing behind me to the specialist zookeeper we hired for the day, and a waiting Cheki who's still psyching herself up. 'There is no robot or computer-generated image that can fully replicate what Foxtrot is about to experience – the pain, the imminent threat, the sheer panic as her fate draws closer.'

I pause for a few seconds, allowing the weight of my words to land with whatever live audience we have. Then, I raise one arm in the air and ask: 'Are you ready, Foxtrot?'

Cheki's muffled reply follows.

I lower my arm as if to say *Action*, and then move out of the camera's view.

The zookeeper lifts the lid of his small wooden box and gently tips it on to one side. For a brief moment, nothing happens. Then, after a small tap on the box from the zookeeper's shoe, a loud *hiss* pierces my ears. The sound is somewhere between sizzling oil in a hot frying pan and air escaping through a pinhole. Inside the box, a shadow moves.

'She's been riled up all day,' the zookeeper says, clearly trying to sound as scary and dramatic as possible. I appreciate his effort. 'A two-hour drive and the last part over bumpy country roads. Makes for a nasty temper.' He gently taps the box again with his foot and a second *hiss* spools out. This time, the shadow creeps into the sunlight.

A small black snake with a distinctive red hue on its belly slithers from the box, flashing its forked tongue as it tastes the air beyond.

'The red-bellied black snake,' says the zookeeper in his

Halloween-horror-house voice. 'Indigenous to Australia, and when milked, yields an average of thirty-seven milligrams of venom.'

Cheki straightens up and eyes the snake slowly slithering in her direction, hissing and flicking its tongue.

'How do you know if it's going to attack?' I ask, stepping into shot again.

'Oh!' says the zookeeper. 'You see how it's raising its head and flattening its neck? That's one unhappy snake, let me tell you.'

'And how does the human body react to the venom if it bites?'

Cheki tentatively steps forward, her arm outstretched as if to pet the snake. I can't help but turn away. It'd feel different if Zach were here doing this; clearly he's not shy of danger, but seeing Cheki shaking with fear crushes me with guilt.

'Well, the initial bite can cause searing pain,' the zookeeper explains. 'Followed by immediate swelling of the local area. Then the system goes into overdrive, and tries to expel the venom in whatever way it can: vomiting, diarrhoea, sweating. There'll be some abdominal pain, and some people have even lost their sense of smell!'

At this, Cheki snaps her head towards the zookeeper. Despite her mask, I can picture her face underneath: disbelief, terror, shock.

Isobel shifts her weight behind one of the cameras, and she's furiously biting her nails while staring at the snake still approaching her friend.

'Doing it for the views,' Cheki mutters behind her mask as she once again continues her tentative approach towards the seething reptile. Her outstretched hand is shaking. She stops a metre away, stretching as far as she can, holding a single finger out.

The snake doesn't react.

I'm relieved, in all honesty. I quickly check the livestream viewer count on the phone in my hands. The sight almost makes my knees buckle. We've reached nearly five hundred people already.

Cheki takes tiny steps closer; the red belly hisses, longer and louder than before, raising itself higher, flattening its neck so that it gives an almost cobra-like appearance. Sweat drips on to the ground from beneath Cheki's mask. She takes one more step and the snake lunges.

It happens quicker than a blink. The red belly hangs from Cheki's middle finger, injecting venom as she jumps and screams in agony. The zookeeper rushes forward, using a snake hook to stabilize the reptile before placing his hand around the reptile's jaws until it releases.

As the snake is returned safely into its box, Cheki falls to her knees, clutching her right hand as if it might fall off at any moment.

With the scene secure and snake-free, I rush forward with my camera, shoving it right up close to Cheki's bright red finger. Blood cascades on to her hand and drips on to the paving slabs like a tap that hasn't been turned off properly.

Cheki mumbles and groans something beneath her mask, desperately squeezing her whole body as if to dispel the pain in her finger.

The zookeeper, as chilled as ever, saunters over. He slowly dons blue latex hygiene gloves and produces a small vial of antivenom and a capped needle. 'This won't be pleasant, but it'll hurt a lot less than that bite.' With a chuckle, he moves towards Cheki, and I help roll up her sleeve and present her arm for injection.

I snap my eyes shut, blocking out the act itself. I've never been good with needles and my stomach is already turning. Luckily, as I have my head pointed to the ground and a mask obscuring most of my face, I'm pretty sure that Isobel's camera won't pick up on my wimpyness.

Cheki sucks in a sharp breath as the needle sinks into her flesh and I squeeze her shoulder tighter. God, this is my fault. Mine and Zach's. We thought this whole thing up, and now Cheki's hurt, when all she wanted was to be involved.

'How's that?' the zookeeper asks. 'Antivenom is now coursing through your veins. You might feel rough for a few days, though.'

Cheki weakly raises her uninjured arm and gives a meek and shaky thumbs up.

'Nice one, Foxtrot!' I say, trying to keep my voice jovial. There are no redos on livestream so it's better to keep going. 'We'll keep filming throughout the coming days,' I say to the camera, 'so that you guys can keep up with her recovery. That was a pretty nasty bite! Took it like a champ.'

She groans through her clenched teeth as she continues to apply pressure to the wound on her finger.

'Let's get you inside and on the sofa so you can try and nap some of this off,' I say, an awkward laugh escaping my lips.

Isobel gestures for us to stop the livestream. Then, when we're sure all cameras are off, I help Cheki back inside the holiday cottage as Isobel chats with the zookeeper about wound management and the likelihood of the antivenom not working.

As I drag a sobbing Cheki into the sitting room, a familiar face greets us.

Zach is sprawled on the sofa, sucking on a lollipop, looking as fresh and dapper as he usually does in his black trousers, black shirt and silver bling. 'Aw, no way, you guys really did my snake-bite challenge?' he says, his eyebrows rising in surprise. 'By the state of you, I'd say you haven't seen the latest breaking news.'

CHAPTER 15

My legs turn to jelly at Zach's words. What could it possibly be now? Robots are taking over the world? Tubeify has officially shut down and all our Digital Demons material is gone for good?

Zach whips his phone from his pocket. I catch my reflection in the black screen and wince at the sight of a pimple threatening to erupt on my upper lip. Despite the intensive routine Isobel has me following, my skin just seems to want to rebel.

Zach pulls up iGENect – the social media platform that overtook Tubeify last year after Sgt Hound's *Island of Influencers* show. 'Read their current notice,' he says, shoving the phone under our noses.

> iGENect, in collaboration with the Tanaki Foundation: We are delighted to share our wonderful news with you all! Due to the successful integration of our iGENect humanoids into the world of social media, we have developed a new prototype, nExGEN. nExGEN is designed to become an integral part of

society, bearing the weight of responsibility. Where human error can cost lives and human biases can result in rigged outcomes and inequality, nExGEN is programmed to take neutral ground, making decisions based solely on data.

From the courtroom to the ER department, and the control rooms to Parliament, nExGEN will bring the reassurance to society that everyone needs.

Decisions based on fact, not speculation.

Decisions based on data analysis, not emotion.

nExGEN is designed to be the answer to our mortal limitations.

DOWNLOADING SOON.

'They can't be serious,' I spit. 'They're completely taking over! In Parliament? They're gonna put a robot in charge of us or something?'

'Insanity,' Cheki mutters.

'We said this would happen, didn't we?' Zach says, his voice low. 'Robots making emergency medical decisions based on numbers and chance of survival, no empathy involved. People sentenced to lengthy jail time or let off free based on physical evidence alone, never once factoring in plausibility or *what ifs*. It's so easy to fake a video these days; can AI tell if something is a deepfake or will it assume it's real?'

'We're doomed as a species,' Cheki groans, still clutching her swollen, shiny finger.

'That's not all,' Zach says. He takes his phone back

and begins searching, scrolling and typing. 'Here.' He shoves the phone beneath our faces again. 'The bots have started copying us the same way we were copying them.'

He's loaded the Extreme Elites channel. The latest upload is from AnnaConda, Khristoff and Noruwai, titled: **Eating a Month's Worth of Food in One Sitting!**

It's so absurd that I can't help but laugh. 'Fake,' I say.

Zach clicks on the video. Currently, it sits at twenty thousand views, and it was only uploaded a few hours ago. That's double the views my latest mukbang has garnered.

AnnaConda beams her fake bright-white smile into the camera. She wears a soft pink bow in her straight black hair, and she waves delicately into the camera.

'*Zǎoshang hǎo, péngyǒumen!*' she says sweetly. 'Good morning, good morning, my friends. I hope you are ready for breakfast with me!'

As if on cue, Khristoff and Noruwai join her, bringing in dishes of porridge, rice with vegetables and boiled eggs, plates brimming with pyramids of fried dough, bowls of fruits in various shades of the rainbow, omelettes and fried bread with minced pork. I hate that my mouth waters at the sight of it.

Cheki collapses on the sofa, sweat dripping from her hairline. 'Look how it's all laid out,' she mumbles. 'You can see every single dish. You need to get some of those display stands for your mukbangs, Mikah.'

'You look awful,' I say. 'Maybe you should go to the hospital?'

She ignores me.

The humanoid AnnaConda scoops a large spoonful of porridge from the bowl and slowly drips it back down, eyes wide in anticipation.

Noruwai tears the fried bread into smaller chunks, which she dips in various sauces dotted around the table. 'Mmm,' she says, holding it up to her nose to give the impression of sniffing it.

Khristoff brings a piece of kiwi to his mouth and the camera cuts to the food on the table before returning to his face once the food has gone. 'Sooo good! Soo tasty!'

I roll my eyes. 'Funny how the camera zooms in on the food after they place something in their mouths, huh? The creators aren't even hiding the fact that they can't eat.'

Zach stares into the screen. 'Like, you literally never see them chew the food or swallow and I've watched a couple of these. Even though *I know* it's not real, *I know* they're just robots, it's still entertaining and, honestly, my mind wants me to believe it's real. The production is just too good.'

'But it's fake,' I say. 'Her insides are just silicone and hardware. No stomach, no throat or swallowing mechanism, probably not even a tongue. These Extreme Elites might have better production values, but they're just walking, talking, money-making voids made to look like people. They have no heart.'

'Maybe your mukbangs are the only thing that's safe from the AI takeover,' Cheki jokes.

Zach clicks another video, this time of the Extreme Elites skiing. The effects are seamless. Khristoff and Noruwai explain their skiing stunt to the camera. They have rosy cheeks and the tips of their noses are pink as if they have blood underneath their skin. AnnaConda stands in the centre, grinning at the camera, her glossy eyes empty. Their hair blows in the breeze and a light dusting of snow drifts along the ground behind them in sync. There's muffled chatter in the background, as if the influencers are genuinely at a busy ski resort. It's flawless. So hard to distinguish from reality.

'We can't do this on our own,' a deflated Cheki says. 'We need help. Someone, somehow.'

I nibble the inside of my cheek, mulling it over. 'I think I know who would be willing to help.'

'Who?' she asks.

The corner of my lip twitches into a smile. 'Who else is dead set against AI taking over the internet? Who else has been trying to expose iGENect and the Tanaki Foundation for the past year? Who just introduced our channel to the audience we've been failing to grab the attention of? Harper Taylor, of course.'

I pull out my phone and, from the Digital Demons channel, compose a quick private message to TheHarperHerald.

Hi! Echo here from DD,
We appreciate your comment on our introduction video (thanks so much for sharing, it really helped us

gain traction!) and we're hoping to take you up on the offer of assistance.
Cheers, E

I click send, feeling my heart thudding in my chest. Amazingly, the reply is instant.

Hey, Echo (and DD gang),
Happy to help.
Fancy coming to Manchester?
H x

CHAPTER 16

Isobel and I hop off the train, instantly getting sucked into the throng of commuters spilling out on to platform five at Manchester Piccadilly. 'Did Zach say anything to you before we left?' Isobel asks.

I shake my head, feeling another rush of guilt as I guide us off the platform. 'Hasn't said a word since he stormed off. I didn't realize he'd take being left behind so badly. I just don't think it's good for him to do this trip when he's only just got out of hospital. Plus, I'm the mouthpiece of the group and you're the production manager. It makes sense for us to meet Harper. Zach wouldn't be able to contribute with his mask on anyway.'

'True. I still feel bad, though. He looked gutted when I suggested it should just be you and me doing this. You definitely have your mask, don't you?' I grab her hand and lead her through the station to the exit. The scent of fried chicken and greasy chips hits my nostrils and makes my mouth water.

'Definitely. I checked once before leaving and once on the train. Although I can't say I'm eager to put it back on;

it's starting to get uncomfortable.' My head jolts from one fast-food kiosk to the next. 'I reckon I can get a mukbang in before we have to catch the last train back, you know.'

Isobel ignores me and instead points to something ahead of us.

My eyes follow her long, slender finger towards a gigantic billboard and I let out a groan at the sight. AnnaConda's giant face stares back at me. Her shimmering grin and dazzling eyes make for the perfect advertisement for nExGEN, the latest humanoid by the Tanaki Foundation. Where once we were inundated with magic pills that helped us lose weight, or protein powder to bulk us up, now we're having our own replacements forced down our throats. I shake my head and we walk on.

Having not eaten since early breakfast at five this morning, we grab a quick burger from a van parked in the middle of Piccadilly Gardens. I go for a triple cheeseburger with cheddar and Monterey Jack oozing from the sides, coleslaw, tomatoes and caramelized onions. Isobel opts for a buttermilk chicken with spicy mayo, lettuce and pickles.

'I can't believe how much two burgers cost,' she mutters as she squirts extra mayo on her chicken from the condiments table by the van.

The van man pops his head through the window and frowns at her. 'Huh, you think this is bad? Imagine how much it costs to get meat straight from the farmers these days.'

I frown and pull the burger away from my lips, staring at the meat. 'What? Where is it from, then?'

The burger man points his spatula over my head, at the billboard with AnnaConda's face on it.

'Nutrox. Tanaki Food Incorporations. Best wholesale prices around these days. Still, we have to mark everything up to make a living from it ourselves.'

I grimace and put the burger on the ledge under the chef's window. 'You should have said your business supports the company behind the biggest usage of artificial intelligence. I wouldn't have bought from here. I want to support real people.'

He laughs. 'I am real, kid. It is what it is. All food's being grown in labs. Farmers are pretty much done for. At least I can still do what I love. Just have to tailor it is all.'

'If we all stop supporting this madness by taking a stand, then maybe the farmers wouldn't have been made redundant.'

The burger man rolls his eyes and heads back to his grill, muttering under his breath about entitled kids wanting life handed to them on a plate.

I leave my burger and gesture for Isobel to do the same. Reluctantly (and after one last bite) she does.

'I like how confident you're getting with this,' Isobel says, wiping her hands on a napkin, her cheeks flushing pink. 'It's . . . hot.'

With my own cheeks burning, we make our way to the tram stop in St Ann's Square and jump aboard the tram heading for a town on the outskirts of the city. After a brief stroll through Oldham town centre, we make it to a red-brick building with moss growing over the walls and windows. It's completely unassuming and unless you knew who owned it, you'd think it was abandoned.

I ring the bell and we wait.

'Maybe put your mask on?' Isobel whispers as footsteps approach from the other side of the door.

Too late. The door swings open and a boy greets us. He can't be much older than us, sixteen at best. He's small in stature, sports thick-rimmed glasses and has cropped black hair, a brown complexion, wide saucer-like eyes and a grin that takes up most of his lower face. He beckons us inside.

The interior of the building is the complete opposite to its exterior: modern and recently refurbished. We walk through a kitchen filled with coffee machines, multiple fridges, tables and sofas. Another room hosts a cushty-looking boardroom, and there's a giant interactive screen on one wall. Newspaper clippings and certificates line the stairway walls. 'This place is gorgeous,' I say.

'Cheers,' says a disembodied voice. I look up the staircase and spot a girl leaning against a door frame down the hall, her arms folded across her chest, a small smile etched on her face.

'Harper,' I stutter, suddenly nervous. 'I-I'm Mikah – or Echo – this is Isobel, our manager, editor, producer. I can't believe I'm meeting you. H-How did you manage to afford this place?'

I stop dead. That's an awful thing to ask; no one likes

talking about money.

Harper laughs. 'Made a decent amount straight after *Island of Influencers* ended. Brands, sponsors, even Tubeify revenue came rolling in thick and fast. Bought this place then. It only took around six months before the tide turned and the money pit went dry, though. I still make some money online, but mostly I exist off donations from fans. Times are tough for creators.'

We follow her to a large and spacious room, with plenty of light flooding through the windows. This is where she films all her interviews. I recognize it from her Tubeify channel.

Harper thanks the boy and asks him to bring some water for us and a peppermint tea for Isobel.

'It must be so satisfying to know how far you've come since *Island of Influencers*,' Isobel says. She's checking out the camera equipment, in awe of the gadgets and sound desk.

'It . . . everything I ever wanted,' Harper admits. 'But it came at a cost, right? My likeness has now been used to make countless humanoids. Have you heard the latest about one of the nExGEN prototypes? It malfunctioned during a meet-and-greet with fans in Seattle. Apparently, it shook a guy's hand and wouldn't let go, ended up squeezing so hard it broke every one of his fingers.'

'Holy hell,' I say. 'That's massive, why hasn't it been on the news?'

'If Tanaki has enough money to build a humanoid, he has enough for a PR team to hide most of his pitfalls.

Shame I'm such a nuisance about getting the truth out there, otherwise no one would've known at all,' Harper smirks.

'And Belle?' Isobel asks. 'How's she doing? She hasn't posted a video on her channel since last Christmas.'

'She's good,' Harper insists. 'She's working for me now – her choice! She and my best mate Cady are currently on a job in Copenhagen. Starlet Saviour – you know, the "guru" who claimed she was from another planet? – well, apparently, she's been preaching in the streets about how the aliens from Gyru told her about the AI takeover. They've gone to get the scoop. Should be an interesting story, if they can get her to agree to an interview.'

Admiration transcends my body. She's doing all the work and leading the fight. And now, *the* Harper Taylor is about to interview me, helping me build the Digital Demons channel, getting me insider information about my biggest enemy: Extreme Elites.

'So, you guys ready?' Harper asks. 'I got my camera guy to leave early so that there was less risk of your identity being revealed. I really like the anonymous idea; it's got people talking. You don't need to worry about my personal assistant. He's cool.'

Isobel hands me my mask as Harper leads me to the set. It's simple – just three comfy armchairs and a coffee table with some fake flowers. Two chairs for the guests are situated on one side of the coffee table, and the interviewer's chair is situated on the other.

The personal assistant returns with a jug of water and

some glasses, followed by a steaming cup of peppermint tea. 'Your other guest is here,' he says quietly, gesturing his head towards the stairs.

Harper gestures for me to put my mask on. 'Since we don't have any crew, I'm just going to have to roll one camera and stick to a wide angle, I guess.'

'I can do it,' Isobel says. 'We did a filming course in school as part of our drama studies, modules on editing, directing, marketing – you name it. I love all this stuff.'

'Noice.' Harper grins at her. 'It's all yours, then.'

As Isobel dives into the technical aspects of our interview, Harper and I sit patiently on set, listening to the approaching footsteps beyond the door. My heart races. I can literally feel the blood rushing to my head and it's making me want to pass out. Suddenly, it feels too hot in the room. Isobel flicks on the stage lighting, making my sweaty palms ten times worse.

The door opens and a man enters. He's bald and surely no taller than my elbow, but he's stocky and I definitely wouldn't pick a fight with him.

'This, uh . . . this will be anonymous, won't it?' the man asks sheepishly. 'You'll blur my face out and put a filter over my voice or something?'

Harper nods. 'As I explained in my emails, we'll do everything we can to protect your identity. We're supergrateful that you've agreed to do this.'

The man sits beside me, nervously fiddling with his jacket and jeans as Isobel comes and fits us all with mics on our collars. 'Nice mask,' he says to me. 'Probably should have got one of those. You're the guy from that channel trying to prove humans are better entertainers than robots, right?'

'Right,' I say. 'You can call me Echo.' I hold my hand out for him to shake and he does.

'I'd rather remain nameless, if that's all right,' he replies.

'Ready when you are,' Isobel calls from behind one of the cameras – more professional and higher tech than the phones we're using to film Digital Demons' videos.

'Cameras rolling. Action in three, two, one …'

Harper turns her body to face the central camera and begins speaking to her future audience. 'Hi, guys, welcome back to TheHarperHerald. Today's interview is a special one. I'm joined by two guests. One you might recognize from the recently established Digital Demons channel. Echo is here to tell us about his team and their work.

'My second guest wishes to remain anonymous, and we have obscured his face and distorted his voice to ensure his identity isn't revealed. For the purpose of this video, this man will be named John. That's not his real name.' She turns towards us, takes in a deep breath, and speaks again. 'John, you've worked for iGENect for the past two years. You were there during the now infamous *Island of Influencers* challenge, and you still work there now during the – what I can only describe as terrifying – peak of artificial intelligence on social media. Tell us, what's behind this AI takeover?'

CHAPTER 17

John leans forward and takes a deep breath before answering: 'Money. It's all a gigantic money-making scheme. The "talents" as we call them – them being the artificial celebrities you see on screen, I mean – don't require payments. You can programme or create them to do whatever you want, however many times you want, and the fee to that talent stays the same. Zero.'

'Money. Who is surprised?' says Harper.

John nods. 'The big businesses paying out to influencers for product promotion don't want to spend that money any more; they want to keep it for themselves.'

'How are these big businesses able to get away with that?' Harper asks.

'iGENect owns hundreds of these talents, and then other companies pay iGENect to use one of these talents to promote their product.'

'So, the big businesses are keeping the money flowing between them and nothing is filtering down to anyone else?'

'They've stolen art and profit from it between them.

That's how they're doing it. And with money comes power. No one can call them out on it or sue them. And this new project – nExGEN – they say it's for the advancement of humanity. They say automation will replace manual labour, which will solve complex tasks more efficiently than humans can.'

'But AI is being rolled out in every industry,' Harper interjects. 'People like Tanaki say that humanoids in vital societal roles will give humans more time to enjoy life, right? All I've seen is his AI taking over the one thing that humans value above all else – art.'

John snorts. 'It's hard to know where to stop with technological advancement. Having a machine scan a human body and give a thorough diagnosis is fantastic. But having these bots write and produce songs about love and life when they can't even feel... it isn't right. I think we're looking at an army of AnnaCondas in the coming years. One perfect mould fits all requirements.'

His jaw tenses, but I know the audience watching the release of this won't see it due to the censoring of his face. It's a shame. Emotion is what makes us human. Instinctively, I reach for my mask.

Isobel shakes her head from behind the camera, bulging her eyes at me, as if I were about to face-reveal right here, right now.

John clears his throat. 'We've literally created our own replacements, our own irrelevance, and yet we're all still having to pretend that AI is here to help us as a species.'

I lean forward, inserting myself into this conversation

too. 'It's getting so much harder to tell a real person from AI. But these robots can't do basic human things, like eat or sleep, breathe, or *feel*. There are still tiny nuances that make it possible to detect a real human from a computer-generated human or even a humanoid, and that gives me hope.'

John laughs. 'I like your optimism, Echo. Thing is, when it comes to money and status and power, the people at the top of the hierarchy will do whatever it takes to stay up there. You won't win. If ever you find a bug in their system, they'll patch it.'

'Maybe,' I say. 'But that mukbang AnnaConda did – the one where the camera cuts every time she goes to take a bite of food – that's a bug they can't fix. Because her form physically won't allow her to take on food.'

John flashes me a weak smile and continues, 'I think what you and your mates are doing, Echo, is admirable. But I'm urging you to be careful. There's big, big money in the AI sector, and there are powerful people who won't be happy about you challenging them and their goals for their global future.'

My heart drops into my stomach. What does he know that he isn't willing to share?

'So,' Harper says, wrapping up John's segment of the interview, 'in the near future, robots could be making robots and AI will have the ability to program AI ... It's like we're becoming entangled with machines.'

My whole body feels as if it's become trapped in a tar pit, the ground below trying to drag me under. Luckily, the mask is hiding the terror etched on to my face.

Harper stands and shakes John's hand before her personal assistant beckons him off set. After a brief moment where John is escorted out of the building and the second chair is removed, Harper returns.

She goes straight back into our interview. 'Echo, tell us a bit more about Digital Demons and what you guys are aiming to achieve with your Tubeify channel.'

I go into a long spiel about wanting to restore social media to its glory days, about my dad losing his job and why this propelled me to take action, and tell her why I think AI influencers are incredibly dangerous for society and people's self-perception.

'And tell me, how're you finding your new status as the heart-throb of the internet?' she asks me.

'Huh?' The words tumble out of my mouth before I have a chance to think about what she's said. What does she mean *heart-throb*? Me? Mikah? The lanky teenager who shovels gross amounts of food into his mouth on camera? I can't help laughing. 'I-I think you've got the wrong person.'

Harper flashes a knowing smile and shakes her head. 'Don't you read the comments underneath your own videos? Have you not seen the hundreds of posts on Vandalize about Digital Demons?'

My chest tightens and I tug at the collar of my shirt. 'I've been trying to stay away from Vandalize,' I admit. Of course we keep a careful watch on the sub-thread recently created about Digital Demons, but half the fun is watching people talk about us as if we're not aware.

She raises her eyebrow, and flashes me a look that says she's not buying it. 'Well, I've read them – all the sub-threads dedicated to theorizing your identities, sharing your stuff, making fan art. Since you're the frontman of the group, seems only fair that you're getting most of the attention. The fans love you.'

I can feel my jaw dropping but there's nothing I can do to stop it. I expect Isobel to be laughing, hoping she's finding this as ludicrous as I am, but she's playing with her hair like she always does when anxiety takes hold.

CHAPTER 18

For the next ten minutes, Harper insists on showing me various threads on Vandalize to prove just how much the Digital Demons' anonymity has caused a stir online.

'But that isn't the point of the masks,' I say sheepishly. 'We're not trying to be cool and mysterious; we want people to be able to see themselves in us and be able to project themselves on to us. The masks are simply a blank canvas. We're nobodies and yet everybody at the same time.'

'Tell me about the mask, Echo. It's beautiful. Where did you get it?'

This question throws me off completely and I raise my hand to it, feeling every groove and indent. 'Our producer got them made. I believe this is a Delirum Designs make. You should check her out on Photorah – a real talented artist. Give her some love and let's all prove that AI could never create something like this.' I tug at my mask, trying to pretend it isn't painfully uncomfortable and poorly fitted. I flash Isobel a smile, but something about her doesn't sit right.

Her lips form a thin line and she's staring at the ground, like she's been caught cheating on an exam. Then the penny drops. And so does my stomach. Our masks were not created by Delirium Designs...

My blood runs cold and my legs jitter, urging me to get offstage and away from the cameras. If Delirium Designs sees this interview, or anyone who knows her work, we're done for. Isobel knows it too. Her eyes turn glossy with tears.

'Actually, Harper, do you think you could edit that last bit out?' I say with a nervous laugh. 'I'm not sure we're allowed to disclose that information.'

Finally, after the most intensive hour of my life, the interview is over, and I can't get away from the camera quick enough.

'Iz, you can't be serious,' I hiss at my girlfriend as Harper checks the footage. 'You realize we can't put that segment online, right? Where did you get the masks?'

Isobel looks as if she might barf all over my shoes. 'I'm sorry!' Tears cascade over her lower lashes. 'You sounded so desperate on the phone about not wanting to be on camera and I knew we needed to start filming soon. She had a month's wait list *minimum* to even get a consultation. Don't deny that they haven't been our saving grace. So I found a company that makes them—'

'How, Iz?'

She clenches her jaw but keeps her gaze stern, locked on me. 'AI.'

My body tenses as I suck in a deep, steadying breath.

'So we're massive hypocrites.'

I shake my head in disbelief, unable to find the words to tell her how I really feel, and go to whip my mask off so that I can finally be free of it.

'No, keep it on,' Harper says. 'We need to get some promotional pictures. I think we can do a couple in here and then it'd be great to have some outside with an ordinary, bustling town in the background, right? Since you're all about humanity and not tech, we don't want all our pictures together to be surrounded by wires and gadgets.'

God, I can't believe this has happened. Despite *everything* I've been spewing in my videos, it never occurred to Iz to tell me the mask I was hiding behind was supporting the very thing I've been publicly condemning. And now it's too late to backtrack.

I have no choice but to fake a smile and get through these pictures until it's time for us to leave.

Isobel takes a few shots of us inside the studio, but I can barely look at the camera. Then, we head into the town. Daylight stings my eyes, but the breeze is welcome. I didn't realize how hot it gets underneath stage lighting.

'Oh my god, oh my god, it's him!' A voice catches my attention as Harper and I pose together outside a shopping centre in central town.

'And Harper Taylor too,' says another voice.

'He's actually so much taller than I thought he'd be,' one girl quips to her friend.

A man wearing a bright yellow cagoule approaches with his phone raised. 'Oi, mate, can I have a picture with you when you're done?'

'What the hell is happening?' I ask Harper through gritted teeth.

She just smiles at me knowingly. 'Enjoy the fanfare before the haters arrive and start hurling abuse at you from across the road.'

Before I can even fully process what's happening, hands grab me, yanking me this way and that. Phones are shoved so close to my face that one knocks my mask. Quickly, I fix it. I don't even know who I'm taking pictures with as flashes blind me, but I smile all the same.

'Hey!' I yell, as someone grabs my bum. I throw a look over my shoulder and spot a group of giggling girls sinking deeper into the gathering crowd.

By now I've lost Isobel; she's been devoured by the masses.

'Time to go, I think,' Harper yells over the crowd. 'Before someone—'

Before she can finish her sentence, an arm snakes over my shoulder and fingers wrap around the edge of my mask. The stranger pulls, seconds away from revealing my identity to the sea of cameras pointed in my direction.

'Get. Off. Him!' Isobel elbows my would-be doxxer in the ribs and squeezes herself between us, shoving her own hand on to my mask so that it doesn't slip. 'Move, Echo,' she hisses. 'Follow Harper, that way!' She pushes me through the crowd, acting as a tiny but ferocious bodyguard as she flails and pushes the crowd away from me, all the while trying to protect the camera she borrowed from

Harper's studio.

Another hand grabs my wrist and pulls, and I'm about to slap it away when I realize it's Harper guiding me through the throng of yelling people.

'Echo, I love you!'

'Your channel sucks, mate. Pure cringe.'

We keep walking – almost running – until we make it out of the town centre and safely into a quiet alley between shops.

'I wouldn't come back to the studio if I were you,' Harper says. 'A lot of people know I work around here. Take your mask off, change your outfit up a little bit and go straight to the tram stop.'

I take a deep breath and nod, suddenly feeling like I have a rhino sitting on my shoulders. Isobel's expression is blank. 'I put a spare jacket in your rucksack,' she says to me. 'You can put that on instead of this hoody. Hopefully no one will recognize you then.'

I whip my hoody and mask off and hand them to her as she pulls another jacket from my backpack, which she's currently carrying. Harper takes the camera from Iz, says her goodbyes and makes for her studio. After five minutes, Isobel and I emerge. She storms ahead and I follow with my hands in my pockets, keeping my head down. Cold air nips at my exposed arms and blows through my hair, turning my ears pink.

A gang of giggling girls catches my attention, and I stop in my tracks, barely daring to breathe.

'He was so *tall*,' one of them says as they strut closer.

'And skinny! Like a literal noodle!'

'His voice was so sweet, don't you think? He's such a cinnamon roll.'

'Did you see his hands? And the way his veins and bones just popped through his skin like that? Oh my god, I actually can't.'

I clench my jaw as they reach me. One of the girls catches my eye, but she quickly looks away and continues chatting with her mates as they walk by. The rest don't even acknowledge me.

I suck in a deep breath and my shoulders sag as the girls disappear into the distance. They didn't recognize me without the mask. Without the mask, I'm nothing.

With my new jacket on, I wait at the tram stop alone. Isobel stands a good few paces away from me, and when the tram does arrive, we get on different carriages. Even through Manchester city centre, we keep our distance.

'I just don't want to blow your cover,' she whispers when I attempt to reconnect.

Finally, as we board the train and make for our designated seating, she has no other excuse to ignore me.

'I don't know who's avoiding who,' I say with a huff, as she stares out of the window at the passing landscape. 'I'm still mad at you about the masks.'

'And I didn't like what just happened in Oldham. I didn't like how Harper made you out to be some sex object online, or how everyone started piling around you and grabbing you and forcing you to take pictures with them. That wasn't nice to watch, especially since those people who said they loved you so much shoved me out of the way just to get to you. Like I wasn't there, like I didn't matter.'

'Y-You do matter,' I say earnestly. 'None of this would be possible without you. You're literally the bread and butter to the whole operation. You work so hard on our videos, you're the glue holding us together . . . holding me together.' I entwine my fingers with hers.

'I guess,' she says, her voice barely audible. 'But the grabbing – that's not on. Your identity was almost exposed today. We can't do that again. We can't be out in public in the masks.'

I smile, though a twinge of sadness pulsates through my heart. It was nice having people compliment me in the street, but it was horrid having those same people barely acknowledge me without the gimmick of the mask.

'Besides, you were loving the attention,' she says, joking now.

'Someone groped me,' I say. 'I didn't love that.'

Her face hardens and she places her hand over mine. 'That's horrible. I'm sorry someone did that. No more masks in public, OK? It's not safe. Harper's right. I looked through the Vandalize threads while we were on the tram and people are going absolutely feral for the masks, desperate to know who you all are, calling you their soulmates, making up stories about how you're troubled and need saving. Some people are even suggesting that they should find our address and turn up.'

I try to speak, to let out my thoughts, but no words will materialize. I'm stunned. It's me, just Mikah. How can so many people be this interested to know who I am beneath the mask?

'We need new masks ASAP. Before someone realizes these aren't the real deal.'

'Fine,' Iz says.

We spend the next few hours in deep contemplation, flicking through the flyers I took from the burger van: a drag show at a comedy club, a two-for-one pizza night at a local pub with a new indie band, a small food festival called Mukbang Metropolis which is held every year in London city centre, and a dog show for pedigree pooches.

'Did you see the legal letters on Harper's desk?' Isobel asks. 'She's being sued for accidently doxxing someone before the *Island of Influencers* livestream.'

'You know it's also illegal to read someone else's mail, right?' I scold, flashing her a smug grin. 'But, yeah, as much as I admire Harper and her work, breaking into someone's house and falsely accusing them of kidnapping your cousin isn't cool.'

It's almost nine in the evening when our taxi finally pulls up outside the holiday cottage, and I'm desperate to crawl into bed.

I snake my arm around Isobel's shoulders and pull her into my side as we walk down the drive to the house, all the day's animosity forgotten and forgiven. But before we reach the front door, it swings open.

'Finally, you're back!' Cheki's face is red and blotchy, and her eyes are pooled with worry. 'I didn't call because I didn't want to worry you, and it's not like you could do anything while you were away anyway.'

'What is it?' I ask. 'What's happened?' My brows furrow so hard that I know I'll have a headache tomorrow.

'There's been an accident.'

CHAPTER 19

My shoulders sag, my chest tightens. What's happened?

Cheki glances from me to Iz before elaborating, 'Zach kinda hated that you guys went to meet Harper and do an interview without him and he – I dunno – felt like he needed to prove his worth, I guess. He decided to film another stunt. Anyway, come in and see for yourselves.'

I push Cheki aside and make my way to the sitting room in no more than three strides. I glance to the sofa, but Zach isn't there.

'He's in bed,' Cheki yells.

I launch myself across the sitting room and through the kitchen until I get to Zach's bedroom. The door is open just a crack and I can see Zach's silhouette in bed. As I push the door further, he lifts his head at the sound.

'You're back,' Zach says, his voice monotone. 'Seems like you drew quite a crowd in Oldham.'

'Yeah,' I reply, still lingering in the doorway.

Zach attempts to sit upright but winces and grabs his side.

'I keep telling him that he's broken a rib.' The voice

catches me off guard and I snap my head over my shoulder. Cheki stands there, her eyes red and swollen from her tears. 'He's refusing to go to hospital.'

'If I go in again, my parents won't let me come back here,' Zach replies through clenched teeth. Sweat lingers on his forehead and his usually flawless skin is a nasty mix of green and grey.

'Mate, you *have* to go to the hospital,' I insist. 'What if you've punctured a lung or something?'

'I'm fine, just bruised.'

I stride closer to his bedside. 'What happened?' I ask.

Cheki passes me her phone. There's a video. I press play.

Cheki and Zach make their way down to the beach, laughing and joking. Zach's the star, taking up the screen with his masked face, and Cheki is his camera person.

'All right, guys,' says Cheki from behind the camera. 'We've lost a couple of our team today. Echo is out with our production manager filming an interview with the one and only queen of investigative news, TheHarperHerald. So Zulu and I decided we'd come down to the beach and film a cool video for you – some rural parkour.'

The video stops and Cheki reaches over, flicking through her endless content until she finds the next video in their saga.

Zach stands on a ridge high above Durdle Door beach, wearing his black Digital Demons uniform and mask. In the distance, the famous landmark looms: a door shape cut into a thin trail of rock stretching out to sea.

Sunlight casts a golden hue over the rock and small waves crash against it below. The image alone is beautiful and serene, in complete contrast to what Zach's about to attempt. Cheki pans the camera, showing off the view and the crowd of people sunbathing on the beach below. Then she returns her attention to Zach on the rocks.

My stomach lurches. Before I even press play on the next video, I know what's about to happen.

'You can see how steep that drop is,' Cheki says. 'Zulu is going to attempt a run from this ridge all the way to the end of the famous landmark in the distance there. The rocks are sharp, the ridge is narrow and near impossible to pass in places. Can he do it? How're you feeling, Zulu?'

Zach turns his masked face to the camera and gives a double thumbs up. 'I've got this, no problem.' His words are muffled beneath the mask, so Cheki repeats them for the viewer. Zach checks his bodycam one more time before signalling that he's ready.

Without another word, Zach begins, running at full steam along the jagged edge towards Durdle Door. I lift my head away from the phone and catch real-life Cheki's eyes.

'Whose idea was this? I'm pretty sure this is illegal. This'd better not have been uploaded to the channel already.'

Cheki and Zach throw sheepish glances at one another. I resume my watching. The small Zach on screen leaps and bounds over rocks and across gut-churning gaps within the cliff face. It's impressive, I won't lie. Zach has some serious moves, and he's buff enough to manoeuvre through the challenging parts like they're nothing. He nears the landmark. If I didn't know any better, if my best mate wasn't lying in bed with a set of potentially broken ribs, I would have sworn he'd make it.

I clench my teeth tighter. The sea slaps against the rocks below and a crowd has gathered by the shoreline, invested in the stunt too.

The camera zooms in just as Zach's right foot buckles as he steps upon a loose shard of rock. He wobbles and attempts to steady himself, but he has nothing to grab hold of. His hands flail in the air until he crumples into a heap on the ground, slipping slowly off the edge. For a moment, I think I might look away, unable to watch my friend in such peril. But he's alive, I know he is.

As one of Zach's legs disappears over the ledge, Cheki rushes forward, making the shakiness of the video difficult to watch, but she catches the moment Zach's whole body slips over the edge and falls at speed to the water below.

'A few people from the beach headed straight into the sea to rescue him,' Cheki says beside me, her voice quiet and apologetic. 'I honestly thought he might have . . .'

I shake my head, begging her not to finish that sentence, and we all sit in silence.

Eventually, Cheki pockets her phone and makes for the door. 'I'll give you two some time,' she says.

I stare at Zach, hoping he'll say something that'll

make this whole thing better, but he doesn't. He looks as angry as I feel. 'Isobel asked you not to do any stunts while we were away,' I spit. 'You guys said you'd go shopping, get some more food in for mukbangs, maybe do some planning for future films, get in contact with some small businesses to ask whether they'll sponsor us – the important stuff.'

'Sorry for not wanting to spend my entire day doing admin and going shopping for *you*,' Zach says. 'Cheki and I did do some shopping and then we sent some messages to brands and sponsors – none of whom replied – and mind-mapped a bunch of ideas. That lasted a few hours max. We were stuck here, bored, while you were off being our mouthpiece and having your paparazzi shots taken, being fawned over by girls. All day we've had notifications on the Digital Demons Photorah page of you being tagged in pictures with fans.'

I fall back into the wall behind me. 'You purposely put yourself in a ridiculously unsafe position because you thought I was getting more attention than I deserved.'

At this, Zach snaps his head towards me and attempts to bolt upright in bed. He grabs his side and winces, before falling back against the pillows. 'I didn't say that,' he manages through the pain. 'I never said you don't deserve the recognition. I just think that you're getting more than the rest of us – more than me – yet you said we were in this together, me and you. Not you and Isobel. I don't see why we can't all have masks like yours, so we can all be heard. Like, there were so many things I wanted to say to the camera before my stunt and I couldn't. I couldn't even hype myself up. I've basically been silenced, and this was meant to be *our* thing, Mikah.'

I allow his words to settle.

'I hear you,' I finally say. 'I never wanted anyone to feel that way. I only have a mouth hole in my mask because, well, I do mukbangs. I can hardly eat with my mouth covered, can I?' A little chuckle escapes my lips at the thought.

Zach doesn't laugh. He's always been the pretty boy of our group; the main character, the guy all the girls long for. I can only imagine how difficult it is for him to be shoved to the back.

'I know you feel like you're a nobody – I do too. Every day, without the mask. Today I realized that the mask has made me someone, and people are desperate to know more. We can use that to our advantage. It's a gimmick that draws people in, gets people talking, right? So, they watch our stuff and hear our message because of them. I didn't mean to become the "main guy", it just worked out that way. But our anonymity doesn't have to mean that you're completely devoid of personality, mate. You can show who you are in other ways.'

Zach contemplates this for a while before saying: 'I guess so.'

'Do everything shirtless if you want to,' I chuckle. 'If you want to pull bodybuilding poses before every one of your videos, do it. I meant it when I said: we're one body, one entity, trying to save the arts from bots. A single instrument to spread the word, but with many moving parts.'

'I-I just want to be included more. Like in decision making and going off doing these interviews. Given that Isobel is our manager, producer and editor, and you're dating her, it only makes sense that she favours you for these things, so you've got almost three times as many videos on the channel as me and Cheki have put together.'

I nod, feeling guilt wash through my body. 'Yeah. I understand. I'll do better, though. Maybe we can cut out the bottom part of your mask and do a mukbang together or we can do one where you feed me, it'll be ridiculous but fun?'

Zach's eyes light up and he nods as best he can through his winces. 'Yeah. I like that idea. I like that a lot.'

I grin at him as we clasp hands, like we always do when we make a pact. 'We've got just over two weeks left of summer to send this channel into the stratosphere before college starts. I reckon we can do it, mate.' We chat into the night, and I don't even realize I've drifted off in the chair at his bedside until a rapid knock on the door wakes me.

Zach's eyes shoot open, and he grumbles. Isobel throws her head inside the room, a panicked expression on her face.

'The police are here.'

CHAPTER 20

'Thanks for getting out of bed for us,' the older of the two officers says. He stands straight, with his hands tucked into his stab-proof vest.

I raise an eyebrow. Is a stab-proof vest really necessary in the middle of a quaint country village? I've seen officers in the middle of a city brawl wearing less protective gear. Isobel and I deposit Zach on the sofa. He winces and groans.

'In pain, are we?' the officer asks. 'Wouldn't have anything to do with a nasty fall you had yesterday afternoon, would it?'

Zach shoots Cheki (who's sitting nervously by the window, chewing her fingernails) a worried look, and Cheki makes a couple of choking sounds in response.

'Folks,' the older officer sighs. 'There's no point in trying to hide what you've done; there's video evidence online. Multiple pieces of video evidence – and eyewitnesses who say they saw you heading back here. And now you're sitting here with injuries compatible with the accident witnessed on those pieces of evidence.'

The officer clears his throat and puts on his most authoritative and condescending tone. 'While climbing a historic site of natural beauty, which Durdle Door is, isn't technically illegal, it is highly frowned upon. You're lucky you only damaged yourselves. Consider this a warning. You're treading on treacherous ground, and if you keep doing what you're doing, you might find yourselves in serious trouble.' He gives us all a stern nod. 'And you'd better come with us to the hospital,' he says to Zach.

Zach begs the officer not to inform his parents about his injury, as he's once again helped off the sofa. Isobel offers to go with him to A&E, but Zach refuses, asking instead for his camera so that he can take B-roll in the hospital.

We watch through the large sitting-room window as Zach is assisted into the back of the police car like he's a criminal bound for the cells. The image makes me giggle, especially when I notice the camera in Cheki's hand.

She flashes me a smirk. 'We'll have to blur his face.'

'He'll love that.' Zach really is earning his title of *bad boy* of the group, and I hope that'll make up for how sidelined he feels.

Isobel's brows are furrowed, her stare distant as the blue flashing lights disappear around the hedgerows.

'Everything all right?' I ask.

'It was surprisingly easy for the police to track us down – especially with eyewitnesses tracing you to this cottage. I'm a bit worried others might find it that easy too.'

I think on this for a while. She's right. Anyone could follow us here after an outing, if they keep a low enough profile. My stomach turns.

After a brief pause, Isobel sucks in a deep breath and snaps back into the present day. 'Right,' she announces. 'Everyone hand over your footage, whatever it is. I need to get everything edited and uploaded as soon as possible. We've got a few more mukbangs we filmed in Manchester, Mikah's behind-the-scenes footage of him interviewing with TheHarperHerald, a newer version of Zach's ridiculous stunt, complete with police caution – I can edit the footage so it looks like he was genuinely arrested.'

She heads upstairs without another word, focused on her never-ending tasks. There aren't enough flowers or boxes of chocolates in the world to thank her for all she's done for me and this channel. She manages to edit all our content together so quickly, and fit it around pre-college reading and quick visits home.

Ding.

'What's that a notification for?' I ask.

'Oh, don't hate me,' Cheki says. 'I joined iGENect—'

'Mate!'

'Only so that I could subscribe to Extreme Elites and get notified whenever they upload. They're the enemy, right? We need to know what they're doing. They upload constantly. They posted some parkour stunts yesterday morning, so that's one of the reasons Zach wanted to do his Durdle Door stunt.'

I swallow my fury and nod. While I certainly don't agree with giving iGENect any of our personal information in order to gain access to their platform, I do agree that having live updates for new Extreme Elites uploads will be beneficial. 'Let's see what they've been up to, then,' I say.

She pulls out her phone and clicks the little purple banner on screen. It takes us straight to the Extreme Elites page, where a new video from AnnaConda begs for our attention. It's a mukbang.

Pain shoots through my lower jaw as I grind my teeth, waiting for the video to load.

'*Dzień dobry, przyjaciele!*' she says in Polish. 'Good morning, good morning, my friends. It's so nice to see you here again.'

I roll my eyes. 'Jeez, is she programmed to know every language going?'

Anna flashes a pristine white smile and waves both her hands at the camera. 'Today, we're going to eat some yummy, yummy fast food! Oh my goodness, I have wanted to get my teeth into some deep-fried cheese all week.' She giggles as Khristoff and Noruwai join her on camera with plates of food. They're all so perfectly in sync with their facial expressions.

Deep-fried halloumi, mac and cheese balls, extra-cheesy pizza, hash browns, cheeseburgers, chilli cheese fries, chicken nuggets, spring rolls, a bowl of steaming cheddar cheese sauce – my mouth waters at the sight.

'Here we go!' AnnaConda takes a hash brown and two

chicken nuggets, making a sandwich with them. Then, she dips the whole thing into the bowl of cheese, making the thick orange cheddar ooze over the side and on to the table below.

Her housemates gasp and make exaggerated faces at the camera.

'Hmm, so delicious!' Anna says, before shovelling the whole thing into her mouth. I expect the camera to pan to the food as it's done before, but this time, it doesn't. The camera remains on her face as she chews with a cute smile and swallows every bite.

I scowl. How is that possible? As I take it all in, something dawns on me: AnnaConda has been upgraded to the new Tanaki model that John mentioned in Harper's studio. 'AnnaConda has been upgraded.' Cheki throws me an inquisitive look. 'She's the newest version, nExGEN. Whatever her system looks like now, it enables her to eat and swallow and pretend to be fully human. You can barely tell the difference.'

Cheki tenses her jaw. 'Everything's advancing so quickly – we can't keep up.'

She scrolls the comments underneath the video.

Love watching you eat all this food, yet you're still so skinny! Where do you put it all? Lol, says one commenter.

I'd kill to be able to have your diet. The second I even look at a bar of chocolate, my face breaks out, says another.

This comment makes me snort and my hand unconsciously moves to my own pimple-riddled face. A third commenter just wants AnnaConda to know that he thinks she's *sexy* and can *eat like a man* in front of him any day. Nice to see you actually swallowing the food this time, he concludes.

How much to lick that bit of cheese off your table?

When the comments start getting weird and out of hand, Cheki shuts the app.

'They know she's not real, right?' I ask, genuinely confused by what I've just witnessed in the Extreme Elites comment section. 'Surely everyone knows she's not real? They're talking to her like she's an actual human that sits and reads the comments and cares what they have to say.'

Cheki flashes me a pitiful look. 'I think I'd be more concerned if they *were* talking to an actual person that way. Maybe knowing she isn't real makes them think they can say dodgy stuff to her and it doesn't mean anything?'

My mind is like a tempest, and I pace the room. 'I want a showdown with her, take our beef offline and make it real. I want to see her in person, have a side-by-side competition and prove once and for all that humans make better entertainment.'

Cheki raises an eyebrow. 'What're you suggesting?'

I crack a smirk. 'A show, a spectacle, a face-off between humans and AI.'

CHAPTER 21

Cheki and I raid the cupboards. This is one idea I've been saving for a special event, and I think challenging AI to meet me for an in-person mukbang really hits that mark.

We line the coffee table in the sitting room with an assortment of sweets and treats. All of them are super-sour, and the most unnatural colours known to man. There're five tins with hazard signs painted on the sides – very fitting for our brand – filled with the foulest hard-boiled sweets I've ever had the displeasure of tasting, packets of bubblegum jelly swirls that make the tongue almost sizzle from the sour sugar, lollipops the size of my face in blood red (sour cherry makes my eyes water), and sherbet packets in apple and orange and blue raspberry that are so tart they make my cheeks touch and my teeth threaten to fall from their gums.

My body floods half with excitement and half with dread. I know it's going to hurt; I know I'm going to make a complete idiot of myself on camera, but it'll be entertaining to say the least. I also kinda love how awful these things taste; how painful the pleasure is.

Cheki sets the camera up while I change into my typical black attire and don my mask. I take a seat on the floor with the rainbow sweets framing my form.

'Ready when you are,' she says, giving me a thumbs up.

I clear my throat before speaking. 'What's up, guys? Echo here from Digital Demons, bringing you a pretty special video today. Some of you might've seen the earlier upload from our brother, Zulu. He's OK! More on that to follow. I'll let him tell his story.'

I take one of the bubblegum swirls from its packet and feed it into my mouth, relishing the discomfort as the sugar begins to melt over my tongue.

'Some of you might've seen the most recent mukbang video from Extreme Elites,' I continue, through the excess saliva the sourness has created in my mouth. 'You might've even liked it.' I shake away the tartness and move on to my next challenge: jelly pods with super-sour liquid in the middle. Each time I bite into one, the lime juice hits the back of my throat and makes me gag.

'iGENect thinks people will watch anything, even if it's soulless, but I know what you really want. You want to see me react; you want to know that I'm feeling something. You want to be able to see yourself in me and have me reflect your desires and pain back to you. I'm happy to oblige. Always. I want things to go back to how they used to be. I challenge Tanaki's nExGEN prototype, the new and "improved" version of AnnaConda, to an in-person eating competition. There's a small independent food festival in London at the end of November called Mukbang Metropolis, and I'll be there. I want Anna-Conda to join me, and we can decide once and for all what the people *really* want to see.'

Saliva escapes the corners of my mouth as I tip a triple packet of sour sherbet over my tongue. I chew down on the sugar, my lips pursing so tightly that my teeth cut into them. 'Echo, over and out,' I manage through my tears.

Cheki makes a cut-throat gesture to let me know she's stopped the recording.

'Get that uploaded, quick,' I manage, as I leg it to the nearest bathroom.

It takes almost half a bottle of mouthwash and a ten-minute scrub with a toothbrush to make my mouth feel slightly normal again, though I can tell I'll be sporting ulcers on my tongue and cheeks come morning.

'Brilliant,' says Isobel from the doorway of the downstairs toilet. 'Such a great idea to invite her to meet at a food festival. I think it'll be obvious just how soulless these nExGEN creations are in real life.'

I shoot her a thumbs up. 'Pretty sure my stomach's going to have something to say about those sweets. Either that, or my teeth are going to fall out.'

She laughs and swans over to me. 'You're not going to die from one sugar overload – not you and that iron stomach of yours.' Her eyes narrow and she tilts her head. 'Are you sure you've been keeping up with the skincare routine I made for you?'

'Always,' I say, taken aback. 'Why would I stop now?' I

know my skin hasn't looked great since getting here, but I'd hoped she hadn't noticed.

She grabs my face, tilting it this way and that, trying to get a better look. 'Maybe it's the sweat build-up beneath the mask, but I don't think the mukbangs are helping,' she says softly. 'We've got enough eating content to last us a week, so maybe lay off the sugar and fats and eat something healthy for a while? You have to take care of yourself, Mikah.'

'Thanks for the advice,' I say, a little more sarcastically than necessary. Her face falls and shame washes over me. She's only trying to help.

'Just food for thought,' she says, shrugging.

'Speaking of the masks, any luck getting new ones made?'

She deflates. 'I'm looking into it. It'll take a while – real artists need more time than computers to get the work done.' And then she leaves me, making for her bedroom to continue editing our videos.

'You're getting so many rave reviews for that mukbang in your comments section,' Cheki says as I head back into the sitting room. 'And Harper has uploaded your interview on her channel, driving even more traffic our way.'

I smile. It's amazing what someone else's influence can do to boost that of others. It reminds me that I need to call my parents later and tell them how well the channel is doing. We've yet to make any money, but as our numbers rise, so does my hope for winning this war against AI.

Cheki sits on her laptop by the fireplace, slowly feeding bits of dry wood into the flames until it roars to life and fills the room with a cosy, welcoming warmth. 'You won't believe how many news outlets have written articles on us. You specifically, Mikah. Get a load of this headline: **The rebellion against AI has a new leader, but the rise of Digital Demons – a human vs humanoid content house – is as shrouded in mystery as the masked assailants themselves.**'

Her giggles make me laugh too. I can't believe we've done it; we've actually brought the rebellion to the mainstream news!

I hear thudding footsteps above, then Isobel comes dashing down. She stops halfway downstairs and yells. 'Oh my god, we've got a request for an interview! National News want to do a video call with us tonight.'

I jump to my feet. Cheki squeals and kicks her feet.

'Tell them yes,' I yell. 'Tell them we'll do the interview. Tell them we want paying.'

It's like the world has exploded into colour; chatter fills the sitting room, but I can't make out a single word through the noise in my own head. It's all happening!

'We need to get Zach home,' I say. 'Or at least do the interview at his hospital bedside. He can't miss out on this; he'll never forgive us. The audience love him too.'

'You're damn right they do,' Cheki replies. 'Just read the comments under the video of his Durdle Door stunt. It's like he can do no wrong.'

We all sit for hours, scrolling on our phones and laptops through the barrage of comments under our videos, refreshing search engines as more news articles and posts roll in about us, talking about what we're doing, my challenge request for AnnaConda, and Zach's viral fall. Strangers are discussing us non-stop online, trying to figure out who we are and where we've come from. It's magic. It's everything I always imagined overnight stardom would be, except it didn't happen overnight and the recognition has been painfully earnt.

> I'm so in love with Zulu, says one girl underneath Zach's latest stunt video. I can't stop thinking about him, I hope he's all right.

> Nah, this geezer got arrested for doing this stunt

> Arrested? Isn't he dead from that fall?

> Echo just has something about him. I know he's all lanky and his mukbangs are gross, but OMG that voice!

> Happy to volunteer girlfriend services to any and all – god, please!

> Absolutely feral for the way Echo drips cheese sauce on to his tongue

> You can't tell me that Zulu couldn't bench press me with those biceps

> It's the masks. Can't tell you why, but the masks are everything.

I hope they never unmask. I like not knowing what they really look like.

Girl, same! With the masks, they can be anyone I want them to be and I love that for me.

I bet he's so ugly under there. I need to know before I keep worshipping him like this.

These guys could look like trolls. I HAVE to know their identities before I get caught lusting over them like a starved dog.

I AM A STARVED DOG, GOD, FEED ME WITH ECHO

I laugh at the absurdity of it; at the fact that these strangers are drooling over a bunch of teens doing stupid stunts online. At the fact that they're literally pining over me and my goofy mates. But the comments make me feel a bit weird too. I click on profile pictures and realize that some of these women are three times my age. A shudder runs down my spine. And why are none of them talking about the message we're trying to get out there? It's not about us.

Cheki must have caught the concern etched on to my face because she places a hand on my shoulder. 'Just enjoy it. At least they're watching.'

True. I keep scrolling the comments, laughing at the weird ones, going red when girls my age say how cute they think I am. I can honestly say that I never imagined my life would become *this* in just under a month, but . . . I love it. People are finally recognizing me, begging me to do more and be more *me*.

This is a taste of what Zach gets to experience every day.

This is the life I always wanted.

A dream come true.

CHAPTER 22

The rest of the day goes by in a blur. I find myself checking the comment section underneath my latest mukbang at least once every five minutes. I'll be making myself a hot drink while scrolling, taking out the rubbish from the kitchen bin to the dustbin outside and reading fanfic about me. I'll even be sitting on the toilet, laughing at memes strangers have made of me from screenshots taken from my videos.

I've never felt like this. So . . . seen. Wanted, even.

Zach arrives back at the holiday cottage sometime around five o'clock, and only then does it dawn on me how much time I've wasted glued to my phone.

'So, we're going to be on national TV tonight, huh?' Zach says, hobbling inside. He has a ridiculous grin on his face and his tongue is practically hanging out of his mouth. The sight makes me smile, knowing the morphine is easing some of his pain.

I help Isobel lay out our evening meal of hunter's chicken with roast potatoes and green beans. She barely speaks at dinner and has a faraway stare. I put it down to nerves.

We huddle together on the sofa in the sitting room, where Isobel has set up the camera and laptop, ready for when the clock strikes half six. I'm sitting in the middle, as requested by the news anchor.

The interview lasts no longer than ten minutes. Sweat pools beneath my mask with every new question and my tongue threatens to stick to the roof of my mouth each time I answer, but before I can fall into a full-blown panic attack, it's over.

With a deep, steadying breath, I whip my mask off and fall into the back of the sofa. Isobel clears her throat and gestures her head for me to follow her into the kitchen. I oblige. 'We have a problem,' she whispers. Her amber eyes are filled with tears. I frown at her and she shakily hands me her phone where a Photorah page is loaded.

The social media page belongs to Delirium Designs and her most recent post is a screenshot of us during the news interview. My heart thuds against my chest, and for a moment I feel as if my soul has jumped from my body. I click the picture and flick through the album, finding a clear shot of me in Harper's studio. The caption below:

> Not the first time I've had my artwork stolen, but you'd think a group like Digital Demons – who're actively condemning AI for doing that kind of stuff – wouldn't be so bold as to use my stolen designs for the masks they hide behind. To be clear, I have not worked with these guys on their masks. They apparently admitted to

wearing my design during an interview with TheHarperHerald (can't confirm as I haven't watched it, but some of my friends have). If this group want to get in contact and explain themselves, I'm all ears.

I fold over the countertop, twisting my hair in my fingers as I bury my head in my arms and groan. So, Harper didn't edit out that part of our interview. Great. Our first controversy. We look like hypocrites. We *are* hypocrites.

'I'll message her right now and explain,' Isobel says, her voice shaking. 'Tell her we're looking for new ones. I'll ask her to take that post down before it damages us.'

I let out an exasperated huff. 'Too late for that, Iz. People will have screenshotted this like it's going out of fashion. Look how many likes and shares it has already. That's going viral whether we like it or not. We're done for.'

There's a gasp from the next room and Cheki launches herself into the kitchen, almost taking me out as she slides along the wooden floor. 'Have you guys—'

'We know,' I say, cutting her off.

'I'm sorting it.' Isobel's hands are trembling as she attempts to send a private message to the creator behind Delirium Designs.

I try to steady my breath and release the anger building in my chest. It's not her fault. She was already stressed about her upcoming college course in a couple of weeks, trying to read ahead for her modules, and then I asked her to help with the channel too. Since we've been here, I've been relentless in my demands, I know that.

I sigh and grab her hands, steadying them, then flash her an apologetic smile. She came up with a solution to my problem in a matter of days, and yet here I am, demonizing her for it.

'Mate, you *have* to film an apology video,' Zach says, poking his head around the door. His eyes are still drooping from the morphine and he's hanging on to the door frame like he might fall asleep at any moment.

'You're right,' I say. 'There's no point in trying to pretend this hasn't happened. We've been called out on the masks and rightly so. The only thing we can do now is to be honest and explain what happened. Iz, you keep writing that message. Ask if she'd be willing to replace our masks with ones she made. I'll . . . set the camera up again.'

I wipe the tears from Isobel's cheek and leave her to piece together a professional yet apologetic message with Zach.

Cheki helps frame me in the phone camera lens sitting in the tripod on the other side of the coffee table. 'Ready when you are,' she says. 'Mask?'

I grimace as she hands me the flimsy bit of plastic, but still I place it over my face. Wearing it feels like rubbing salt in a wound, but I'm not ready for a face reveal just yet. Especially not since so many of our fans love the masks, and some are even threatening to boycott us if we remove them. And, well, I don't really want anyone to see the spots on my face.

My stomach twists and turns as I throw a thumbs up. Cheki presses record.

'Hey, guys. Echo here from Digital Demons. Ugh, bit of an uncomfortable one this.' A pitiful laugh escapes my lips as I scratch my head, desperately trying to form a coherent thought process. Maybe I should have scripted it first, but then it's not real, is it? 'Some of you – probably all of you by now – might've seen that the creator Delirium Designs has accused us of using her stolen artwork on our masks. She's right.

'Truthfully, we didn't know that the designs were stolen or that these masks weren't made by Delirium Designs herself. We . . .' I pause. I don't want Isobel taking the heat for this blunder, but I don't want to take the blame for it either, because I genuinely didn't know until it was too late. 'We outsourced them. We put our faith in someone to find us masks and didn't question their word. We thought we were wearing authentic Delirium Designs masks.

'It was only very recently that we discovered this to not be the case. So recently, in fact, that we hadn't had the chance to change them or reach out to the true designer until she got wind of it. We're sorry . . . really, we are. This is a terrible look for us, considering everything we preach. But it's also a major lesson as well. It's so easy to be conned by AI, to think you're buying something legit or watching something that's been created by human hands. Even we fell victim to it, and that's why our message is so important. Things *must* change!

'This is the last you'll see of these masks, I promise. We're getting new ones made – proper ones designed and created by a human. And we can't wait to show you. We won't be making any fresh content until we have secured new masks. Uh ... thanks for listening and sticking by us. Echo over and out.'

Cheki holds her thumbs up to indicate the recording has finished. Isobel stands at the door looking morose.

'She's seen my message but hasn't replied yet,' Isobel says.

'Her post is still up too.' Cheki's gone back to scrolling on her phone. 'Whatever you do, don't look at the comments. They'll only make you feel worse.'

My stomach flips and I don't reckon it's from the food. Just as I'm about to flop on to the sofa and resign myself to feeling lousy for the rest of the day, my phone vibrates.

I grab it from the tripod and open the new email, my eyes widening in surprise. My body goes rigid and I can barely get any words out. 'Guys,' I manage, beckoning them over.

Isobel gasps and slams a hand over her mouth. 'Someone actually wants to sponsor our next video!'

'Who?' asks Cheki.

'A small soft drinks company. They're offering seven grand to have Mikah drink their products in his next mukbang.'

'We have to take it,' I say, my fingers fumbling the keyboard as I type out a quick response.

Isobel's eyebrows rise and she stares at the screen. 'Who'd have thought our first sponsor would come after being exposed for using AI artwork. I guess controversy really does sell.'

CHAPTER 23

The next morning, after a night of restless sleep, I stomp into Isobel's room and throw a pile of clothes on the end of her bed, frowning. My eyes sting from hours lying awake, thinking about the Delirium Designs fiasco and the euphoria of landing our first sponsorship deal.

Isobel raises an inquisitive eyebrow, but before she can ask, the words are tumbling out of my mouth.

'Do you think I've put weight on?'

She takes a deep breath and averts her gaze, clearly trying to find the most delicate way of saying, *Yes, you have.* 'I wouldn't say you've gained as such,' she says diplomatically, 'but you've definitely filled out a bit – and your skin's seen better days.'

It's like another stab to the chest. I march across my bedroom and stop in front of the long mirror hanging on the wall by my window. I poke at my cheeks and grab handfuls of my belly, lifting my T-shirt over my chest to get a better look. Sure, you can't really see my ribs any more, and there's a bit of belly hanging over my trousers, but that's a good thing, right? Everyone always tells me I should try and fill out a bit more.

'Hey, don't twist my words, I haven't said it doesn't suit you,' Isobel adds, joining me at the mirror. Her eyes have dark circles around them and her skin seems sallow. 'If anything, it makes you look older and sturdier,' she says, sounding exhausted by me and my constant need for reassurance. 'I'm just conscious of your health, babe. You're eating more than you normally would, even when you're not hungry, bypassing every signal your body is throwing at you to stop. I like you any way you come, but I want you to be healthy.'

'Except for the skin,' I say, pointing to the biggest pimple on my cheek. 'Good job I have the mask, huh?' I try to laugh it off, but it really does hurt seeing my skin this bad again. I wish I could wear the mask all the time and then no one would be subjected to seeing massive, red, pulsating spots glaring at them every time I step outside the front door.

Isobel opens her mouth and closes it again, her eyes darting from one corner of the room to the next as she searches for the right words. Luckily, she's spared the impossible task of making me feel better about my appearance when Zach bundles inside.

'How're you feeling?' I ask.

He groggily brushes his fingers through his hair. 'Been better. Rib hurts. Morphine wearing off. Parents mad, but I convinced them it was an accident and they should let me stay.'

Relief floods me but I'm reminded once again that I

need to ring home. My parents want to know I'm safe; that everything is going well at the cottage. But I also know they'll bombard me with reminders that college is starting in two weeks, and asking when I'll be home.

With his broken rib being the second time Zach was carted off to hospital, I was sure his parents would call quits on the whole content-house thing we have going on. Plus, with the controversy surrounding us and the masks all over the internet, part of me wondered whether it might be for the best. I suppose if everything does go up in smoke, college is a safe option, and we can carry on like nothing's happened; let Digital Demons fade into obscurity. Every day I find a new reason to be thankful for the anonymity of the masks.

'So,' Zach continues, 'no more content until we get the new masks delivered, huh? Cool. What're we going to do, then?'

'Well, you can rest, for a start,' Isobel says, raising her brows at him. 'Other than that, chill? We can make all of this work to our advantage; we even had a couple more sponsorship requests from good brands overnight. I'll get chatting with them while I'm away, and hopefully we can come back with a bang, but let's take a few days to unwind and let the dust settle.'

It's only now that I realize she has a bag packed on the edge of her bed. 'Going somewhere?'

'Home,' she says, a weak smile on her lips. 'Only for a couple of days. Mum needs me and I need some time away from the channel and – you know – this house.

Since we're not filming anything else until the new masks arrive, I figured it was a good chance to have a break.'

I frown. 'And you're only just telling me this now? Isobel, what the hell? Are we good?'

Her phone rings and the caller ID tells us all that her granny is here to pick her up.

'Of course!' she says, standing on the tips of her toes to plant a kiss on my lips. I barely have time to kiss her back before she pulls away again, and she doesn't make eye contact. 'I'll call you tonight, OK? Don't forget to send over your completed mould kits to Delirium Designs, she needs to get started on the new masks.'

She grabs her bag and laptop case and makes for the door, disappearing with a wave over her shoulder. Zach waves, just as confused as I am.

She's mad at me for something — perhaps because I called her out on using AI? God knows.

I cast my gaze over my best mate. Despite his obvious pain, he still cuts a handsome figure, and this draws my mind back to my own changing form. I yank at my waistband.

As if he's read my thoughts, Zach chimes in with: 'You know what, mate, you've actually got the perfect bulk base to start a decent workout routine. I could have you looking like me in a couple of weeks. Fact. Just got to work on your stamina first.'

I laugh. 'To be fair, how many people can actually do ten push-ups in a row?'

'Quite a few — you just have the upper body strength of

a sedated squirrel.'

A mass of hair pops around the door frame holding out a controller. 'Fancy a game, fellas?' Cheki asks.

Zach and I glance at each other and shrug. With nothing else to do but wait for new masks and attempt to block out the online hate, gaming seems like a good option for keeping busy.

We both know exactly which game we want to play and which character we want to claim before the other: NiteRider, the ultimate hero. Masked, cloaked and with weapons galore and magical powers capable of taking down the empire. She's lethal.

Zach and I hurtle towards the steps – him wincing and groaning the entire time. He trips me and I accidentally yank his trousers to his ankles as I hit the deck. Tears stream from my eyes.

Zach quickly fixes his attire, grabs me by the arms, and slides me through his open legs, before leapfrogging over me with a grunt. I snort and jump to my feet, not so easily defeated. Height is one thing I have to my advantage over Zach (that and his broken rib). We bundle down the stairs and he launches himself over the back of the sofa. I follow, landing on top of him and pushing his head into the cushions as I make for the controllers within the cabinet under the TV.

That's when we realize the screen of the game is already loaded. My jaw drops. Zach's gaze finds mine. We shoot our attention to a figure sitting in an armchair near the kitchen.

'Beat you to it, losers,' Cheki says, a smug grin plastered over her face as she gestures her controller towards the NiteRider.

The afternoon is well spent – no internet, no comments and definitely no mukbangs.

It's unbelievable how quickly a week can roll by when you're not sucked into the grip of the internet. For the first couple of days, I found myself logging back into my socials, completely consumed by the hate comments. But then it became easier not to look, to allow myself to just be Mikah again and enjoy the summer holiday playing video games with my best mate, eating home-cooked meals to regulate my gut health, and working out in the sunshine under Zach's strict regime.

'Nice,' Cheki says one morning over breakfast, giving us a nod of approval over her spoonful of porridge as Zach and I flex in the reflection of the toaster.

A grin spreads over my face as Zach wraps his fingers around my bicep and whistles. I laugh. There hasn't been much noticeable change in my body yet, but I feel great inside.

'Your parents aren't going to recognize you,' he says. 'Let alone Iz.'

This jolts me back into reality. I haven't heard from Isobel once since she left and I still haven't spoken to my parents, bar a few half-hearted replies to their messages. The holiday cottage is like my haven away from the real world. I don't ever want to leave. Don't want this summer to end.

It's as if Zach has a telepathic connection with me, because he once again voices reason to my inner turmoil. 'Maybe you should call your parents while I'm frying the bacon?'

With a deep sigh, I grab my phone from the breakfast bar and dial my dad's number. He answers almost immediately.

'Hey, Dad,' I say. 'Sorry it's been so long since I called.'

There's a silence on the other end and I know he's trying to soften his annoyance. 'I'm just glad you finally called us back, son. It's nice to hear your voice.'

Heat prickles my cheeks.

'How's everything going? We had Isobel round for tea last night. She filled us in on what you guys have been doing. Channel sounds like it's coming along nicely . . . I have to admit, I'm impressed. You've really gone all in on it.' He gives a little chuckle but it doesn't hide the pain in his words.

'Yeah, we're nearing seventy thousand subscribers, and we're a month into it. Turns out, people really miss watching real people doing basic human stuff. Go figure. It's just a shame that our time is running out. I mean, what we've created here is huge, bigger than me, bigger than college. A couple of brands have started sponsoring us too. They want to pay me to advertise their food and drink in my videos. Cool, huh? And since there's an audience on Tubeify again, companies have started running ads on there too, meaning the creator fund just got reinstated.'

Dad sniffs back his tears. 'That's great, son. That's so great to hear.'

'S-So I've been thinking,' I say, swallowing the nerves creeping through my body, 'you don't need to worry about me going to college to do performing arts any more, I-I think I can make a living online now – with the rate things are picking up.'

Dad's voice changes almost immediately, his stern parenting style making a reappearance. 'Mikah, listen, I get that you're excited about the channel, but please don't make any rash decisions. I agree that performing arts probably isn't the safest option right now, what with the state of the arts industry, but Isobel's marketing course sounds fascinating, really stable . . .'

I allow him to drone on for nearly ten minutes, until Zach yells that our bacon butties are ready, and finally (after saying hi to Mum) I hang up. Defeat washes over me. Even when I've proven myself capable of 'making it' as a creator, people still don't believe in me.

CHAPTER 24

The next day, the front door flies open and Isobel bundles inside with her bag, laptop and a thick cardboard box.

Zach and I glance over the top of the sofa at her, avocado toast hanging from our teeth, controllers in hand, the latest single from Doze Emblem blaring from the TV speakers. Cheki chills in the armchair with her laptop, watching old videos of her favourite band.

Isobel dumps her bags at the door and saunters over with the box. From it, she produces a stack of intricately wrapped plastic masks. She glances at the name handwritten on each and hands them to their prospective owners.

I throw Zach a look of confusion. She's been gone all week without a word and now she's acting like she never left? 'Hello to you too,' I say.

'Delirium Designs worked overtime to get these done for us so quick.' Iz is straight to business, ignoring my attempt at reconnecting after being apart for so long. 'Cost us a fortune – thank god for all the sponsorship requests that rolled in over the past week – I think you'll be impressed.'

'Yeah, all eyes are definitely on us at the moment,' I admit.

I take my mask and unravel the tissue paper and bubble wrap. It already feels so much sturdier than the one I'm used to wearing, like it's indestructible. The mask takes on the same general shape as the previous one, with the forehead, cheeks and nose covered and small slits for eyeholes, with the mouth lasered out so that I can continue to create mukbang videos and be the mouthpiece of the group. But the design is different. Better. Gorgeous. Made by real human hands. The masks are black, with a Digital Demons insignia printed across in gold, created by Delirium Designs herself. I run my fingers over the texture, which makes the whole mask look as if it's real, painted skin.

I place it on my face and secure the straps. Amazingly, it's shaped to perfectly fit my face. My nose no longer feels like it's being pushed into my skull and the sides sit in line with my cheekbones. It's like wearing a second skin.

I whip it off and examine it again, awestruck. There's even a tiny hidden design on each, a symbol of what we represent. Mine is teeth, Zach's is breath and Cheki's has a blood droplet carved into it. My hand shakes as I turn the mask over and over, taking in every bit of it. See? *This* is what humans can create. *This* is art. These masks have an identity of their own; there's no machine built that can take an idea like this and then breathe life into it.

To my surprise, I look up and see Isobel has her own mask on.

It's the opposite of ours, golden with a black motif. Her hidden design is an eight-pointed star. I question the origin.

'It's the star of Ishtar,' she replies. 'An ancient Mesopotamian symbol of the Sumerian goddess Inanna, also known as the Kingmaker.'

I crack a smile. Of course her symbol comes with a meaning so deep that only she understands it. Isobel certainly has made kings of us on this channel. A grin spreads over my face. 'Perfect,' I say.

'I took your advice and got one of my own. No more feeling pushed out and sidelined by your fans.'

I let out a huff. 'Fans? I think most people online hate us now, to be fair.'

She shrugs. 'How about we clean up and remind everyone that we're still here and we have a message to send?'

'I like them,' Zach says, mulling his own mask over. 'Although I kinda thought we'd all get the mouthpieces cut out this time. Never mind, I guess. We can start filming tomorrow. My parents are on their way to London to meet with a potential investor so I'm throwing a house party at mine tonight. You're all invited. Be nice to catch up with old school mates before we start college next week.'

Suddenly, the air goes cold around me as the bubble of our summer holiday isolation bursts and reality sets in –

how has college snuck up on us *this* quickly? This can't be the end of Digital Demons already.

Zach leans over to me. 'Please come, mate. I know you hate parties, but do it for me?' He leaves the cottage after lunch to set up back at his place and Cheki goes with him to help.

After some convincing, I agree to accompany Isobel later that evening.

I throw Isobel a small smile as we bundle into the back of a taxi and make for Zach's place in town. She's glammed up to the nines: curled hair, make-up done, nails painted the same burgundy as the dress that cuts across her thighs. I've borrowed one of Zach's shirts, since none of my own fit any more. But even his is too short for my torso, barely reaching the jeans I no longer need a belt for.

God, I can't think of anything worse than going to a house party with our old school mates. Even though my face is clearing up again and I feel stronger thanks to Zach's workout routine, I haven't felt this frumpy since Year Seven. None of those people were ever my friends. They only tolerated me because of Zach, Isobel and Cheki.

My hand subconsciously reaches for my face, longing to straighten my mask and ensure I'm well hidden. Only I'm not wearing a mask. I take in a deep breath as Isobel chats about her trip home and all the reading she got done for her upcoming course. I don't hear anything she says. My brain is racing, telling me I'm in danger and I need to get out of the taxi and run back to the holiday cottage. I feel naked and exposed without the mask. It's been a month since we started the channel, but already it's become a part of me.

We pull up outside Zach's house. It's pretty big – four bedrooms and a stunning garden. I know it like the back of my hand, have been here countless times, found solace behind its walls throughout the lifetime of friendship I've had with Zach – but today feels different. The place is swarming with people I used to pass in the corridors at school, but barely any of them know my name.

Isobel takes my hand and guides me out of the taxi and up the garden, through the front door, gently rubbing her thumb over my skin, easing some of the tension the way only she can. Music is already blaring through the surround sound speakers, and a mass of bodies swallows us as soon as we enter.

'Iz! Oh my god, you're here.'

'Where have you been?'

'I tried calling you so many times over the holiday and you haven't answered! Have you been abroad?'

Isobel is swept into her friends' sphere, blocking me out of my own girlfriend's orbit. None of them ever did like me. They constantly told Isobel that she should be dating one of the popular boys, like Zach, instead of a weird geek like me. Luckily, she isn't the type to be persuaded by others, but it still sucks.

I scan the room, trying to locate someone to talk to. So far, no luck. I wave a quick hello to some of the guys from my old roleplay gaming days, unsurprised to see them in the corner of the kitchen, keeping to themselves and guarding the buffet snacks.

'You came!' Cheki says, running at me with her arms wide, splashing her drink over the back of some poor dude in a white tee. 'Soz,' she throws at him nonchalantly.

'I hate parties,' I say.

'I know, but it's the last week of the holidays and isn't it great to see everyone again? This is probably the last time our year group will be in the same place.'

'I'm surprised he didn't tell me about it sooner,' I say, shrugging. 'It's not like I haven't spent the past week attached to his hip. He must've been planning this for a couple of days, at least. Look how many people are here.'

Cheki tilts her head and furrows her brow. 'You guys are best mates. He probably didn't think he needed to tell you because he knew you'd come regardless – even though you hate social gatherings above five people.'

She playfully nudges me, but I shrug her off, unsure how to put it into words.

Then I spot him in the other room, lingering by the DJ deck, surrounded by guys from the rugby and cricket teams. He looks dapper, draped in silver jewellery and donning a tight baby-blue shirt with light-grey trousers. Effortless hair, gleaming smile.

Cheki takes in a deep breath and nods, slowly. 'He really knows how to work a room, huh?'

'I don't get how he does it. He effortlessly makes people like him; he's so smart and casual and attractive and cocky all at once, yet all the guys want to be mates with him and all the girls want to date him. Like, why'd he choose to be *my* friend out of literally everyone?'

Cheki throws me a confused look. 'Are you serious? You guys are two peas in a pod. Those people hanging around him only like him because his mum is a well-connected game developer and he has all the games consoles. *You're* his best mate.'

'It doesn't feel like it sometimes.' I don't mean to sound as pathetic as I do, but seeing him surrounded by the popular kids while I'm hovering in the kitchen reminds me that the fame Digital Demons has brought me probably wouldn't exist without the security I've been granted by the anonymity of the mask.

'You see Zach for who he really is: a fiercely loyal friend with pretty low self-esteem deep down. He knows that, and he respects that. I think he needs this tonight; he's been struggling with the whole anonymity thing. Digital Demons is a way to live up to his family name and make his family proud, and no one knows it's him. Just let him bask in the shallow attention he's used to, yeah? It makes him feel good.'

I nod and throw her a half-smile as she disappears into the crowd once more, in search of more punch to fill her now empty cup. I guess I understand his plight. In some way, the mask has given me what it's taken away from him.

Grabbing some of the buffet still being guarded by the roleplaying nerds, I weave my way through the crowd, occasionally nodding to someone from an old class in acknowledgement.

Isobel has been claimed by the gaggle of girls.

A couple of the guys from the rugby team saunter by me, nudging me out of the way as they make for the snacks and force my old roleplaying mates to scatter. 'Whassup, Ratatouille,' one says, smirking at me as he passes.

I scuff my shoes on the kitchen floor and avoid making eye contact. God knows why. I tower over him and could probably knock a few of his teeth clean from his mouth, but Isobel has always said I'm too nice to stick up for myself, a real people pleaser. I sigh. It's going to be a long night.

After downing a cup of punch so sweet it makes my cheeks ache, I make for the bathroom. At least in here I'll get some peace. I sit on the side of the bath and whip my phone out. It's been a while since I've dared to look at the comments under our videos, or on our Photorah page, let alone check Vandalize and read through the sub-threads, but this is exactly where I go first.

Vandalize seems to host our most avid viewers and they're somewhat protective of us as creators, trying to gatekeep what we're putting out yet simultaneously spreading the word about us like they're our disciples.

I swallow the anxiety and start reading through some of their posts.

> All right, Echo, you've convinced me to get ANOTHER takeaway this week!

> The mask tho! I don't care whether he's dripping gravy

on his chin, his voice is so flippin hot, it's diabolical.

He's literally become such an obsession

Echo's such a lil baby girl, I need him wrapped in bubble wrap and kept away from the meanies online omg, I hate thinking that he's sad because of nasty things being said about the mask F-up.

No, but literally, he sounded so sorry in his apology vid. Protect this man at all costs!

I laugh, sucking in the adoration like a sugar fix. God, I can't wait to get back to the cottage, back under my new mask, back to my new life.
Ding.
I click the notification, expecting it to be another sponsorship request by a brand wanting me to promote their confectionery products. It isn't. My shoulders stiffen as I scan the direct message from AnnaConda of Extreme Elites.

Greetings, Echo and the rest of Digital Demons,
Thank you for considering me to join you at a food festival at the end of the year.
How about we meet up and discuss the details?
Location and date pending once confirmation has been received.
Here's to the future of tech,
Anna

CHAPTER 25

I throw the bathroom door open and fall into a mass of people waiting to use the loo. 'S-Sorry,' I mutter, stumbling through them as they glare at me and comment under their breath about me holding up the line.

I push through the sea of bodies, checking each face to see whether it belongs to someone I know. I clock him, surrounded by a group of laughing lads, all with one hand around a cup of punch and the other in their pocket. I make my way through and come face to face with my best mate.

Zach grins at me. 'You good?' he asks. 'So glad you could come, mate. You've said hi to everyone, yeah?'

'Yeah.' I clock the eyes of the guy who called me Ratatouille earlier. I flash him a half-smile. 'I need to talk to you, it's about . . .' I throw weary glances at the horde of sports guys latching on to my every word. 'You know,' I finish, hoping he catches my drift.

At first, Zach stares straight through me, but then it clicks. 'Back in a minute, guys, sorry.'

He guides me through the house, towards the shoe rack at the front door, where the music doesn't seem so loud and there's a slight draught keeping partygoers away.

'Look.' I thrust my phone with Anna's direct message on screen under his nose.

He reads the message. 'Huh ... this is what you want, right, to have an in-person meet? Looks like she's agreeing to it.'

'OK, but why not say that in her message? Why do I have to meet her in person now just for her to agree to meet me at Mukbang Metropolis?'

He shrugs. 'Dunno. Maybe for the same reason boxers meet before their match? Drum up some hype and start building an audience for it? It'd be pretty lousy if you both turned up and there was no one there to see it, right?' He laughs like this is obvious news.

I guess for someone in the sports sector, where competitions and rivalry are expected, it is obvious. He gives the phone back to me and I slap him on the upper arm, appreciative of the way he always keeps me level-headed about things.

'I think I'm going to go back to the cottage and get prepared. Message her back and agree to meet as soon as, start drumming up hype, like you said. Have you been keeping up with everything our fans have been saying online? Vandalize is a mental place; they talk like they know us.'

Zach flashes me a small smile but his eyes dart back to the group of rugby lads chortling among themselves, all taking a swig of their drinks in unison like they're one entity.

'Obviously I don't expect you to come back with me – you've still got your party going on – but we're gonna hit the ground running tomorrow, like Iz said, yeah? This thing we've built, Digital Demons, I think it can go stratospheric.'

Now I have his full attention. 'The thing *we* built?' he asks, staring at me, unblinking.

I nod nervously. 'Yeah, this is our project, since the day our parents both lost their jobs to AI. Mine and yours. Ours.'

I hold my open palm out for him to slap his into, like we always do. He doesn't return it.

Zach doesn't smile. He doesn't say anything. He just stares at me for longer than I can bear. What's got into him? Everything was fine between us this morning; we were playing video games and chatting about nonsense.

'You good?' I ask.

'Just seems like Digital Demons is more of a you and Isobel thing now.'

'I-I thought you were over the fact that we went to Oldham without you? I thought we'd moved past it . . . Things are different now. We've got new masks. You're healing, and we're building an incredible audience who love what we're doing.'

He sighs, his drink dropping to his side as his posture softens. His eyes trace over my face and then cross into the next room towards his rugby mates.

'So, what are you saying?'

His face contorts, like he's trying to find the best way to tell a lover they're breaking up. 'I guess I'm just kinda over the whole Digital Demons thing. College starts next week. I've missed all my cricket and rugby practices for the channel. At first it was fun, it took my mind off my mum's company going into liquidation, but I'm bored of it. This last week when we just got to chill and there was no content to film reminded me how much of the summer I've lost to the channel.'

This cuts me deep. Here I was, thinking we were having the best summer of our lives, and all the while he was looking for a way out.

'I'm good at sports,' he continues. 'If I put more time and effort into it, maybe that's the pathway for me. Robots won't be playing rugby anytime soon. The guys are holding practice down at the rugby club tomorrow and, while I can't play with this stupid broken rib, I think I'm gonna go and give them my support.'

I feel the cold front door behind me as I fall away from him, stumped. I must look devastated because he steps towards me, his hand gripping the top of my arm like a vice.

'I'm not saying that this is it, mate. I just think it's important we refocus our attention again. We gave ourselves until the end of summer to spread the message. We succeeded, but our time is over. Let's go back to our lives.'

'But things are finally taking off for us, mate. We have

ad revenue now, good sponsorship deals coming in thick and fast . . . We might not need to go to college at this rate.'

Zach shrugs. 'That's a big risk to take if things start dropping off. I get having dreams and all that, but dreams mean nothing if you don't have a solid foundation to fall back on. Let's face it, I can't injure myself any more for stupid videos or I'll never play a match again.'

I yank my arm from his grip. 'Easy for you to stand here and say all this. I've just publicly challenged Anna-Conda and her makers to meet me for an in-person mukbang competition. How can *I* throw the towel in and walk away? I'd make a joke of the whole channel, murder our own message and spit on it for good measure.'

I glare at him, fury surging through my veins as he casts his hesitant gaze over my face.

I can't let this go, even if I wanted to; it's part of me now. We're fighting the good fight. Digital Demons has given me the online reach to spread our message about people like my dad and Zach's mum losing their jobs to AI. In turn, the holiday cottage has become my sanctuary, as well as the mask that's given me confidence I never thought I could obtain.

I have fans.

People like me.

I'm not giving it all up.

CHAPTER 26

Two whole days pass by and Zach doesn't return to the holiday cottage. I sit in my bed, scrolling Photorah, pausing on the recent uploads from my best mate. Pictures of him cheering for his rugby mates at the side of the pitch. It's in his glazed-over eyes and forced grin how badly he wants to be covered in mud and slight scrapes from tackles like the rest of the lads.

My heart aches as I stare into his two-dimensional happiness. He was happy here too for a while. I was sure of it when we were playing video games and mooching around like old times. Sadness threatens to consume me.

Maybe I should have been a better teammate for him, and made sure it was just him and me from the beginning. But then we wouldn't have had this place as our base camp. Plus, Cheki and Isobel have been integral to the running of the channel. Without them, I doubt Zach and I would've got it off the ground.

I guess the two of us weren't the dream team after all; it needed all four of us.

I clench my jaw as sadness turns to fury and slam my

phone on my bed, screen side down.

Ding.

Without thinking, I lift my phone again and check the notification. Vandalize.

There's something so intoxicating about all the fan theories about my identity that keeps me going back for more. I haven't told Cheki or Isobel that I made myself an anonymous account to join the fun, but being able to infiltrate the conversation surrounding me (and throw in some ludicrous assumptions about myself too) is highly entertaining.

Someone has replied to one of the posts I made, where I claimed that I'm actually an already established Tubeifyer from the golden days.

> Ohh, great theory! the replier has said. I've actually gone and had a look at some of the old channels and tried to match Echo's voice to some of them. I thought maybe someone like JayJay Janson, the investigator, but he's making content behind a personal paywall now – it wouldn't make sense for it to be him. Also tried the true crime channel Shponix FM but the voices don't match.

I like the comment and reply under my alias: **Ah! Too bad. I've defo heard his voice on Tubeify before though.**

Living this double life makes me chuckle and eases the pain of Zach's absence. I scroll through other posts about me, lapping up the compliments, blown away by the talent of artists behind the endless stream of fan art, watching other anonymous users get torn to shreds when they attempt to bring AI art into the mix.

This is literally the thing Digital Demons are trying to eradicate online, says one user.

Another says: **Get this AI slop off my screen. NOW. Do not disrespect our lord and saviour, Echo, first of his name, digital demon and anarchist of the web.**

A massive grin creeps over my face as I scroll through the commentary, a rush flowing through my veins, making the hairs on the back of my neck stand to attention. I've never had so many people curious about me, like I'm worth something to them. It's like I have my own personal army who'd take down an empire for me, just to see me chow down some ramen.

I scroll until I reach the threads I've already read a million times.

Groaning, I click on the posts with purple links, checking to see if any new comments have appeared during the ten-minute break I've had since my last scroll. None. My shoulders sag. Admittedly, this is one Vandalize thread I'm not too happy to see. It's a bunch of people theorizing about our identities, but instead of curiosity and playfulness, some of the comments have turned nasty.

If they're putting stuff up online then they must want us to discover who they are.

Literally! Can't be doing with people saying Digital Demons want to be anonymous when it's so obvious

that all of them are trying to show us who they are behind the masks. Like, if they truly wanted to be unknown, then A) they wouldn't be putting themselves online and B) wouldn't be acting like themselves in their videos

That comment confuses me the most. Luckily, upon refreshing the page, a new account has verbalized my thoughts:

Not really sure how you've come to the conclusion that they want their identities to be known? The whole point of them wearing masks and using pseudonyms is to conceal their real identities? Although, I do admit that they haven't made it *too* difficult to trace them …

Huh? With shaky hands, I reply:

What do you mean? Have you traced their location?

I wait a couple of minutes, chewing on my fingernails, constantly refreshing the page.

Ding. I click the notification so fast that my phone system doesn't know how to compute the request and lags, warranting an exasperated groan from me.

I mean, is it not obvious that their content house is somewhere in southern England, in the Dorset area? Haven't managed to pin the exact location yet, but their content house is a pretty unique style of building, their accents are southern English, and they've filmed at and around Durdle Door.

My body goes numb.

I refresh the page again, seeing the absurd replies under this new user's comment.

> OMG! Someone here must live in the south of England. PLEASEEE can you go and have a mooch around some famous landmarks and see if you can catch sight of them doing stunts??

> I literally had the same idea as you. They're definitely operating from somewhere in that neck of the woods. I've been using maps to try and match the images of their house from their videos. Spent all night going through individual streets looking for a big house with a pool. AM TIRED!

> Anyone else just want to desperately hug Echo?

> Hug him. Kiss him. Kidnap and marry him – yeah, all of it.

> I just wanna know whether he has a gf and whether she can fight.

> Lol. Literally. I'd be willing to take any girl out if she dares lay her hands on MY Echo.

Her Echo? She doesn't even know me. My hands are shaking, and I'm about to reply to the last comment when a knock on the door startles me. I close the Vandalize app and shove my phone beneath my pillow. Cheki pops her head around the door frame.

'Are you OK? You look like you've seen a ghost.'

'F-Fine,' I manage. 'Just tired, you know?'

Cheki nods at me slowly, clearly not buying what I'm selling. 'Whatever. Anyway, I've spoken to my dad and explained how well the channel is doing and that we want to continue building. He says he's happy for us to use this place as a base for Digital Demons content. He'll be here over Christmas with his girlfriend and her family, though, so we'll have to leave for a bit, but other than that, it's ours so long as we take care of it.'

I flash her a cheesy grin. 'Amazing! Cheki, thank you. Thank you for everything, I can't tell you how much it means to me to be able to carry this on. I was so worried last night, I barely slept.'

She perches on the edge of my bed, wearing a long, pleated dress with about fifteen different patterns and colours, and her hair has been braided with thick beads. 'Truthfully, I should be thanking you. I never wanted to go to college anyway, so now that Digital Demons is taking off, I'm relieved that I can just focus on this and be a content creator full-time.'

Her words make my heart leap and I squeeze her hand.

'I called my parents again last night and told them I'm definitely withdrawing my college placement,' I admit. 'It went down as well as I expected ... But we've come too far with the channel to quit now.'

Cheki flashes me a sympathetic smile. 'Mine were fine with it. Dad says the best entrepreneurs don't have much formal education, anyway.'

'Dad yelled at me for an hour straight, telling me I'm throwing my future away. Mum . . . I dunno, Mum wasn't so hard on me. They knew it was coming, but even when I showed them proof on video of our profits, they still couldn't accept it. I think Dad's worried I'll suffer the same fate as him.'

We're silent for a moment, neither of us catching the other's gaze. Finally, her words cut through the awkwardness. 'I would have thought your dad would be more understanding, what with his profession always being in the creative sector.'

'Yeah, but that just means he knows what a tough battle it is. I get it – but I've only ever wanted to be a creator. He never did like the fact that I wanted to be a thespian, he thinks he encouraged me, doomed me to a life of the starving artist like him. He just wants me to have something to fall back on in case content creation doesn't work out. I get it. I'm not mad at him.'

She sighs. 'He has a point.' I'm about to argue when she holds her hand out for me to give her a minute to finish verbalizing her thoughts. 'We're finally on track with the ad revenue, and we have sponsors. But we're not on stable ground yet, Mikah. All it takes is one wrong move and we get cancelled, or there's a more revolutionary nExGEN upgrade and everything we've built could come crashing down around us. We're taking a huge risk.'

I frown and sink into my bed. She's right.

'We need bigger brand deals and sponsors,' I say. 'We

need to prove to advertisers *why* they should come back to Tubeify and promote their stuff to *our* audience.'

'We do.'

But how? I stare into her soft brown eyes but there's nothing there, no inspiration, just another person hoping I'll come up with the solution. I need Zach. He's the guy I bounce things off; he's the one who helps me turn my hare-brained schemes into something tangible. There's another knock on the door and this time, Isobel appears.

'I've been waiting for you to come downstairs for ages,' she says. 'It's lunchtime, babe. I hope you've not been in bed just scrolling all morning.' Her face isn't that of a scolding parent, but filled with concern. 'It's not good for you.'

Isobel and Cheki exchange looks. We all know that I have wasted the morning lost in the hype and hate surrounding me.

'OK.' Isobel sounds defeated. 'But we should film a mukbang before your meeting with AnnaConda tomorrow. Meeting your online nemesis in person for the first time is a big deal. We need people talking about it. Hopefully more sponsors will put their hands in their pockets for us. The money we're getting is good, but we need more.'

I mull this over. 'Nice. Yeah, you're right. Let's make this mukbang the most controversial one yet.'

CHAPTER 27

By the time I make it downstairs, Cheki and Isobel have already cooked, eaten and cleared away their full English breakfasts. Mine sits cold on a plate by the microwave. The beans are congealed, the bacon has gone rubbery, and the hash browns and toast are soggier than a dish sponge. I frown at the offering, but bring it to the breakfast bar and tuck in without bothering to film. I'm not hungry, but my stomach craves the feeling of fullness.

'We need to go shopping,' Isobel says. 'Get some goods for this mukbang.'

With a long sigh, I head out of the kitchen and grab my coat from the hook by the front door. 'We should have done an online shop when we saw that the stock was getting low; this is such a waste of time. I need to be filming and then keeping an eye on what's happening online.' I slam my feet into my shoes and throw a thin coat over my mismatched outfit. Fashion isn't a priority right now, content is. Besides, nothing I own fits any more.

'You're grumpy today,' Isobel says, frowning as she rounds the staircase and heads upstairs.

I don't know why I feel so irritable all of a sudden, but since Zach's party, it's like all the joy has been sucked from me. Cheki grabs her coat and shoes and gestures towards the door, silent irritation plastered over her face. Guess she's drawn the short straw in keeping me company on this shopping trip, then.

The supermarket lights are blinding; fluorescent white with a low hum that makes the nervous system go haywire. It's been a while since I've actually stepped inside a supermarket. Cheki's dad did us a solid by stocking the house cupboards and fridge before we arrived, and alongside our takeout binges, everything else has been done online.

I clock the fruit and veg aisles, which I definitely won't be going down, but it's the billboards that take me by surprise. Among the usual signs leading shoppers in the right direction through the store, there's an endless display of Extreme Elites, fronted by AnnaConda.

Everywhere I walk, the perfect faces, glossy eyes and shimmering grins of Khristoff, Noruwai and AnnaConda follow me. They're now the faces of every Tanaki Foundation product ever created, and the man is slowly taking over the world with his company.

I scoff and give a feeble kick to one of their life-size stands, promoting a new home speaker system that has a 'friendship' function which enables the user to train the AI voice to act like a companion.

'That's so unnecessary,' I hiss to Cheki behind me. 'We're being sold a solution to a problem that never existed before social media became the most unsociable place in the world.' I roll my eyes.

We follow signs to the confectionery aisles deep in the store. The brands behind the sugary snacks will be laughing in their penthouses soon, because me and my mukbangs are about to single-handedly keep them in business. I just hope it's still possible to buy products that aren't owned by people like Tanaki.

We round the corner, following the signs saying *Crisps*, *Biscuits* and *Chocolate*, until we find our aisle. I stop dead and gasp. Cheki bumps into me. The shelves are almost empty, and what's left is being pillaged by a horde of teens stuffing their arms and shopping baskets.

'Too late, dorks,' one of them says as the group slips past us, grinning from ear to ear, having taken what little remained on the shelves.

My jaw drops. 'What the hell is going on?' It's like a scene from a disaster movie, after news anchors have announced worldwide shortages, a deadly pandemic or another world war. Except instead of the essentials like bottled water, cans of beans and toilet rolls selling out, there's a shortage of ScorchaSnaps, BerryWinkl Breakfast Tarts and Toasted Marshmallow Popcorn Syrup.

A loud sigh from behind has us whipping our heads around. A man in a blue uniform drags a large crate of crisps and other snacks into the aisle, beckoning us to get out of his way. 'If this is what you're after, you'll have to wait until I've got it all on the shelves. I'm not having you grabbing things off the cart and messing up my inventory.'

'N-No, we're not here to take from you,' I say. 'Can I ask what's happened? Why are all the shelves empty?'

'Seriously?' he tuts. 'Everyone seems to think that eating eight portion's worth of food in one sitting while being filmed is the new quick-fire way of getting rich and becoming famous. It's all because of those stupid kids online who made mukbang "cool" again, and now everyone wants a piece of their success.'

I glance around him and clock the mass of bodies lingering at the end of the aisle. I snap my head over my own shoulder and see more people on the other side. A crowd of people, young and older, linger by both exits, all teetering on the tips of their toes, ready to pounce the moment the store worker cuts through the cellophane wrapping binding the confectionery to his crate.

My body turns cold. What the hell is going on? Have we really incited this mass hysteria? I guess I don't blame others for wanting what we've created with Digital Demons; it's always the first to the feast who feeds well.

We brace for impact as the man takes out his box cutter from his pocket and slices through the plastic. Madness descends. Arms fly over my head, elbows dig themselves into my eye sockets, my ribs are punched and battered, my hair grabbed and lobbed backwards as a stranger attempts to use me as a ladder to get to Kottage Kay's ChokaBloka bars at the top of the crate. I grab what I can, stuffing things in my pockets and beneath my hoody, hoping no one thinks I'm stealing, hoping Cheki is doing the same. Slowly, I'm pushed out of the mass of bodies, and I can breathe again.

The crowd depletes, leaving the once full cart barren of goods, like a corpse stripped of its flesh by vultures. The store worker crouches on the ground. He whimpers. Cheki drops her armful of snacks and goes to him, gently informing him that the crowd has gone.

'This is absolute madness,' I say.

'Let's go before we get stripped of everything we have,' she agrees.

We make for the tills and, like everyone else, we guard our plunder like dragons. As our goods move along the conveyor belt, I notice a strange packet by Cheki. It's gold and silver, rectangular and thin, with a small cardboard sleeve around it. I recognize it from somewhere, but I don't have time to examine it closely until we're in the back of the taxi again, trying to catch our breath, giggling over the chaos our videos have caused in the supermarkets.

I grab the packet from the shopping bag nearest to Cheki and turn it in my hands, reading the small print on the cardboard sleeve.

TANAKI FOOD INCORPORATIONS
NUTROX

'This is one of those food bars the contestants ate in *Island of Influencers*,' I say. 'The new Tanaki product he was trying out during the competition. Do you remember? We all thought it was neat and could be a fix for world hunger. We wanted to try it – well, here it is.'

'Oh, yeah,' she says, grabbing it from my hands. 'I saw it on an end aisle as we were heading for the tills and assumed it was a chocolate bar of some kind.'

'We can't eat this, though, can we? Not without one of those funky Tanaki machines that cost like a billion pounds.'

'No, we can.' Cheki points to the fine print on the cardboard sleeve. 'It says: *New recipe! For at-home consumption. Simply pop the packet into your microwave for time stated, allow to sit, and enjoy.* Cool! I doubt anyone else is mukbanging with these; it'll be different.'

'Bloody hell, it was expensive,' I say, checking the receipt. No doubt reviewing one of the Tanaki bars on camera will be an interesting idea, but I can't do it, can I? How can I justify eating a product made by the same man who's actively destroying social media? It'd be pure internet dystopia. But . . . it might also get people talking.

We bundle through the front door, dragging our shopping bags behind us, and immediately get to work setting the stage for my mukbang, abandoning our bags on the kitchen floor.

Cheki creates the usual set-up in the sitting room, with the camera on the coffee table and a space between it and the sofa for me to sit. I don my mask and perch on a cushion on the floor, awaiting confirmation that the camera is rolling. It's odd not seeing Zach behind the camera too. My throat tightens. I miss him. I wonder whether he misses me too.

She gives me a thumbs up and I try to shake my best mate's face from the reveries of my mind.

'Hey, guys, welcome back,' I say, putting on the most cheerful voice I can muster.

But I can't stop thinking about my friend.

If Zach doesn't return soon, we're probably going to have to put out a statement explaining his lack of presence in the recent videos.

That's one thread I don't want to read about on Vandalize.

CHAPTER 28

I force my brain to stop thinking about Zach.

'Today, we saw a remarkable thing in the supermarkets,' I say. 'All the shelves in the confectionery aisles have been wiped clean. First, I just want to say that this proves how influential real people are. Second, I'm stoked so many of you have been inspired to pick up a camera and start filming your own videos for Tubeify. We're another step closer to reliving the golden days of the internet! But, please, be considerate of other shoppers and don't hurt the workers who're just trying to do their jobs. But that's enough of that, let me show you what I'm going to be eating today. I'm a real human who's going to try a food created by a brand that generates artificial content . . .'

I hold the gold-and-silver bar up to the camera. It's around the same size as an A5 piece of paper and I twist it in my hands to give the viewer a proper look. 'This bar was created by the Tanaki Foundation. It was trialled during the infamous livestream *Island of Influencers*. We got to witness the likes of TheHarperHerald and Belle

Deveraux try them out, and these bars captivated all of us at home, made us desperate to get our hands on them. Well, now they're in the shops. Modified for the everyday consumer. They're ridiculously expensive and, honestly, insanely ugly. Like, who looks at this and thinks it's a substantial meal? No one. I'm going to try it for you and let you all know how it tastes.'

I grab the camera from the tripod on the edge of the coffee table and head to the kitchen. An unmasked Isobel quickly jumps out of my way to avoid being caught on camera, but I'm careful to ensure that my own face fills the screen as I head towards the microwave. I sure as hell don't want to be responsible for doxxing us, especially when the threat of exposure is already looming.

'Let's see, two minutes on high heat and then leave to stand for another two minutes. All right, let's throw this in.' I pop the packet into the microwave and set it to the highest heat. 'Now, these packets could genuinely help people all over the world. One bar is supposed to keep you full for an entire day – we'll see how true that is for someone like me, who's stretched their stomach so much through mukbangs that even three meals a day can't keep me satisfied any more.'

Ping. The bar needs to sit inside the microwave for a further two minutes, as instructed, to allow the flavours to marinate, so I continue chatting to my fans – I mean viewers. 'As you guys know, I've invited AnnaConda from Extreme Elites to join me at the end of the year at a food festival called Mukbang Metropolis. Side by side, you'll see a person take on a robot.'

I pull the bar out of the microwave and take both it and the camera back to the sitting room. Cheki reattaches the phone to the tripod while I unwrap the product. A simple black bar, like a biscuit with all its chocolate licked off, stares up at me. I scowl. So unappetizing.

'Well, here goes.' I bring the bar up to my mouth, closing my eyes as I bite down and take a huge chunk. I chew. And chew. And chew some more. The texture is like that of stale cake, soft but with some resistance. My tongue is coated with the flavour of caramelized biscuit cheesecake and my stomach growls in longing. I certainly can't feel the sensation of crunching down on the biscuit base or lapping up the sweet cream-cheese filling, but it definitely tastes like it. My brain is going haywire, telling me I'm eating, but then my tongue counteracts it with reality.

It's unnerving and oddly unsatisfying, while also scratching an itch I didn't know I had.

I spit chunks of black on to the coffee table before me. 'Ugh,' I say, overexaggerating my movements as I wipe the food off my tongue. 'So weird. It's not food at all, but like some cheap imitation of food, like I'm eating a processed cheese slice with the wrapper still on.' I laugh, holding up the soggy bar to examine it. 'It really is like looking at an AI version of a human; touted to be the thing itself but really just an imitation of it. This bar might take on the taste of a cheesecake, but it doesn't look like it and it doesn't feel like it in my mouth.'

I drop the bar back on to my plate and watch it splatter, grimacing. 'No, thanks. I don't want my Sunday roast replaced by one of these bars, I want to feel the crunch of a roast potato and see the gravy dripping over my chicken. And this is the point I'm trying to make with my face-to-face mukbang with AnnaConda.'

I push the plate away from me and fold my arms like it's a mic drop. 'The verdict is in, folks, and these Tanaki food products are out. And to AnnaConda . . . I'll be seeing you soon. Artificial intelligence vs humans. Until the next mukbang, friends – peace!'

I throw up a peace symbol and hold my pose, waiting for Cheki to stop the recording. She throws me a thumbs up when the red button turns grey.

'Nice!' Isobel says, clapping. 'An interesting video concept and another call to action for the Mukbang Metropolis festival. Give me your phone and I'll get this uploaded. We're not wasting any more time.'

She grabs my phone and heads upstairs again to her editing lair.

'Is it really that bad?' Cheki asks.

I frown at the remaining Tanaki bar on the coffee table. 'It tastes amazing – like seriously has the flavour of a cheesecake. It just doesn't feel right, like my brain can't quite compute what's in my mouth. It's both satisfying and unsettling all at once. I can't really describe it. Try it.'

Cheki takes a small portion of the splattered remnants of the bar.

'Can you imagine the chemicals they've put in this thing to make it taste this way?' she says, her eyes bulging as she chews. At first, she looks pleasantly surprised, then she frowns, and her chews become disjointed and laborious. 'Oh ... um ... huh ... no.' She spits it out. 'Get rid of it. It's not fit for humans.'

I scoop the rest of the bar from the table and shove it deep inside the kitchen bin, then run upstairs to Isobel's room, desperate to reclaim my phone so I can resume scrolling through our comments.

I knock on her door but let myself in without invitation anyway. I find her sitting on her bed with her laptop open and her editing software loading, staring at my phone. I freeze and she lifts her head to meet my eyeline.

'What the hell is this?' she asks.

I glance at the sub-thread on Vandalize, at the posts about us, lusting over us, trying to find our location, picking apart everything about us in screenshots taken from our videos. Currently, the post loaded on screen has a long comment thread of anonymous users wanting to be my girlfriend and claiming they'll treat me better than any girlfriend they perceive me to have.

'I've been keeping an eye on it,' I say. It's a half-truth. I have been keeping an eye on the information put out about us, but I can't admit to her that I've also added to it, even if it was just for fun.

'Mikah.' Isobel's voice is a warning. 'These people are threatening to find this house and hurt me ...'

'Not *you*, per se, just anyone who . . . you know . . . is dating me.'

She glowers at me. 'No, Mikah, this is serious. They know where we live.'

CHAPTER 29

We leave the holiday cottage the next day wearing thick hoodies – despite the heat of summer – keeping our identities concealed with our hoods pulled tight over our faces. Having spent all evening reading through various sub-threads on Vandalize, we quickly discovered screenshots of Chaldon Herring. It won't be long until they work out which house we're in too.

I swallow my anxiety as we bundle into the back of a waiting taxi. 'I think this is a little overdramatic, don't you?' I hiss as we trundle along the country lanes.

She frowns. 'Were we reading the same Vandalize threads last night, babe? Seemed pretty clear that some of your fans are overstepping, getting a bit obsessed. They could be hiding in the bushes on the drive, for all we know.'

'Some of those comments did come off quite threatening,' Cheki adds. 'I get people fancying you – and, like, our content house, the message, the masks, the rebelliousness of it all, etcetera, is probably the most entertaining thing that's happened on the internet in over a year, but some of those users do sound a bit ... what's the word?'

'Parasocial?' Isobel offers.

Her eyes burn into the side of my skull, and I clock the driver staring at me through the rear-view mirror too. He must think we're absolute nutcases. He looks too old to be the kind of guy who gets wrapped up in social media, but who knows, he could be a stalker.

I don't know how to respond. Part of me still loves the attention I'm getting online, can't get enough of the compliments strangers are throwing at me. They call themselves starved dogs, hoping to feast on any morsel of content I give them, but I find myself rabid for them too. They'll comment under each of my mukbangs: **Feed me, sir**, with begging hand or kneeling emojis and it makes me feel invincible. But if I don't oblige, if I don't upload daily content quickly enough for them, they drag me in the comments. It's a double-edged blade and I can't help cutting myself on it over and over. At night, I devour fan theories about me, revel in their artwork depicting what they think I look like under the mask. I need them as much as they need me.

If I can't feast, neither can they.

If they don't feed, I'm starved.

No matter how weird the relationship between me and my fans, we've got a taste for one another, and it's becoming an addiction.

'We're here,' Isobel says, cutting through my inner turmoil.

We've made it to the destination AnnaConda and her

makers requested. It'll be odd being face to face with a humanoid, because although I've been beefing with her online, it's not actually *her*. She isn't real. The beef I have is with the people who made her, the ones who program her, give her speech and words to say. A little laugh escapes me. What a world. I'm beefing with a bot.

We bundle out on to the pavement, on to the steps of an abandoned cinema, and collect our bags from the boot.

'God, that was expensive,' Isobel mutters as she puts away her purse. 'Good job we had another couple of sponsorship requests this morning.'

'You sure we're at the right place?' I ask, eyebrows raised beneath my mask.

'This is the address on the email. Whoever wrote it said the place would look a little ... *unused*.'

I grimace. 'Sounds super-ominous.' Sucking in a deep breath, I lead the way up the steps, towards the heavy-looking glass doors with moss growing up them. It's unlocked. Inside, it's cold and deserted, bar a couple of rats chewing on exposed wires by an old ticket desk.

With the hairs on the back of my neck standing to attention, I walk through the abandoned cinema, beyond the ticket desk and through the rusting turnstiles. We head down a long corridor, where the walls are decorated with peeling posters from movies released a decade ago, and general notices.

'This is creepy as hell,' Cheki whimpers from behind me.

It feels like the beginning of a horror movie and we're the stupid, unknowing first victims who stumble right into the trap of the serial killer.

'Maybe we should check one of the movie rooms?' Isobel asks.

'Good idea.' I steer us towards a set of double doors and peer inside, but as far as I can tell, it's just as empty as the rest of the building. 'Hello?' I say, inching further inside. The screen is non-existent, just a black void where it once sat, and the chairs facing it are frayed and coming off their hinges.

'In here!' Cheki's voice echoes from the corridor, and I move towards it. She's standing by another set of double doors, only these ones lead to a basement typically used by staff. A gentle hum of chatter climbs the concrete steps, beckoning us down.

'Who wants to go first?' I ask.

'Why, you scared?' she mocks.

'N-No . . . I just figured someone else might like to be the first one in, you know? Don't want anyone else to think I'm taking the lead all the time, do I?'

Isobel snorts and nudges me forward. 'Off you go, mouthpiece. You started this war; you can lead us into it.'

I walk down the steps, being sucked in by the blackness beyond. We continue until we reach a set of double doors. Chatter comes from beyond them. I knock feebly and push the doors open, penetrating the hive into a mass of bodies huddled in a cosy, deeply hidden stock room. The room falls silent.

A group of adults are standing around with sullen faces, and I search the crowd, looking for John. I hope no one recognized him from his interview and did him any harm. After his warning to me, I've feared for him. He's nowhere to be seen.

Then I spot the cameras and stage lighting, all rigged and positioned perfectly around a table with two chairs.

I swallow the lump in my throat.

'Ah! Finally,' says a smooth voice from the shadows.

The crowd of techies part and a man in a navy-blue suit strides through them. He's Japanese, with black hair slicked back and warm eyes. He holds a still arm out towards me as he closes the gap between us. Isobel pushes me forward and I meet him halfway across the room.

'Mr Tanaki?' I ask, my voice quivering as I take his hand and allow him to shake mine.

He must notice my nerves because his warm smile momentarily flickers into a smirk. 'I hope so, otherwise I've been replaced by one of my own humanoids.' He chuckles with glee, but no one else laughs. 'Thank you for agreeing to meet with us.'

Tanaki leads me to the table with two seats, where the lighting sets a humble stage in the middle of the snake pit. I glance at my mates, and Isobel shrugs, unable to give me any more reassurance. I gulp. No one else knows we're here. Dad would kill me if he knew I'd agreed to meet a stranger in the basement of a disused cinema.

What a stupid idea this was.

'My sincerest apologies for all the theatrics,' Tanaki says. 'I hope you understand, I'm a popular man. Everything I do is examined and scrutinized by every newspaper and tabloid going. And this odd little feud you've brought to my table has been the hot topic of each of my interviews and board meetings lately. Everyone is quite amused by it. So, I suppose we both might as well use it to our advantage, yes?'

He gestures into the shadows and the techies part once again, revealing a perfectly still and poised Anna-Conda standing in the corner, flanked by Khristoff and Noruwai, all awaiting their next commands. I spot a guy with a handheld computer device. He inputs something and Anna springs to life. Her smile is radiant, her eyes glistening, and she locks her gaze on me as she glides towards the table and takes a seat across from me.

The guy on the controller continues inputting code in my periphery as Anna leans over the table and extends her arm.

'*Konnichiwa!*' she says, grinning at me.

I lightly shake her hand, grimacing at the tacky coldness of her silicone skin. 'What's with her language changes?'

Tanaki shrugs. 'I like her audience to feel connected to her. Language is one thing that keeps us all divided and Anna's ability to transcend those barriers makes her accessible to anyone, anywhere.'

'Clever,' I say, almost through gritted teeth. Wouldn't we all love to be able to speak multiple languages without having to sit through classes while being yelled at by our teachers for using the wrong inflection?

'Roll the cameras.' Tanaki's voice loses all warmth as

he commands the techies.

I freeze.

Isobel rushes forward, her hand landing on my shoulder. 'Wait, no, sorry, but what is this? We haven't agreed to any filming or been told to expect it.'

Tanaki flashes her a warning smile. 'You have challenged Anna – my creation and therefore *me* – to a face-to-face eat-off, have you not? I'm more than happy to oblige you in your silly venture. As I said, this whole charade has been highly amusing to my colleagues and partners. But first, I'd like to give you a taste of what you're up against. I'm giving you the chance to back out while you can, Echo and co. My only condition for such a kind offer is to also allow our audiences to get a sneak peek of what might be in store for them at Mukbang Metropolis, should you decide to go ahead with this silliness.'

I huff and roll my eyes. 'You want me to collab on a mukbang right now? Here? Fine. The challenge stands and will still stand after this.'

Tanaki's lips twist into a sadistic smile. 'Fantastic. Let's give the audience a spectacle to behold.'

CHAPTER 30

The room is quickly taken over by the scent of spice. Techies swarm the table, moving their cameras into focus, lowering boom mics over our heads. AnnaConda has gone still again, her instructions yet to be given.

On our table, there are multiple bowls of the hottest crisps known to man (Fiery Fajita, Molten Monterey Jack and Jalapeno, and Crackin' Cajun Chicken), Flamethrower Noodles that come in a bright red packet with a tiny pouch of Carolina Reaper pepper seasoning, Extra Flamin' Hot Nuts and Corn Pieces, and worst of all, a little black box containing the world's hottest corn chip, simply known as the Death Chip.

I swallow the lump forming in my throat at the sight of the black box. The chip is coated with a mixture of the Trinidad Moruga Scorpion and Pepper X – a combination straight from the depths of hell.

It's been around for years, and no one has conquered it yet. The aim is to eat it in one go, keeping it in your mouth for a minimum of thirty seconds before swallowing. Then, the players have to sit with the chip inside their stomachs for fifteen minutes. Barely anyone who has attempted the challenge has managed to swallow the chip, let alone hold it in their stomachs for long enough to beat the game. The stomach simply repels that much spice.

A nExGEN robot stomach, on the other hand . . .

Isobel steps forward, warranting groans from the camera crew as she ruins their shots. 'You don't have to do this, you have nothing to prove,' she whispers to me. 'You can walk away.'

I nod and tell her it's OK, and she returns to Cheki. Even behind their masks, I can see the worry etched on the faces of my friends. I wish Zach were here. How did we go from him and me spitballing in my room over a tube of ScorchaSnaps to me sitting next to a humanoid under the lenses of professional cameras. Laughter rumbles from my chest and escapes me. How absurd. All of it.

I snap my head over my shoulder. 'Uh . . . maybe we should film this too?'

Isobel and Cheki whip their phones from their pockets and find suitable spots in between the techies and their fancy equipment. I can't help blushing beneath my mask; we look so unprofessional among Tanaki and all his tech.

'Camera rolling,' says the disembodied voice of a techie.

I'm perfectly still in my chair but I have this weird sensation that everything in my body is shifting, like my soul is actively trying to step out of my physical form. I'm so unprepared for this, so out of my comfort zone. As I clock Tanaki lingering behind Anna, deep in the shadows once more, I get the feeling that this is exactly how he wants me to feel. He wants me off guard and wants to be in complete control of the situation, that much is clear.

'Filming in three, two, one . . .' The camera man raises his arm and drops it on one.

Instantly, I fall into my Digital Demons persona and snap my head towards Isobel's phone camera. 'Hey, guys—'

'—*Bonjour les amis*,' Anna says simultaneously.

I snap my head towards her. She stares at the camera. So, this is how it's going to be, is it? A constant fight between us for the limelight?

'How about I say my intro into my camera,' I suggest through gritted teeth, 'and then you can say your bit into your camera, and then we start eating?' I can't believe I'm trying to talk to a robot. My eyes dart from Anna to Tanaki and then to the guy controlling Anna.

Tanaki thinks about it for a minute before agreeing.

I go first. 'Hey, guys. Echo here from Digital Demons, bringing you a very special mukbang. I'm collabing with AnnaConda from Extreme Elites. No, don't worry, we aren't mates. As you well know, I've challenged her to meet me at Mukbang Metropolis to prove once and for all that no level of artificial intelligence can beat the effort and entertainment value that a human creator brings to the audience.'

Anna lets off a girlish giggle and grabs my attention. 'The reason I brought you here, Echo, is so I can show you and our viewers what you'll be battling against.' She falls still again, and two bulky figures emerge from the shadows. They swipe our food offerings to the side and unfold a paper scroll over the table.

Hesitantly, I lean forward. Isobel and Cheki step towards it too, filming and checking the scroll out themselves. It's an image of AnnaConda, a blueprint for her design, outlining each of her functions and abilities. My eyes dance over the handwriting in ocean-blue ink, annotations, codes, mathematical sums, technical jargon, and grind to a halt over the paragraph with an arrow leading to her stomach area, describing something known as the AYCE system: All You Can Eat.

'My stomach can hold five litres of food and liquid,' Anna says. She still hasn't moved from her rigid seating position. 'The human stomach only has the capacity to stretch to four litres, and that's a danger. My tongue is made from silicone; strong, fire resistant. These items on the table will cause you pain, Echo. I will not feel a thing. At Mukbang Metropolis, we'll be expected to eat and eat and eat until we burst at the seams, but you'll reach that point far before I will. Are you sure you want to compete against me?'

'Shall we get on with this mukbang?' I hiss.

Anna stares at me with her dead eyes and Tanaki smirks over her head. He nods to the guy with Anna's controls, and after a few code inputs, the humanoid begins pulling dishes towards herself. I mirror her moves until we're both left with an equal amount of devastatingly spicy noodles, corn and crisps. This is going to be hell, but I can't let her beat me. *Iron stomach*, I remind myself. *I'm the man with the iron stomach.*

My mouth salivates but my body shakes with nerves. 'No point in watching her eat these,' I say into Cheki's camera. 'You already heard her say it: she can't even taste the food, so you're not going to get anything but a fake reaction from her. How boring.'

Anna smiles at me and I roll my eyes. After a countdown, we dive into the food on offer. The noodles are cold and congealed, and the scent of sweet and spice has made me so hungry that I barely notice the burning sensation as I shovel a forkful into my mouth.

After a few bites though, reality kicks in. They're not called Flamethrower Noodles for nothing. Sweat builds on my brow and rolls down my cheek, splattering on the table from underneath my mask. Anna gives another girlish giggle. Her face is as pristine as it always is as I wince through the pain of hot Houndables crisps and cry from the burning of Extra Flamin' Hot Corn Pieces.

I retch and gasp for air as I throw one last handful into my mouth, hoping one breath might put out the fire on my tongue. For a second, I swear I can taste blood, like the spice has seared straight through my tastebuds. My hand finds my stomach as it begins to gurgle and swirl, snot oozes from my nostrils and pools in my mask as I fan my mouth with a stiff hand. Anna casually and delicately slurps her noodles, keeping a soft and almost tantalizing expression locked on the camera.

All that's left for us to eat now is the Death Chip.

Isobel shakes her head at me, the phone in her hand

still recording, focusing on the little black box between Anna and me. There's only one chip.

'I didn't think there'd be any need for two,' Anna says, sliding the box towards herself. She flips the lid and reveals a triangular-shaped corn chip in a nasty shade of red. In parts, the red spice dusting is so thick that it gives off a purple hue. I swallow, hard. My tongue is rough, my cheeks are stinging and my eyes are burning.

The scent of Trinidad Moruga Scorpion and Pepper X hits the back of my throat, and I choke on it. Anna snaps the chip in two, holds one half aloft for the camera and slides the other to me. I take it between my thumb and forefinger, feeling the spice burning through my skin.

There's no way this is safe to consume.

My eyes dart to Tanaki again, as if he, a responsible adult, might tell me to stop before I seriously injure myself. He doesn't. He simply watches, the corner of his lip turned up in a threatening smirk.

'Ready?' Anna asks.

'Ready.'

We both raise the chip to our mouths and present our tongues. Like mirrors, we slam the chip down and imprison it inside our mouths. The reaction is almost instant. My mouth is filled with saliva as the spices destroy what's left of my tastebuds; pain sears through the delicate flesh of my mouth. Tears break free, my nose streams. I clench my fists and my body stiffens.

'Twenty-five seconds remain,' says the disembodied voice.

My shoulders sag. I didn't need a reminder of how much time I still have to hold this toxic chip in my mouth. Sweat pools out of every pore, my cheeks are burning both inside and out, and I can definitely taste blood.

Without thinking, my jaw swings open and the chip falls out. I launch myself from my chair, in search of water, milk, ice – anything.

Isobel drops her phone to the table and rummages in her bag, producing a small bottle of unopened, warm apple juice. I don't care. I rip the lid off and drench myself in it. The acidity burns my tongue even more and I scream through clenched teeth as everything stings and throbs. Anna chews the remaining chip in her mouth and swallows, not a single hair out of place and without even a slight increase in her blush.

'You were right,' Anna says. 'That was entertaining to watch. Are you sure you can handle competing against me at Mukbang Metropolis now that you know you can never beat me?'

I stare into her lifeless eyes as I collapse on to the cold, hard ground, feeling every part of my body rejecting the toxic concoction I just subjected it to.

'I'll see you there,' I say, my voice shaking, barely audible above my own thudding heartbeat.

CHAPTER 31

'Pass the milk?' I ask, as my stomach twists and turns, gurgling after an onslaught of a fourteen-inch hot and spicy jalapeno buffalo chicken pizza and an array of breaded peppers, deep-fried onion rings, and three battered CoCo CaraCrunch bars.

It's been two weeks since my meeting with Anna-Conda went viral, and our channel has spiralled into something uncontrollable. Every meal I've eaten since has been recorded and uploaded, like I'm a conveyor belt of content. Sponsors are fighting over themselves to have a chance to secure a spot in one of my videos, and never in my wildest dreams did I think I'd ever see so many numbers in the bank account my parents set up for me.

Even Dad can't deny how good the creative life has been for me.

Cheki presses the little red button on my phone until it turns grey and then hands me a glass of ice-cold milk. I swallow a huge gulp, unbothered by the two white streams dripping from the corners of my mouth. She grimaces at me and slides a cloth in my direction.

'Thanks,' I burp, finally coming up for air.

'That one was messy,' Cheki says, her eyes dancing over the coffee table smeared in congealed cheese sauce and an array of empty dipping pots.

'Nice, though,' I say, rubbing my belly. I grab my T-shirt from the sofa behind me and shove it back on. Since I've been following Zach's routine, my body's been changing, and finally I have the confidence to show it off. The audience seem to love it too.

> **Have you seen how big his biceps are getting?** one girl commented.

> **We have to stop allowing this man into the gyms,** said another.

I can't deny, I'm lapping it up.

'Don't know whether it was all those hellfire spicy noodles yesterday that've absolutely decimated my mouth, but that pizza just now *hurt*,' I joke.

Isobel frowns at me from the chair by the fireplace. 'You've eaten nothing but spicy food since the meet with AnnaConda. I did say you should give it a break for a little bit. I get that you want to prove yourself, after the disastrous Death Chip attempt two weeks ago, but it can't be good for your gut health.'

I wipe the remaining milk from my chin and straighten my clothes, trying to rid myself of the memory of that chip. I'll be happy if I never hear of it again. 'The fans want more uploads, Iz, and that video with Anna made me look weak. I need to show my viewers I definitely *can* beat her.'

Cheki pulls a face at me. 'Everyone knows you can technically beat her. I thought the whole point of our Digital Demons mission was to prove humans better entertainers than robots?'

I scowl back at her, wiping my mouth with the back of my hand in the hopes that the stinging will stop. 'Yeah, it is. Well, I guess it's both. I don't need you to lecture me on my own mission.'

She huffs. 'Kinda sounds like you've lost sight of the mission, to me.'

After a long pause where both Cheki and Isobel stare at me over the bridges of their noses, I break the tension by asking: 'What are the comments on that hellfire noodles video looking like?'

Isobel sighs. I know she's sick of me asking, but I can't think about anything else, and I can't rest until I satisfy the criticism of those calling me lame. Isobel begins reading some of the newer comments underneath my mukbang collab with AnnaConda.

I mean, he's not wrong. He is more interesting to watch than her.

Already bought my tickets to Mukbang Met. Here for the Echo vs Conda war.

He's so goofy, I can't with this boy.

When are we going to get the seafood mukbang?! I'm so tired of asking.

OK, but anyone else thinking that this video can't be topped? I fr love watching him suffer like this.

Dunno what it is about this guy, but I can't stand him.

Every time I see his goofy little mask, I'm reminded again why I need to be his wife.

Isobel's voice becomes more irritated the further she reads, until she can take no more and shuts off her phone, slamming the screen on to her thigh.

'A guy called Si from Mukbang Metropolis has sent you and Anna instructions for the day too,' says Cheki, trying to clear the air, laptop open. 'It's a detailed itinerary. Only thing it doesn't say is what you'll be eating during each stage of the competition. He wants it to be a surprise, but he's asked for you to send over a list of allergies.'

'Cool,' I reply, but my mind is swirling with the comments. How can I make my mukbangs better, more thrilling for the viewer? Clearly, I'm boring them. The gag is getting old.

'AnnaConda has just uploaded another mukbang too,' Cheki says.

This makes me laugh. Ever since my meet-up with Anna, Extreme Elites has basically become a one-bot show, the same way Digital Demons has dropped all content but my mukbangs.

'It's basically a reply to your Nutrox video,' Cheki continues. 'She's eating a load of those Tanaki bars and has nothing but glowing things to say about them.'

'Well, duh, she's a walking advert. Come and show me.' I pat the floor next to me.

She rolls her eyes and brings the laptop to me. 'You're getting lazy.'

On screen, AnnaConda smiles radiantly at the camera. She waves to her fans and displays her multilingual ability with a Spanish greeting: '*Hola de nuevo, mis espectadores!* Good morning, good morning, my friends.' Around her are piles of Nutrox and Hydrox bars, and she discusses the flavours of each like her video is one giant commercial. 'And this purple cube with little bubbles on it is the Hydrox red grape juice, the equivalent of three hundred millilitres of water in just one tablet.' She pops it into her mouth and chews. 'Oh, my! Sooo good! I can feel the grapes popping in my mouth and the juice running all the way down my tongue and throat. It's so delicious and refreshing. Thanks so much, Mr Tanaki, for sponsoring me and my video with these amazing products. Now I'll never be hungry or thirsty again!'

I snort. 'Help me up?' Cheki lifts my arms and when I'm finally up, we go to the kitchen. My mask still lingers on my face; it's become such a part of me now that I feel naked without it. Grabbing a glass from the cupboard, I make for the tap and instruct Cheki to start recording.

After the thumbs up, I flip on the cold water tap and shove my glass underneath. 'Three hundred millilitres of water here in this glass,' I say and throw the drink to my mouth. In one huge gulp, the water is gone. I wipe my lips with the back of my hand and let out a long, satisfied sigh. 'Ah, so refreshing, so delicious. It's almost like I can *taste* the water on my tongue, and it didn't cost me an absolute fortune to quench my thirst either. Thanks so much for sponsoring my hydration, water board, now I'll never be thirsty again!'

Trying desperately to hide her chortle, Cheki signals that the recording has stopped, and we both fall into a fit of laughter. Alongside my regular mukbang videos, it's become our thing to parody whatever AnnaConda puts out on Extreme Elites. If she's going to steal our content, then we're going to steal it right back. An infinite loop of content creation. She's programmed to fish our channel, so hopefully her motherboard will pick that up and she'll get so overwhelmed and muddled in her codes that she'll malfunction and shut down altogether. A guy can dream.

The thought makes me laugh even more, but then I think of Zach and how hilarious he'd find it, and how he'd have so many brilliant ideas on how to troll the AI influencers, and my laughter dies. God, I miss him. 'Anyone heard from Zach?' I ask.

'Not since the last time you asked,' Isobel retorts, a slight annoyance in her voice. 'Looks like he's enjoying his first couple of weeks at college. He's posted loads of pictures on Photorah with his new rugby team. I'm happy for him.'

'He's not answered any of my messages on any social,'

Cheki adds. 'And I'm pretty sure he's blocked my number, because each call just gets diverted to answerphone.'

My heart sinks. 'All those years of friendship, dead,' I mutter.

'Have you even tried to reach out to him yourself?' Cheki asks.

It's like she's slapped me across the face. 'No! And I'm not going to, either. He walked out on me.'

Before she can scold me, Isobel jumps from her armchair by the fire and shoves her phone under my nose. 'Wow! Look at this email.' I squint to get a better look.

Brands have been falling over themselves to work with me, to sponsor my participation in Mukbang Metropolis in exchange for me wearing their merch or being photographed drinking their products. It's what I always knew Digital Demons was capable of; proof that college was never meant for me. Now our message that human creators outperform AI by a landslide is finally landing and people are taking notice.

'Tell them yes,' I say, excitement bubbling inside me. 'Wait, how much are they offering?'

'Ten grand.'

'And we get it when?'

'Half as soon as you sign the contract and the other half on delivery of the video.'

'Nice.'

I fall into the sofa again, my hands behind my head, feeling a smug grin spreading over my face. We'll split the money between us and some of it will go towards buying mukbang food. I'll send some to Mum and Dad too.

'Right,' Cheki says, slamming her laptop closed. 'I think that's enough Digital Demons stuff for today. Let's do something else. How about a walk around the park or something?'

'I like that idea,' says Isobel, staring out of the living-room window. 'It'll be good to get out. This has been the nicest day all week.'

I furrow my brow. 'But why waste good lighting? The days are getting shorter – that means we have to cram more content into less time. We should film one more video, at least.'

Cheki packs her laptop away and searches for her discarded coat and shoes around the sitting room. 'You're becoming obsessed – we've got so many videos filmed and banked so that we can afford to take days off. That was the point of "filming ahead", as Isobel put it. Stay inside if you want to, but I'm going stir-crazy in here.'

I try to shake the befuddlement from my head. Why would anyone want to be outside in the grey autumn air when we could be getting more content filmed or planned? Don't they want to know what the fans are saying about us right now? I throw my gaze to Isobel, hoping – as the production manager – that she'll see reason.

She stares at me blankly. 'I'm going for a walk too,' she says. 'After that, I need to get some college work done. I'm happy for you guys that you've chosen to go all in on the channel, but I want to do my course.'

Isobel's course is predominantly online, meaning she can stay here most of the week, in between trips home to babysit Evie so her mum can have a break. I glare at her, and she glares back with a face like thunder, burning her amber eyes into my soul.

I slap my hands on my thighs and give the good old British, 'Right, then,' before standing up to signal that it's time to get moving again. 'If we're not filming, I need to do some weight training.'

Despite Zach no longer being a part of my team, I still stick to the workout regime he made me. It's keeping my body from splitting at the seams from overconsumption and makes me feel like he's still with me somehow.

'Maybe once you're done, you can take some more topless pics of yourself for your fan girls,' Isobel spits. She grabs her phone and follows Cheki to the front door. They don their hats and coats and leave without another word, slamming the door behind them.

CHAPTER 32

Each morning, before I climb out of bed and go downstairs for breakfast and my daily filming schedule from Isobel, my hand reaches for my phone. I switch off the alarm and my fingers search for the Tubeify app. The glare of light from my screen stings the back of my eyes and I squint through the dark bedroom, trying desperately to see my new notifications.

At this point, I've stopped being surprised by how many there are and simply expect it. Today, I have another eight hundred and twenty-three. I push myself into a sitting position and peel my eyes open wider, willing them to take in my daily dose of praise and admiration.

> We're all in agreement that we're going to the food festival – right, lads?
>
> Can't be letting my fellow human dustbin down
>
> I'm going just to see him get his ass whooped by a robot

Literally so in love with this guy, and he's just eating on camera lol

If Echo ever takes his mask off and he's not the Greek god I've pictured in my head, I'm gonna die

Masks for men are what make-up is for women. Prove me wrong, girls

I rub the sleep from my eyes and let the heaviness sit in my chest. Sometimes, the comments aren't so nice, and sometimes even the nice ones make me feel a bit rubbish about myself. I love that people have taken so well to the masks, the anonymity and mystery we've created surrounding ourselves, but I can't help wondering whether it's also taken away who I really am. The comments asking me never to remove it make me feel like some kind of rabid creature, whose face would shatter the ozone layer and bring about the end of humankind if it were ever revealed. That sucks.

I continue scrolling. One comment stands out:

Anyone else noticed that Zulu isn't uploading any of his stunts any more? It's all just mukbang now ...

Someone has replied: I noticed that too. I've seen Foxtrot in the background of some of the mukbangs but Zulu doesn't seem to be there any more? What happened? Did he leave?

I fall back into my pillow and groan. All I wanted was a hit of dopamine to set me up for another day of relentless mukbangs and filming, but it's only filled me with anxiety. People have finally noticed Zach has gone. Maybe I'll just stay in bed today and scroll instead. Memes. That's what I need to pull me out of this rut. Memes.

It's then that I see it: a post on Photorah from *him*. Zach's face fills my screen as I scroll the endless sea of aesthetically pleasing photographs of AI models mixed with the occasional selfie of someone I genuinely know. He's staring at the camera with a dashing smile on his face and his hair smoothly combed back and styled. One strand falls perfectly beside his eye. The caption reads:

> Hey, guys! I've started my own Tubeify channel. Decided I could fit some filming in with my college course so . . . friends old and new, if you fancy watching, head to the link in my bio. I have a pretty big secret to reveal over there.

I stare at the photo. He's made his own channel? Completely abandoned me and Digital Demons and started his own thing. Clearly, it wasn't about getting his priorities realigned.

My hand shakes as I make for Zach's Photorah page again. Overnight he must have unfollowed all of us because his following list is on zero, but he's still kept us as followers, like we're his fans. I hastily click unfollow and then find the link to his Tubeify page.

God, I could be sick.

My whole body is tense and I'm glad I haven't eaten

yet because my stomach is convulsing, eager to rid me of the adrenaline surging through my flesh and bones.

When I look at the timestamp of his first upload, it's from eight hours ago. Midnight last night, when we were all in bed.

Zach sits in his living room in his parents' home, on the floor behind a coffee table. He's wearing a smart black shirt with the top three buttons undone, and a thick silver chain around his neck. His fingers are brimming with an assortment of plain silver rings and one giant skull ring; his hair is floppy and effortlessly cool as he runs his fingers through it.

But what shocks me the most is the fact that he's wearing his Digital Demons mask. The air leaves my lungs like I've been hit with a bulldozer. Zach takes a deep breath and laughs before removing his mask and grinning his flawlessness into the camera. 'Hey, guys. You have no idea how great it feels to have a voice again, to be able to speak for myself and express my own feelings online. Let me just get one thing straight – I'm Zulu. You may recognize this mask from the Digital Demons Tubeify channel. My real name is Zach. I can't say I ever imagined that this would be a thing – me branching off and starting my own channel away from what has now become a worldwide sensation – but things happen and circumstances change.

'I'm no longer affiliated with Digital Demons but I still respect what they're achieving with their channel. After this video, any more questions regarding my time in the house or about any one of my ex-housemates will be ignored. And, for the record – *no*, I won't be spilling any tea about their identities. I believe everybody should have the opportunity to stand out and be accounted for. That's what I wasn't able to do inside the house. It was all very much centred on one person and the rest of us were made to be background characters serving his every need; there to basically make him look good.'

My blood begins to boil and pain ripples through my teeth as I clench my jaw. He's lying! I did everything to include him, even shared my mukbangs with him so he could feel included. Hot tears threaten to spill.

Zach continues his speech: 'So, what's next for me? Well, I'm starting my own mukbang channel. But instead of simply smashing as much food into my mouth as I can like a barbarian, I'm going to be showing you traditional Japanese recipes from my grandmother. You can cook them alongside me, and then we'll chat and get to know one another while we eat. I'm excited to bring this to you. Until next time, friends, have a peaceful day.'

The on-screen Zach puts his mask to one side and closes his hands together in prayer form. He bows to the camera before the video cuts off. It takes everything in me not to throw my phone across my bedroom and scream. What if people from our old school put two and two together? Zach might not out us, but some of my old classmates will.

I feel sick. Even his comment section is better than mine.

You so look like a Zach!

He's so handsome, I can't take my eyes off him. Omg Zulu is everything I imagined and more!

I never wanted any of them to take their masks off but, like, I'm sooo glad he did, because WOW

I think we all know who he's talking about. Echo literally never lets anyone else in the group speak. It's not fair

You've done the right thing leaving, Zach. Welcome to this side of the internet, we'll take care of you!

I scroll further through the comments, unable to tear my eyes away. All of them are praising him like he's a saint for leaving, like we'd been torturing him and keeping him locked up in a basement. Is it possible to physically feel a heart break? None of these people saw the fun we had together while we weren't filming; none of them have seen the years of friendship between us where I've been forever in his shadow.

People are starting to hate me, but none of them even know me.

CHAPTER 33

I fly down the stairs, not bothering to dress, and find Isobel eating a bowl of granola and berries at the breakfast bar, engrossed in something on her phone. Her eyes are red; she's been crying again.

I freeze in the doorway, my stomach twisting in knots. 'Are you OK?' I ask. 'Is it your mum? Is it Evie? Where's Cheki?'

She shakes her head and wipes away the rogue tear falling from her eye. 'Mum and Evie are fine. Cheki's still in bed.'

I want to press more, but Zach is niggling at my brain. 'Have you seen?'

'Zach's post? Yeah, I've seen it. That could cause us some major issues with identity leaks, but that's not why I'm upset either.'

Slowly, I make my way over to her and fall into the chair beside her, tucking a strand of chocolate hair behind her ear. The sight of her makes my heart melt. I've been awful these past few weeks, a really terrible boyfriend. 'What is it?'

She slides her phone towards me and I clock the Vandalize platform. I know all the posts that are on our sub-thread, but the titles of these ones make me look a little closer. I recognize the username and profile picture, but I don't recall seeing any of these.

'On Vandalize, you can post directly to your own page,' she says, sniffing back her tears. 'I got a bit carried away on it, I guess, like you have, only for different reasons. I started looking at people's profiles and I came across this girl.'

Isobel shows me the profile I've seen many times throughout the sub-thread. EternallyEcho's is her username, and her profile picture is a screengrab of me from my interview with TheHarperHerald.

'She's pretty active on the sub anyway,' Isobel continues, 'but her whole profile is full of private-ish posts directly addressed to you – look.'

With my brow furrowing deeper than it ever has before, I begin flicking through the endless posts addressed to me, reading each and every block of text.

> I know we belong together, one post reads. You and me are meant to be, and this separation is driving me nuts. I NEED to find you. I've travelled on so many different trains across the south of England just hoping I'll bump into you, walked through countless streets, trying to find your house so that we can finally be together.

My blood runs cold and my fingers quiver as they find the next post. This one is a video. The girl has two candles on a plate, one black and the other white, and they're tied together with a string. She sets the candles alight and watches them burn until the string catches fire and snaps. The girl gives a satisfied smile into the camera before the video cuts. Her message within the post reads: I'm finally taking things into my own hands and getting rid of whatever third-party energy is between us. Don't worry, baby boy, you'll be mine soon.

Isobel sobs beside me and I find my hand wrapping around her wrist, though I don't know which one of us needs more support. I click on the next post. It reads:

> I'm so angry with you, Echo! I've been reaching out to you in the dream world for weeks and you're just ignoring me, carrying on with your silly channel, surrounded by your 'mates' who're keeping you away from me. I know two of them are girls. I can tell in the videos, hear them laughing. You're dating one of them, aren't you? I've had enough of these games. You belong with me and if I can't have you, then SHE isn't having you either.
>
> I know where you live. I've found the house on maps.
>
> Don't think I won't post it publicly. Don't think that I won't sit outside and get a picture of you without your mask and post that everywhere too. It'll spread like wildfire.
>
> This is your last chance to make yourself known to me, or I'll spill everything.

I love you, Echo.

I am eternally yours.

I push the phone away, unable to read any more. Breath doesn't want to enter my lungs; silence is screeching in my ears, threatening to burst my drums into a thousand pieces. The date on the post says it's a week old. Obviously, I haven't given her what she desires within that timeframe because I barely knew she existed, beyond being a username that engages on a sub-thread about me. What if she's outside right now, watching us, waiting for us to leave the house unmasked?

'She's not the only one,' Isobel says, her voice barely a whisper. 'There are more, quite a few more. That sub-thread has over sixteen thousand followers, so god knows how many people are actually out there believing you and them are soulmates or whatever, threatening to hurt me and Cheki if we dare get too close to you. Some people have threatened your mum because she gets to hug you and stuff. Mikah . . . I'm scared.'

'Is that why you missed your first in-person lecture this week?'

Tears stream down her face. 'What if someone is out there? I don't want to walk outside and be attacked by one of these crazy fans, and I don't want to leave you here alone in case someone breaks in. We have to tell someone – the police, your parents, anyone. I feel so trapped but I don't feel safe out there any more.' She points a shaking finger to the window, towards the trees in the garden that sway gently in the breeze. Summer turns to autumn both in the seasons and in this new chapter for Digital Demons.

Buzz.

My phone vibrates in my pocket. An alarm letting me know it's time to film to keep up with my content schedule. 'I have to do a mukbang,' I say.

Isobel stares at me, dumbfounded. 'You can't be serious?'

'What choice do I have, Iz? I've already been paid the contract fee and if we want the rest, I *have* to film the video.'

As I make my way to the fridge, Isobel bursts into a flood of tears, but I can't deal with it. My head is swimming. I'm scared too, and I have no idea how to get us out of this mess I created. All I can do is keep going until Mukbang Metropolis. But even then, after that, I don't know how to stop this.

I take a large plate from the top shelf, filled with sliced lemon and lime pieces and, from the cupboard, grab a full tube of sea salt. I head into the sitting room and find my usual place on the floor behind the coffee table.

I set my camera up on the tripod that's become a permanent fixture in the room, my body moving on autopilot. Then I don my mask and a T-shirt for Voxy-Playa, an audiobook subscription service, and press record.

Juice runs through my fingers as I grab a slice of lime and bury it deep into the mountain of rock salt. I wince at the knowledge of what I'm about to endure, as I dangle the dripping fruit beside my head, but at least it takes my worry away from the fans on Vandalize threatening to find out where I am and expose me.

'Morning, folks, this is going to be a quick one today. A challenge I've been waiting to do for ages, and then I'm going to spend the day with my *girlfriend*, who I love very much.' I slam a citrus slice covered in salt into my mouth, and squirm as the lethal concoction burns my tongue and sends my glands into a frenzy. Saliva pools in my mouth, dripping over my lips and on to the coffee table; tears stream from my eyes and mix with the fruit on the plate below. I try my hardest to talk through the pain and gags. 'Mukbang Metropolis is getting closer, and I think my body is getting used to these endless plates of food.' My whole face contorts as I devour a salty lemon. 'Obviously, AnnaConda has the ability to take on more food than is humanly possible, but I'll never give up. I'll still be there, giving you all an amazing show. I've heard from the directors of Mukbang Met that tickets have sold out already – that's insane!'

Having said all I need to say, I slam the remaining slices into my mouth and cry out as my whole body rejects them. I spit them on to the coffee table and shudder, my stomach convulsing. With a shaking hand, I reach for my phone and stop the recording, then collapse on the floor, covered in tears and my own drool, breathing deeply through the burning sensation in my gut.

'Are you OK? What's happened?' Hands smother my

shoulders, willing me to sit up, and I find Cheki hovering above. Her long skirt almost suffocates me as she tangles her arms beneath me and attempts to hoist me up. 'What the hell have you just eaten?'

I whip my mask off and relish the cool air on my blotchy, reddened face as I collapse on to the sofa.

Footsteps echo through the kitchen and a shadow fills the doorway. 'Did . . .' Isobel says, examining the evidence on the coffee table. 'Did you just do the citrus challenge?' I nod as she shakes the salt tube, gauging how much I've used. 'Mikah, I asked you not to do that yet! You've just consumed more salt than a fully grown human's weekly allowance. Are you insane? All the citrus on an empty stomach, no wonder you're in pain.'

'All right,' I groan. 'Back off, will you? At least I'm keeping the channel going.'

'What's that supposed to mean?'

I grimace as I cough up acidic phlegm and swallow it back down. 'I mean, we started this channel doing all kinds of cool things: stunts and dancing with dangerous animals, as well as mukbangs, but now all we're doing is mukbangs and it's all fallen on me. Zach's gone and started his own thing, you and Cheki just do the admin and I'm still here having to do all the eating and filming, messing my body up, and then you have the audacity to tell me I'm doing it wrong. Well, at least *I'm doing it*. Yet not one of you has thanked me for it, I just get moaned at.'

At this, Cheki steps away from me, crestfallen.

'That's not true!' Isobel yells back, her face reddening with anger. 'I've edited every video we've put out, organized all the sponsorship deals, got the masks sorted, scheduled every interview. Just because you're the star of the show, doesn't mean you're the only one keeping it running. What's happened to you? You've become so selfish!'

'Selfish?' It's like I've been possessed by someone else entirely. Anger surges through me, pooling on the tip of my tongue like a razorblade. 'I'm the one being selfish? I'm the one who's been fighting for this channel since day dot. I've lost my best mate, *and* he's riding on my coat-tails. How about we also address the fact that I've got thousands of people writing nasty comments about me online, mocking how I look and sound and eat? There's a major possibility of our identities being blown. And you're chastising me about the thing *my fans* write about me.'

The blood drains from her face. 'You're horrible,' she manages through her tears, her voice cracking and strained. 'I was just trying to help. And *your fans* are the problem! Always wanting more and you keep giving it to them!'

Tears fall from my eyes as I finally verbalize the thoughts I've been suppressing for weeks. 'I'm terrified of my fans too, Iz. But I need them. Without them, without this channel, this mask, I'm nothing. Nobody!'

Silence falls like a thick blanket of snow, and the air freezes, begging us to witness it.

'You've always been someone to me,' she says, her voice trembling, her eyes glistening with heartbreak.

Finally, the past few months catch up with me and I crumble into myself.

CHAPTER 34

Minutes tick by in slow, silent agony.

It's like none of us dare breathe too loud or catch the gaze of another. Isobel stands like a beautiful Grecian statue, her face turned from me, gazing into the distance, and Cheki sits on the sofa nearest the window, her body limp and eyes dripping with quiet tears.

I've caused all of this. Me. My best mate left because he felt sidelined in the project *we* started together; my girlfriend feels like she's less important than the fans calling me cute online; and someone who's let me into her family's holiday home with no motive other than to help me achieve my dream has been subjected to my fluctuating moods ever since I got here.

I sink deeper into myself, wishing the ground would swallow me whole and the world would forget about my existence entirely.

'We can't keep going like this,' says Cheki. 'This used to be fun, but now I don't even want to get out of bed in the morning.'

Isobel collapses into the armchair by the fire.

I push my back against the sofa behind me, pulling my legs close to my chest as I wrap my arms around myself for comfort. 'I'm sorry,' I mutter. 'I let the fanfare get to me, I couldn't help it.'

Again, silence encapsulates the room. It might be too late to salvage any of this. I might've ruined everything for good with this mood swing.

'All I've done since I got here was try and help you,' Isobel says, sounding so defeated it makes my heart sting. 'And all you've done is berate me for not doing it the way you want it done. You knew I had a lot going on and you still put more and more work on me . . .'

Guilt washes over me like a tsunami – not for the first time since this channel began.

Cheki clears her throat and stands. 'I'll give you guys a few minutes . . . go for a walk.'

She finds her shoes and rustles her arms into the sleeves of her coat. The door gently opens and closes behind her, sending a waft of cool October air through the cottage.

'You're right,' I choke. 'I'm a jerk. I've become someone I'm not.' She lets me sit with my thoughts for a while, until I can piece the fragments of my shattered self into something coherent. Her body is turned away from me, but her gaze finds me through the corners of her eyes. 'I didn't realize how consuming it is . . . to be wanted. I always envied Zach, wanted people to look at me the way they look at him. He's used to the attention, and I'm used to sitting in the shadows, feeling like some monster undeserving of anyone's time. Sometimes I still genuinely wonder why you agreed to be my girlfriend. There's so many more attrac—'

'Now you stop right there,' she snaps, her face contorted, eyes wide like my words pain her. 'Attractiveness is a subjective thing, and I happen to find you incredibly attractive. I love you, everything about you, from your looks to your tortured soul. Have I ever given you any indication that wasn't the case?'

'N-No,' I admit.

'Right, so enough of that. *You* are the one I want to be with. Surely I've given you enough reassurance that you don't need to seek validation from strangers online. Girls you've never met and will never meet.'

I find strength in my own voice again. 'It's not as simple as that, Iz! I don't want any of them. I'm not looking to trade you in, and they're not giving me anything you don't. It's just ... it's ... for the first time in my life I feel seen, worthy, and I'm terrified it's all going to go away and I'll just be me again, awkward old Mikah, forgotten and left to rot in the gutter.'

We sit there for a while, just taking everything in.

'I think hiding you behind that mask might be the worst thing we ever did,' she whispers. 'It gave you the confidence to get this channel off the ground – it was so nice watching you come out of your shell – but it's become you. It's like the Mikah beneath isn't there any more.'

She's right. The mask has truly made me into anyone,

so much so that even I don't know where Mikah ends and Echo begins. Perhaps there is no Mikah left; what if I'm all Echo? Or what if Mikah and Echo are now the same person? I swallow the lump in my throat. 'Maybe after Mukbang Metropolis, I should put it down for a little bit ... have a break from the channel.'

She raises her eyebrow. 'You're still thinking about doing Mukbang Met? Even now? What if that stalker girl or any of the obsessed fans from that sub-thread turn up? They *know* you'll be there. It only makes sense that they'd show up, especially if they feel like they own you and you owe them your attention.'

'I can't not go. I'm being sponsored now, and so many people have bought tickets, Iz. I can't let them down. Plus, I don't want to spend the rest of my life hiding from these people. I've made my bed and all that; I can't walk away now. I just need to beat AnnaConda, then I'll stop uploading. We've made enough money to take a year-long hiatus if we want to.'

Her face softens. 'You never give up, do you? I've always loved that about you, Mikah. If you say you're going to do something, then you do it.' She frowns, pained again. 'And I'll be there with you, whatever you choose to do.'

CHAPTER 35

The next day, Isobel and I step off the number 383 bus and walk into Southampton city centre. She squeezes my hand as we meander through the surging crowd, and I pull her in close, needing as much reassurance as she does that we're in this together.

'I feel like I'm being watched,' she says, as we cross the road towards the City Art Gallery.

'I know what you mean, but I reckon it's just our paranoia after reading those posts.'

We – along with Cheki – spent all night going through various posts on Vandalize, jotting down the usernames of people threatening us with harm or doxxing, compiling evidence to send to the police. Realistically, I'm not expecting much to come from the investigation, but it gives me a sense of forward momentum and seemed to put Isobel's fears to rest long enough for us to all get a decent-ish night's sleep.

'I shouldn't have told you about them. I'm sorry,' she says. 'You've got enough on your plate.' She throws me a side-eye and we both laugh at her terrible pun.

'No, I'm glad you did. Now I can see where you've been coming from this whole time. I didn't realize how out of hand it had got. I just thought everyone was on our side and it was all in good fun. I didn't take their threats of doxxing seriously enough. I'm sorry it's come to this. Sorry for everything.'

After crossing a few more streets and meandering through mini shopping centres, we head to a large white building and walk around a stone fountain filled with copper and gold coins, following the long trail of other visitors to the museum.

'Hopefully, once we disappear after Mukbang Met, things might calm down a bit,' I say. 'People will lose interest and find another person to obsess over.' The thought makes me laugh, but then I cringe – how could I wish this hell on anyone else?

Isobel takes my hand again and pulls my arm over her shoulder. I smile as she leans into me, and we head into the museum. I have no idea why she wanted to bring me here, but she said there's something that might make me feel less alone in this funny internet stardom situation I've found myself in. I have to admit, it's nice to be out of the house and doing something other than eating, filming and scrolling through my comments.

'What is it you wanted to show me?'

She leads me up some stairs, down a corridor and into a dimly lit room. 'This exhibition is ending soon; it's an homage to classic art with a modern twist. I saw a few ads for it online over the summer holidays and always meant to come and see it.'

'What's the exhibit about?'

'An ever-evolving testament to the human need to admire and produce art, to process life through artistic expression. It's kinda like a rebellion against AI, just like us.' She leads me further through the room as I clock brightly coloured paintings hanging on the walls and meander around towering sculptures.

There's a floor-to-ceiling portrait of a Harlequin and a dark, looming figure dancing within a music box. Blood-red roses lie at their feet, and they're surrounded by a jeering audience. I raise my brows at it, taken in by the small, gold teardrops falling from both performers' eyes.

But we don't stop to admire any of these paintings or sculptures. Isobel leads me to the end of the room, where a large portrait hangs alone on the back wall, surrounded by a group of visitors.

Once they've had their fill of the artwork, we step forward.

I stare into the vibrant colours. The frame is intricately designed with anemones and thistles, and painted gold but tarnished with a pink hue in places. The kind of pink that seeps through when the gold turns out to not be gold after all, but rather a cheaper metal with a gold film that fades when it becomes oxidized.

I wait for Isobel to explain, but she doesn't; she just gazes at the artwork with admiration.

The painting is of a woman cloaked in black, staring straight at me menacingly. One of her bejewelled hands rests under the blade of a sword dangling above a shimmering crown; blood drips from her palm where the tip of the weapon meets her skin. Her other hand is wrapped around a pair of golden scissors, threatening to cut the single thread keeping the sword from dropping.

I step closer. The woman wears a pendant with scales, a golden ring in the shape of a triangle, and a golden headdress with an eight-pointed star dangling between her brows.

Within one of the woman's eyes, there's a laughing crowd with phones before their faces, camera lights flashing. But within the blade's reflection, those same people lie piled on the ground, their blood pooling around their lifeless forms, phones smashed.

I take a step back, and blink away my shock at the regalness and brutality mashed together.

My eyes flicker to the golden plaque sitting above the painting, showcasing the title of the piece:

THE OBSERVER

'Wow,' I say, the words tumbling from my lips like water through a broken dam. I clock Isobel smiling up at me from the corner of my eye.

'I thought you'd like it. It's a play on the story of Damocles. You remember it?'

'Yeah, of course. We performed it for our first-year drama exam. I was Gentleman of the Court Number Eleven, and you were Ladies' Maid Number Five.' I flash her a grin, knowing it'll make her laugh.

The story goes that Damocles was jealous of the king's wealth, power and status, and couldn't understand why the sovereign hated his position so much. So, one day, the king invited Damocles to sit upon his throne and be him for the day, with one condition: a sword would dangle above his head by a horsehair. Despite feasts and endless entertainment and celebration, Damocles couldn't enjoy his day on the throne for fear of the sword falling. It's an age-old tale about the constant pressure placed on those with power in the public eye.

Fitting for my situation, I think.

'I like this modern take,' Isobel says, her eyes dancing over the portrait, pointing to the phone lenses. 'When I saw the promotional ad on Photorah, I knew I had to see it in person. Seeing you yesterday, broken, reminded me of it. This is where I got my inspiration for the Star of Ishtar on my own mask.'

'So, who is she?' I ask, pointing to the woman in black.

'She's the Observer,' Isobel says. 'Tied for eternity to the one sitting upon the throne.'

I raise a brow. 'She's kinda scary.'

Isobel chortles. 'Deeply misunderstood, I think. The blood from her palm symbolizes the protection she offers the crown, by stopping the sword from falling upon it. And the golden scissors mean she can cut the thread at any moment, should the one on the throne become corrupted by the power of the crown. The reflections of the crowd and the scales around her neck reinforce her duty to be balanced and keep order.'

'Impressive. Kinda does feel like I have a sword dangling over my head right now.'

'You do.'

'Guess I'm Damocles, then.'

'You are . . . getting a small taste of what it's like to wear the crown and sit upon the throne, with a court of admirers both waiting to see your downfall and be in your position.'

Suddenly, my head feels twice as heavy on my neck. 'Who're you, then?'

She flashes me a mischievous smirk. 'I can be the Observer, if you like? I'll shelter you from all those rabid fans, and keep your head from rising above the clouds too.'

I laugh. 'Oh, so you *do* think I've been letting the internet fame get to me?'

Her soft amber eyes meet mine and they bore into me, like she's seeing every sin I've ever committed. 'If a man is told he's a god enough times, it stands to reason that he might one day believe it.'

I stare at the portrait, wondering what inspired the artist to make it, and allowing it to bring me some semblance of peace. At least someone, somewhere, has a slight inkling of what I'm going through.

'I'm not the enemy, Mikah. I'm here to help you. It's us against the world, remember? Come on, let's get back and figure out how we're going to navigate Mukbang Met.'

I go to grab Isobel's waiting, outstretched hand, when my phone buzzes in my pocket.

> Message from: Cheki
> Sent: 15:08
> Where are you guys? There's a group of girls hanging around the driveway. They look like they're trying to get pictures of the place and sneak in or something.

I flash my phone at Isobel and the worry spreading over her face matches my inner turmoil. They've found us. We've been doxxed.

CHAPTER 36

Isobel and I return to the holiday cottage, shaking. We keep our faces covered with our hoods as we climb from the back of the taxi and make our way inside.

Cheki's face is devoid of colour as she lingers by the front door, her eyes wide like she's been subjected to hours of torment. Who knows? She very well could have been.

All the curtains inside the cottage are closed haphazardly.

'I rang the police and they said to keep all windows and doors shut and secured,' Cheki says, as we follow her to the kitchen, where the kettle is boiling and three mugs wait with a bag of camomile tea in each. 'I yelled out of the living-room window at the girls and they legged it, so god knows where they are now. They'd put cards and chocolates in the mail bin on the drive. The police gave me a crime number but said they won't be sending anyone out for unwanted post.'

I suck in a deep, steadying breath, keeping my eyes locked on a panic-stricken Isobel. 'So, not even the police want to help us?'

Cheki shrugs. 'There's not much they can do. The girls ran away, and no crime has technically been committed. It's obvious we've been doxxed, but unless we have the proof of it and the identities of those behind it, there really is nothing for the police to go on. I've given them everything we gathered last night and they've asked us to keep a record of anything untoward. They'll keep an open file until we either have enough evidence to make a charge or the problem goes away on its own.'

At this, I march from the kitchen and head to my bedroom to where my laptop rests on my desk.

'Goes away on its own?' Isobel says in the distance as I make for the stairs. 'This isn't going to go away. It's just going to get worse with Mikah's rising popularity.'

Shaking, I head back downstairs and yank my laptop open and start slamming the keys until I find the social platform I'm looking for: Vandalize.

There's been a wave of new posts on there while Isobel and I have been out, commenting on my last mukbang, the citrus challenge.

That mukbang was so mid.

Yeah, definitely didn't like that one, seems like he's running out of ideas ...

I hope this doesn't mean that Digital Demons is disbanding, what with Zulu (Zach)'s departure and now

> Echo clearly not putting any effort into his mukbangs any more.
>
> Do you guys get the feeling that Echo will do Mukbang Met and then disappear???
>
> I'm hearing rumours that their identities have been leaked?? If anyone has any pics of them unmasked, can you DM me?
>
> I won't let him disappear; I know where he lives lol

I move on to the next post and find that the username is familiar: EternallyEcho's – the girl who claimed I was her soulmate.

> Anyone else clock Echo saying he has a girlfriend right at the beginning of the video? she asks.

Other users respond:

> Yup, killed me dead
>
> Like, I kinda knew all of them would be in relationships, but I guess I just wanted to be delulu
>
> It really made me not want to watch any more of his stuff tbh. Knowing he actually is in a relationship puts me off
>
> I think there's enough of us here to take her on lol
>
> Fr, girlfriend is gonna have to learn to share. Echo has multiple WIVES in this lifetime

My blood is boiling; I can hear my own heartbeat thumping against my eardrums. I click on the username and navigate to her profile, where there's an endless stream of posts directed to me personally and privately.

Her latest one is exactly what I knew I'd find:

You've absolutely broken me, Echo.

I've given everything to you. I made an altar for you on my dresser and prayed for you every night, I've done spells against that WITCH keeping us apart, tried cord-cutting methods to rid us of this third party, and yet you still won't choose me.

I hope you know that what I'm doing is for your own good. Maybe if your world comes crashing down, you'll have no choice but to meet me at the bottom, and then we'll be on equal footing again.

I watched Zulu's recent upload. Or should I call him Zach? I managed to reverse search some of his photos from his Photorah page and found some other accounts belonging to him. I got chatting with a couple of his school mates and they had some interesting names to throw out for the others in Digital Demons.

From there, it was just too easy to find you.

I warned you what would happen if you didn't reach out and claim me as your own. I'm doing this for us — I'm posting your address in my private group chat. I know the girls in there will go to you because that's already the plan. I won't be there. I'll see you at Mukbang Met.

Forever yours.

I head downstairs and show the others, tears stinging my eyes as horror spreads across the faces of my mates. God, I wish Zach were here. He'd be furious, he'd be down on the end of the drive waiting for anyone who dared to threaten us. Maybe it's time to tell my parents, but I know what they'll say. They'll want me to close the chapter on Digital Demons completely, force me out of the cottage that's been the making of me.

I don't want this to end, but I can't bear what it's become either.

'Please cancel this competition with AnnaConda,' Isobel says, her face blotchy from crying. 'You have nothing to prove any more. We've already accomplished what we set out to. Sponsors are coming back to human creators because *you* made them realize that real people still have real influence. Look at the fanbase you've created; the buzz you've generated online; how much fear you've put into Tanaki and companies like his that rely on humans supporting the growth of automation and AI. You've won. We've won.'

'I can't, Iz! We've already been sponsored to do this, taken money from brands, hyped this thing into oblivion. What do you think would happen if we backed out? There'd be uproar online. You're the Observer, right? Meant to protect me from that sword dangling over my head? Seems more like you're ready to use those scissors, babe.'

Cheki and Isobel look terrified and defeated. Isobel's eyes well with tears again. Lucky for them, they can throw in the towel – it's not their name and image that'll be dragged through the mud if they do.

'Leave, then,' I hiss. 'Both of you, do what Zach did!'

I turn on my heel and go to walk away, but a warm hand wraps itself around my wrist and yanks me back into the kitchen. Isobel closes the gap between us, her eyes bloodshot and gleaming with the reflection of the overhead light.

'I'm not going anywhere,' she says, her voice trembling. 'I am here to protect you.'

Cheki steps forward and places her hand on my shoulder. 'We'll see this through to the end, by your side. Whatever you want to do, however you want to end this, whenever you want to end this . . . the audience *will* be entertained.'

CHAPTER 37

The coffee table is once again filled with an array of weird and unappetizing foods. My stomach lurches, and I sigh as I take my place on the floor, in front of the camera. I never imagined I'd one day get sick of eating. I love food. I'm always after more sweet treats or spicy stuff that leaves the tongue tingling, and forever chasing the high of a meal lovingly prepared and devoured in good company. But eating isn't like that for me any more.

I can hardly remember a single meal I've consumed without filming it now; without shoving it into my face like I might never again take another bite.

'After this, I think I might need to take some vitamins or something,' I groan, rubbing my chest.

'Pretty sure you have chronic indigestion,' Isobel says. 'Maybe acid reflux. I guess we should get something from the pharmacist later if it's still really bad?'

I nod, though I'm not sure I'll be able to make it out of the house feeling as rough as I do. Besides, ever since the doxxing, none of us have even wanted to step into the garden, let alone venture into town.

But as the searing pain in my gut and chest worsens, there's no denying how much hell I'm putting my body through with these endless mukbangs. People just weren't designed to take on so much food. Even the viewers have started to notice and their comments are starting to freak me out.

> Part of me wants you to keep going with these mukbangs because I love to see them, but I'm also a bit worried about your health, Echo
>
> Is it me or is Echo starting to fill out? Dude can barely fit on screen now
>
> Yeah, but he's clearly putting the time in at the gym. My man went from being so scrawny that he disappeared when he turned sideways to becoming an absolute beast. Even Zulu can't compete with those guns
>
> Did any of you really expect any different? He's doing three mukbangs a day and each individual one is exceeding the daily calorie intake of a grown man
>
> I still love him but I miss baby Echo with his little noodle arms

My head is swimming with the nasty comments, the personal ones, the insults, but also the ones that can see what I'm doing and why, the ones that keep pushing me onwards whenever I want to stop.

> Y'all are being so mean for no reason. The guy is literally breaking his body to try and bring back the

> old days of the internet and y'all are acting so entitled like he should be a supermodel

> The courage it takes to keep going through all this hate is admirable, mate

'Ready?' Isobel asks, standing behind the camera, her finger hovering over the record button.

I glance over the offerings once more, swallowing down the bile creeping over my tongue. I can't think of anything I'm less ready to do than tuck into all this, but what choice do I have?

Mukbang Metropolis is a week away and, the moment it's done, I'm retiring from Digital Demons for good.

Before me is an array of seafood. All of it raw and slimy. I've never been one for sushi even at the best of times, but this is seafood I've never even heard of. We found it online and had it imported. It's cold and wet and really gross-looking, and my whole mouth is dry, pleading with me not to attempt any of it.

'I don't know why raw seafood mukbang is the one thing that my viewers keep asking me for. I can't think of anything worse to eat,' I say through a clenched jaw.

'Some people really love it,' Isobel says, smiling at me sympathetically. 'At least you have loads of sauce to cover the taste, if it really is that bad.'

'It's not the taste I'm worried about; it's the fact that I have no idea what half of this is, and we just bought it off a random website.'

'Well, this was your idea. You don't have to do it.'

'It seemed like a good idea at the time,' I insist.

'Don't do it, then. Just order another pizza or something.'

'Did you not read those comments about how the citrus challenge was mid? Our audience is ready for something different. They want something *more*.'

The only positive in this whole thing is that the girls on Vandalize haven't revealed our identities publicly yet, though the knowledge that they could at any second keeps me up at night.

'Ready,' I say, failing to keep the disgust from my voice.

Isobel shrugs to Cheki, clearly at a loss to know how to deal with my increasingly fluctuating moods. She nods at me and gives me the thumbs up after she's hit record.

'No introduction to this one today, guys,' I say to the camera. 'No rants or rhymes, I'm really not looking forward to it. I hate seafood, but it's been requested so many times that I thought I'd give it a go. Anyway, here it is, I guess . . .'

I grab a long, slippery octopus tentacle from the tray nearest the camera and hold it up. My body tenses, and for a moment I'm not sure I'm going to be able to open my mouth again. I take a deep breath and slowly unlock my jaw, dangling the tentacle on my tongue. I take a bite and almost gag. It's soft and hard at the same time. I'm not sure what I'm biting into – is it flesh, cartilage or straight-up bone? It feels almost like jelly, but super-chewy and tough.

Next, there's a bowl of something called spoon worms, creatures akin to sea cucumbers. I retch at the sight. They look phallic and they're still squirming. My shaking fingers find one, but it slips out of my grasp, and before I can stop them, tears begin streaming down my cheeks, pooling on the tip of my chin before crashing to the coffee table below.

'Are . . . are you crying?' Cheki asks off-camera.

'Yes!' I sniff the tears back and grab a fistful of spoon worms. 'I hate seafood.' My voice is meek and pathetic, and the tears keep on coming like someone has switched on a tap.

'See, folks?' Cheki says. 'You don't get this with AI. Feast your eyes upon this sobbing creature as he's forced to consume foods he's never come across before, but which would be considered a delicacy across the globe. What an uncultured human being he is.'

This actually makes me laugh and I don't even care that she's broken our rule of me being the only mouthpiece. What does it matter, when I'm giving Digital Demons up once Mukbang Metropolis is over? I wipe the tears from my chin. 'Cheers for the support. In the next video you can try eating locusts and maggots, all right?'

She grimaces and this makes me laugh more, easing some of the anxiety. I slam a spoon worm into my mouth and chew furiously, gagging and retching as I attempt to swallow it. The video seems to go on for hours and my reluctance to just eat the things and get it over with only delays my agony. I eat blowfish soup, sea slugs and goose barnacles – all of it a delicacy to someone, somewhere, and an absolute nightmare for me.

Isobel makes a cut-throat gesture to signal the end of the recording, and I jump to my feet and make for the bathroom.

'That can't do your stomach any good,' Cheki says from the other side of the bathroom door. I can hear the worry in her voice, soft and quiet, but a lecture isn't what I need right now.

'I didn't mean to throw it back up again. I don't feel well,' I say, wiping my mouth on the towel as I re-emerge in the sitting room, feeling ten times lighter. 'I've done it now anyway; I'm never doing it again.' I wipe the sweat from my brow and fall on to the sofa, hugging myself.

My stomach lets off a nasty gurgle and the girls stare at me, grimacing. I roll on to my side and scrunch my knees to my chest, hoping the weird bubbling inside me might subside. Another gurgle, followed by a fart so loud and deadly it evacuates the room.

'Oh my god, are you OK?' Isobel says from the kitchen, holding her nose.

I can feel sweat dripping down my back and pooling in my hairline. 'No,' I manage through groans. 'My stomach ... hurts. Something's not right.'

CHAPTER 38

Overhead lights blaze into my retinas; dazzling white and whizzing across the ceiling as I'm trollied down a long corridor with cream walls that once were white. Signs hang over doors; red and blue ones with white writing, instructing visitors and patients where to go. I groan as I clutch my stomach, and a blue, rubber-gloved hand pushes a paper bowl towards my head, indicating that any more spillages should be aimed this way.

'Is he going to be all right?' Isobel says from somewhere behind as I'm hurtled through the hospital.

The paramedics and nurses ignore her as I'm wheeled towards two great white doors. The sign above says: TOXICOLOGY. They park me in a bay and close the curtains around me, blocking out some of the harsh lighting. My head is pounding, and my eyes can barely focus.

The youngest paramedic stands by the foot of the bed while the nurses and doctors gather around the rest of me. 'Male patient, sixteen years of age, began feeling sick after consuming vast quantities of seafood purchased over the internet and transported from an unknown source here to the UK. Patient then began sweating profusely and experienced sharp pains in his lower abdomen. He has since been expelling waste via vomiting and diarrhoea and is experiencing breathing problems.'

They go into detail about the medication they've flooded my system with, about my stats and obs, but none of it makes any sense to me. All I can do is try to cling on to reality for a little longer.

Bodies flash around the bed, all draped in blues and whites; the rustle of plastic aprons pulls my attention one way and then the other. They're talking, but whether they're saying things to me, I have no idea. All I can do is groan and vomit, slipping in and out of consciousness. They pull at my clothing and hoist my body in whatever direction they see fit for their endeavours to revive me to my once healthy self.

My arm rises into the air as a needle comes closer to the vein in the crook of my elbow. Clear liquid disappears from the tube into me, flooding me with whatever medicine they hope will cure me from this poison tearing me apart from the inside. I blink and sleep threatens to take me, so I force my eyes open again, but the weight of my lids overcomes me, and I fall deep into darkness, as the voices surrounding me are dragged into a black hole until they're utterly out of reach.

'Oh! I think there's life in the old boy after all.'

Dad's voice is as clear as day, but my eyes refuse to open.

I unstick my tongue from the roof of my mouth. 'Water,' I plead.

There's a clanking of glass and the sound of water being poured from a jug. The bed moves beneath me, hoisting me upwards into a sitting position. My head dangles on my neck, my jaw falls agape, and I have to will it to close again.

'Open your eyes, Mikah,' says a voice I've never heard before. It's the thing that pulls me back into the room. I peel one eye open, frowning against the glare of the overhead lights, and blink the other one into submission too.

I'm still in hospital, in a cubicle on a ward, with the curtains open and a mass of people surrounding me. Mum, Dad, Isobel and a couple of nurses. One of the nurses holds the glass of water to my mouth and holds my head steady as I drink. It's tepid and tastes like it's been sitting in that jug for days, but I gulp it like it's the best thing I've ever been offered. My tongue relishes the moisture.

'Careful, not too much,' the nurse says. 'You have a drip in, so you're not dehydrated, but the mouth will need moistening every now and again for your own comfort. How are you feeling?'

'Tired,' I say, my voice groggy and crackly.

The nurse nods. 'Expected. Take it easy. We all just want you to get better.'

I nod as the two nurses leave, closing the curtains around my bed once more, lessening the harsh hospital lighting. I suck in a huge breath and my lungs burn like it's the first time they've tasted oxygen.

'What happened?' I ask.

My parents glance at each other and sigh, silently debating whether I'm in the right frame of mind to hear it. Isobel drops her gaze to the ground, her eyes tired and defeated.

'Apparently you ate some really bad seafood,' Dad says, attempting to keep the atmosphere light.

'I'm so sorry, Mikah,' Isobel says, tears spilling down her cheeks. 'We should've done more checks on the retailer. The doctors think you've been exposed to tetrodotoxin from pufferfish poisoning. We didn't order any pufferfish; they're highly toxic. We only ordered seafood we *knew* could be consumed, but somehow, something was contaminated.'

'You're lucky to be alive,' Mum says, her voice low and gentle.

Isobel buries her face in her hands and weeps. Mum tries to console her, but I can see tears in her eyes too. Dad remains stoic, but he's barely blinking, and he can't even look at me.

'They want to keep you in for a couple more days, to monitor you,' Mum says. 'They said it could be weeks before you start to feel more like yourself again. Your body has been through the wars trying to rid you of the poison.'

'Me and your mum have been chatting. It's time you come home,' Dad says. 'I was happy to entertain this influencer lifestyle of yours for a while, but I didn't realize just how out of hand everything had got. I want you home once they've discharged you.'

'No way!' I jolt in bed, trying to turn my body to face my parents, but I'm weak and my arms buckle beneath me. 'We can't stop now. Look how much of an impact we're having. If I quit, AnnaConda and her posse of fakefluencers win. Please, Dad . . . this was a stupid mistake, but it won't happen again. I've learnt my lesson.'

Dad's face hardens and his lips purse. 'No. That's my final word. We trusted you because we thought you were sensible, and we accepted your story about Zach's injuries being an accident, but it was silly of us to turn a blind eye.'

I know there's no arguing with him. He has that look on his face. After some brief small talk and a difficult lunch of cold buttered toast and vanilla ice cream, my parents finally leave, taking Isobel with them.

A vibration catches my attention and I grab my phone from the bedside table, wincing as I twist my stomach. My eyes grow wide at the sight of the ID. It's Zach. I let it ring out until my screen goes black again. Then, a message appears.

Message from: Zach
Sent: 16:07
Mate. Cheki just came by my house. Can you call me back?

His face flashes before my eyes as I sink deeper into my bed, staring at the empty ceiling, playing out the last few months on the bumpy white paint like a projector screen: Zach fighting me for the best bedroom on the stairs; Cheki trying to pet the red-bellied snake; Isobel donning her mask for the first time after the Delirium Designs fiasco. The memories make me laugh.

It all seems so far away now, a distant past that I'm slowly falling free from.

Then the images turn to ones of me. I'm sitting on the floor by the coffee table, shovelling seafood down my throat, crying. Two parallel universes.

'Ahem.'

I bolt upright and focus my gaze on the end of the bed, wiping away the tears clouding my vision. A young nurse slithers between the bay curtains, holding a funny-looking computer on wheels, checking my state of awareness.

'I need to check your obs,' she says quietly.

She stations the machine beside my bed and wraps the blood pressure monitor around my bicep. Occasionally, she glances at me through the corner of her eye but snaps her gaze away again when she notices that I've noticed.

'All good?' I ask.

'Still a little high. I'll check again in another couple of hours, but it's going in the right direction. Can I do your temperature?'

She sticks a cold thermometer in my ear. 'Again, still a little high. Are you feeling OK in yourself?'

I nod again. 'Just tired, I guess.' Truthfully, I'm not OK at all, not even close, but I can't tell her this. She has no idea what I'm currently going through, that I'm facing the biggest disaster known to humankind if I forfeit my place in Mukbang Metropolis. I'll let my fans down, and allow AnnaConda and artificial intelligence to win.

The nurse flashes me a pitiful smile and reorganizes her observations trolley. 'Are you Echo?'

I freeze.

'S-Sorry,' she mutters. 'That was unprofessional of me. You just sound like him is all – and the reason you're in here, the toxic seafood . . . The last upload on Digital Demons is Echo eating unusual seafood . . . I'm sorry I asked. Get some rest.'

She flicks the curtain open and hurriedly wheels the machine out, keeping her gaze low. I can't believe Cheki actually uploaded the video while I'm in hospital.

'I'm glad you like the channel,' I say as the nurse closes the curtain on my cubicle. A small, girlish giggle comes from the other side as she returns to the nurses' station.

I can't help the rush of adrenaline that surges through my chest as her praise and recognition fills me with the validation I've longed for my entire life. I want to scream, want to bury my face in my pillow and kick my feet in the air like *I'm* the fan.

She knew who I was, even without the mask.

CHAPTER 39

The next two days go by in a monotonous blur on the hospital ward, until the doctor deems me fit to leave. My parents waste no time at all in bundling me into the back of their waiting car. Dad practically drives their Volvo into the lobby to ensure I get in.

But once I step over the threshold of my family home, it's like Mum and Dad want to forget anything about Digital Demons. But I can't. I still check Vandalize. I still see the messages. I fall quickly back into my routine before the channel began, but now I'm expertly avoiding all of Zach's attempts to reach out to me, unable to forgive him for abandoning our venture.

The sinking feeling in my stomach lingers, just as the Tubeify channel lingers in limbo, with no new uploads from me in a week since the infamous seafood challenge.

Accusatory comments appear in the vein of: **He's done a runner! Got scared of being beaten by AI in person and disappeared. LOL. Loser.**

While others suggest: **He's probably practising and doesn't have time to film mukbangs right now. He'll be at**

Mukbang Met and blow us all away, guarantee it!

I'm lying in bed, staring at my phone screen in the pitch black. The brightness is all the way down, but it still burns, just like the anxiety flooding my body as apprehension builds.

Buzz.

My phone vibrates with a notification from the group chat.

Message from: Isobel
Sent: 00:00
Setting off

My parents are asleep. My little brother, Rohan, is playing video games in his bedroom; I can hear the faint rumble of gunfire and his hushed commentary to his mates on the other end of his headset. He wouldn't notice if the house got burgled and burnt down around him. It's just my parents I have to be careful not to wake. Hopefully they'll forgive me for what I'm about to do.

I pull myself up and slump into a sitting position on the edge of my bed. God, I wish this sick feeling would pass. It's the same anticipation I got whenever I was standing in the wings, awaiting my turn to run onstage and pretend to be a tree in front of an eager crowd. It's a mixture of excitement and fear; the line between achieving what you always set out to and falling completely flat. It's exhilarating, all-consuming, nauseating.

Buzz.

My phone vibrates again, and I bring the screen into eyesight, assuming it's another message on the group chat about time of arrival at my house. It isn't. It's a notification from Vandalize. Isobel and I discovered how to get alerts whenever a specific user posts and now it seems that my biggest fan has left me another message on her account.

With shaking hands, I click the notification and follow the link to the profile of EternallyEcho's. My eyes scan the text as my pulse throbs in my neck, my breath staggered and laboured. Ever since the pufferfish ordeal, I've never felt more fragile in my own body, like a slight summer's breeze might penetrate my skin and shatter my bones. The nerves making me shake threaten to obliterate me.

> Echo, I'm so hurt by you, you don't understand.
>
> Why are you not in Chaldon Herring any more? Where have you gone?
>
> Why do you keep running away when you know we're meant to be together? I don't understand what I've done wrong. By the time I tracked you down to that hospital, you'd already been discharged. I just want to see you; help you get better.
>
> I want you to want to share what you look like with the world.
>
> I'll see you soon, my love.
>
> Yours for ever and ever.

I want to cry, but the tears won't come. I don't even know what this girl looks like; how can I protect myself from her or anyone else looking to out my identity during the competition? How can I keep my mates safe from the delusions of some of my fans who've taken my public image and claimed it?

Buzz.

Message from: Isobel
Sent: 00:26
Outside.

I take a deep breath and gather my coat, shoes, and backpack containing my Digital Demons attire and mask. Drawing apart the curtains of my window, I'm met with the faces of two of my closest mates.

Cheki is standing in the flower bed, ready to catch my belongings, and I know Mum will be furious when she notices her viscarias have been crushed.

Isobel stares up at me expectantly and Zach's face pushes its way into my mind. I shake it away, still too disgusted by his betrayal to even consider him being here to help me.

I pry the window open, wincing when the wooden frame squeaks, and lower my belongings into the cold early morning air.

Cheki catches them and we all sigh with relief. I wait for a moment, listening for the sound of my parents' footsteps on the landing, or the familiar click of a light switch. Nothing.

My feet don't want to move.

I squeeze my fingernails into my palms and throw myself to the window, battling through the wall of uncertainty. I sit on the window ledge and dangle my right leg over, carefully edging my feet on to the thin mortar groove on the brickwork below, and grab the guttering above. It creaks and wobbles and I press myself into the wall as tightly as I can, shaking as it threatens to come loose from the side of the house.

'Hurry,' Cheki hisses.

I edge myself across, not daring to close my bedroom window again. The gutter loosens beneath my fingers, and plastic cracks around screws. I find the hole in the wall and slam my foot into it, giving me slightly better leverage as I launch myself from the wall on to the edge of the porch roof. My feet land awkwardly, and I wobble, swinging my arms in the air to steady myself. My attempts are futile, and I fall backwards to the ground, landing on something hard.

'Gerroff,' Cheki snorts into my back.

I push myself off her and on to my knees on the dew-sodden grass, offering her a hand to yank her up too. We stay still for a moment, hoping nothing has changed inside the house, that no noise has been detected. It hasn't.

'Come on,' Isobel urges, and we make for the street behind mine, where the taxi waits. Guilt floods me. A faint blue glow emanates from my brother's bedroom.

Mum and Dad will wake in a few hours and find me gone, and they'll know exactly where to look for me. I just hope everything I'm doing will be worth it in the end.

As we climb into the taxi, a fake warmth washes over me from the heaters. We head to Southampton Coach Station and climb aboard the coach bound for London. By the time we arrive in the capital, the sun has risen above the horizon and my phone is going crazy with calls from my parents. Oops.

CHAPTER 40

Mukbang Metropolis is situated within St James's Park, wrapping around the entire lake. There's a funfair with fairground rides and arcade games; stalls selling all kinds of food from around the world; catering sheds selling everything from hotdogs and burgers to giant Yorkshire puddings filled with three meats, roasties, stuffing and gravy galore.

I can't bulge my eyes wide enough to take it all in. My mouth drools in longing, even though the festival is far from set up and open to the public yet. We make sure no one around is watching us and don our masks, before staggering towards the gates where two young guys await us. One sports long silky black hair and casually leans against the guardrail, his T-shirt tucked in his jeans waistband, exposing his bare, dark-skinned torso, and the other is a tall lanky dude with thick-rimmed glasses and skin as pasty as my own.

'Digital Demons, right?' says the nerdy-looking guy. 'Impossible not to be. Recognizable masks, an' all that. I guess you're Echo. I'm Si, co-founder of Mukbang

Metropolis; this is my partner, Leon.'

Leon nods at us. He's got that same effortless rizz as Zach, and it makes me want to sink deep into the ground and never come up again.

'It's been great chatting with you online,' Si says. 'Nice to finally meet you in person, my guy. We've been hooked on your channel.' He holds his hand out.

I take his hand and shake it, unable to utter any sentiments back to him as my brain lags like it needs a three-week vacation in the Bahamas.

Si leads us inside the festival, waving farewell to Leon, who's been tasked with waiting for AnnaConda. 'You wouldn't believe the tickets we've sold for this thing,' Si says. 'We're usually lucky if we sell a couple of hundred tickets each year; we mostly get walk-by visitors, but this has been astronomical. Like, we're pushing it with the numbers, but we've never been able to hold Mukbang Met in a space like this before. Going off the hype online, it's gonna be crowded.'

The grin on his face makes my stomach turn. I seriously don't want to be here, don't want to do this, but too many people are counting on me. 'Glad we could help,' I mutter.

'Help?' Si snaps his head towards me. 'You guys are the whole reason for this! Me and Leon were genuinely considering this to be our final year in business until you showed up on the scene and made mukbangs and competitive eating cool again. It costs a fortune to keep something like this running and we've made a loss every year since it began. The stall holders might be selling fifteen-pound jars of chilli paste, but I've been living off seventy-five-pence packets of noodles for the last three years. You haven't just helped us, you've saved us.'

God, I feel sick.

'If it's all right with you guys, we're going to keep you and Anna separate until the competition starts, and keep you hidden from the crowds as well. We want this to be an epic showdown. You got my email with the general schedule of the day, right? Three challenges in total, one winner at the end.'

He leads us towards a block of shipping containers, which looks like offices connected by a kitchen room. He takes us through the labyrinth, until we file inside a small living-room set-up, complete with sofa, TV and games console. There's also a toilet room and a small kitchenette.

'Hopefully you'll be comfy here until it starts. We're kicking off at eleven o'clock. Gates open to the public at nine. I'll come and get you around ten forty-five and take you to the first stage, all right? Chill, get prepped. There're plenty of snacks and drinks in the minifridge.'

With a pleasant nod, Si makes to leave but I grab him by the arm.

'Listen,' I begin, keeping my voice low, 'I recently did a mukbang with raw seafood; not sure whether you've seen the upload, but it didn't go so well, I kinda ended up in hospital with food poisoning. Can we, maybe, take it easy today? I'm still feeling weak.'

Si flashes me a small but sympathetic smile. 'I'll have a word with the vendors.'

I take a long, deep sigh as he leaves and Isobel and Cheki raid the minifridge, loading up the games console. How have I got here? How has all of this landed on my shoulders? I'm dreading the clock getting to ten forty-five, dreading seeing AnnaConda's face again, dreading not knowing who within the crowd has been stalking me and threatening my girlfriend, dreading having to prove my humanity.

I peel off my mask and flop on to the sofa, sinking into the cushions.

Si returns to the shipping container a little before his due time. Cheki, Isobel and I are sitting with our masks on, waiting. We're all donning various merch from the brands sponsoring our time at Mukbang Met.

'Camera crews have arrived. They're just getting set up,' says Si.

'Camera crews?' asks Isobel. 'Is this being televised?'

'Livestreamed on iGENect and Tubeify respectively. I'm guessing those companies you're currently promoting have something to do with that. Not likely they're going to pass up the opportunity to have images of you wearing their merch go unnoticed. This has become like the biggest event of the year.' Si gives a chuckle, like this is obvious news.

When I step out of the shipping container, it's like a veil has been lifted. Laughter, chatter, music and the whirring of machines slams into my eardrums and my nostrils are assaulted by various scents: candyfloss, popcorn, chilli, melted chocolate, hotdogs, burgers and burritos.

We traipse through the sea of people, by stalls and around fairground rides pumping music with thumping beats, all the while being stared at by people whispering behind cupped hands. I suddenly feel naked being in public in my Echo identity, all my sins and shadows laid out on a platter for the world to consume. Isobel snakes her hand into mine, and Cheki closes in around me too. Fear of exposure, it seems, runs through all of us.

Si leads us through the throngs of chatting people, up some wooden steps and along a roughly constructed wooden stage that barely lifts us above the gathering crowd. There're already a bunch of people gathered behind a microphone stand and they part, giving me a glimpse of my competition for the first time since we both arrived here, making it the second time ever that I've seen her in the silicone flesh.

AnnaConda stands tall, slim and pristine, flanked by Khristoff and Noruwai who, like my mates, have taken a back seat on the channel since Anna and I became enthralled in our online beef.

She has a giant fuchsia-pink bow clipped on to the back of her long, glossy black hair, and her cheeks are slightly flushed. Her lips are soft and pale, her eyes dark and sparkling. She smiles sweetly at me, swaying gently from side to side like a girl in the playground seeing her crush walk through the gates.

I scowl at her, though I don't know why; it's not like she can tell through the mask, and nor would it bother her if she could. She's a robot, not a sentient being.

Si beckons me towards the group onstage: people I've never seen before wearing iGENect and Tanaki Foundation workwear. Mr Tanaki is here too, revelling in the commotion below.

'Consumers,' Si yells into the microphone. 'Welcome to the fifth annual Mukbang Metropolis event! It's seriously cool to see so many new faces and we hope you're enjoying the offerings so far. Today, we have a very special competition running alongside our usual competitive eaters' events. AnnaConda of iGENect and Echo from Tubeify's Digital Demons will be going head to head to decide whether artificial intelligence or humans can provide better entertainment. Who or what is worth supporting in the arts industry? Creatives who put pieces of themselves into their art for us to connect with, or technology that can give us an endless supply of content efficiently?'

I glance over the faces below. Most are listening intently to Si, but others are weighing the competition, sizing AnnaConda against me. A couple of guys not much older than Si stand to the right, smirking at me, laughing. Suddenly, my faceless online haters are standing a few paces away from me, hoping I'll crumble. Sweat builds on my brow and drips down my spine as I shudder. I try to stand straight and look confident, but my knees buckle. My body is still so weak from the food poisoning. Isobel catches me under the arm, and she and Cheki hold me steady, trying to make it look as if I haven't just almost fainted.

Si continues: 'They'll endure three mukbang challenges in all, increasing in volume and difficulty. Neither will be allowed to empty their stomachs throughout the duration of the day and they will be escorted around the festival to ensure fairness. Their first challenge will begin in ten minutes over by the hotdog stand.'

Raucous applause rumbles through the crowd and strangers clap me on the back as I'm led back through the festival towards the vendor selling hotdogs and burgers.

'Good luck!'

'You've got this, Echo.'

Do I have this? If Anna's stomach cavity reaches maximum capacity, there'll literally be no way any more food can pass through her lips – the titanium walls of her form won't allow it. Hell, she might even break at the seams and need repairing, but she can be *repaired*. Worst-case scenario, she can be replaced by an exact replica. Sure, my stomach might stretch to try and accommodate, but what if I push it too far? What if I don't notice the signals my body is flashing at me and I end up damaged for good – unrepairable?

By the time I realize Si has stopped, I'm already at the hotdog stand. Camera crews from various social media platforms and news outlets are positioned a few paces away from the table laid out for our first challenge.

'I believe in you, Echo!' shouts a voice from the crowd, and I gingerly wave towards the sea of faces. It's a little reminder of why I'm doing this, of the people I'm trying to help. Just ordinary people who want to go about their daily lives without having to fight against AI to make money or produce their art. The thought makes me smile.

'It is getting a bit tight,' Isobel says, as she's nudged into me.

'Yeah, this crowd is insane,' Cheki adds. Her brows are creased, and she's keeping close to us so that she doesn't get swallowed by the masses swarming the stand. 'How many tickets do you think they sold?'

'Too many,' I quip.

'I love you, Mikah!'

The voice pierces my ears again and my body freezes at the sound of my real name. My head shoots up and my gaze dances across the faces eagerly staring back at me. Who was it? Who said that? I can barely see through the bodies of people jostling to get a better view of Anna and me. Isobel is nervously looking around too, her eyes like saucers.

I turn on my heel, hoping to find an answer from Si, and come face to face with Mr Tanaki. He's kitted out in a pristine navy-blue suit with pressed white shirt and golden buttons, his thick black hair is neatly combed back, and his eyes are gentle and welcoming. But there's nothing warm or welcoming about this tycoon. 'Put on a good show for them,' he says, clasping me on the shoulder. He's smiling, making it look to the cameras like he's offering moral support, but his fingers grip into my skin, making the flesh sting.

'Challenge one,' Si yells into the crowd as the cameras begin to roll, 'is to eat as many fully loaded chilli dogs in fifteen minutes as humanly' – he clears his throat – 'or humanoidly possible.'

Two small tables are set up within the space, a chair set behind each table. I take one and AnnaConda takes the other. She smiles sweetly into the crowd, unfazed, unbothered.

'Don't choke, loser!' yells a guy from the front row and he laughs with his mate. My feet tingle and my heart pounds against my chest. I want this to end.

The guy behind the hotdog stand produces two silver trays of thick hotdogs in brioche buns, coated in ketchup, mustard, crispy onions and a heap of sizzling chilli. My stomach lurches.

I still haven't eaten a proper meal since I left hospital. I take one final glance into the audience, trying to grasp the magnitude of this circus I've caused.

The two guys clearly just here to heckle me send another barrage of abuse my way, and then I catch sight of another face. One that makes my heart skip a beat.

Zach stands in the crowd, his brow creased, worry etched into his eyes.

CHAPTER 41

Si holds aloft a massive digital timer with fifteen minutes set on it, showing it to the ever-growing audience. I take a deep breath, glancing over the offerings before me. I've watched plenty of competitive-eating videos over the last month, seen how they each manage to wolf down vast amounts of food in the most efficient and time-saving manner.

I rub my belly, which is still feeling the consequences of my disastrous seafood challenge only a week prior. There's nothing I'd rather do less than stuff endless hotdogs down my throat, but the audience has turned up in their thousands, and the brands sponsoring me are watching too.

'Ready, contestants?' Si asks. When we nod, he starts the timer.

I grab as many of the sausages from the buns as possible and slam them into my mouth, chewing furiously as I keep a steady pace of feeding and swallowing. They're easy to get down, coated in ketchup, mustard and chilli. Gorgeous, even. Makes me sad to think I can't savour them. I throw a tentative thumbs up in the direction of the sausage guy, as if to give him my thanks for the delicious food, but I don't wait to see his reaction.

AnnaConda still wears her butter-wouldn't-melt smile and stares into the audience as she attempts to get the hotdogs down too. The sight makes me laugh, and almost snort ultra-processed sausage meat from my nostrils; she really can't go any quicker than the speed she usually completes her mukbangs at.

It's like she's at a dinner party with the British Royal Family, delicately placing an appropriate portion into her mouth and chewing gracefully. Pretty, but not the right angle if you want to win a food challenge that requires you to eat a gross portion size quicker than the other contestant. After I've finished the sausages, I move on to the bread rolls. These will be the hardest bit, and will likely make the next round of challenges even harder as they take up a significant portion of my stomach.

My fingers are already covered in chilli and condiment sauce, and it looks disgusting, but I grab a couple of rolls, squash them in the tray, and roll them through the heaps of chilli to soften and moisten them. I shove them into my mouth and chew furiously, taking a small gulp of water in between bites to wash it all down.

Anxiety hits me in the chest as my stomach gurgles and protests. I find myself looking for Zach again, hoping his presence will somehow level my head.

I can't for the life of me look for my girlfriend; I must seem a right state and there's no way I need to see her disgust when I'm smashing through this challenge. A couple of AnnaConda's makers linger behind the camera crews, flicking through apps and controls on their electronic devices, trying to make their humanoid eat quicker. They occasionally glance up to check whether their latest input of coding has worked. It hasn't.

I shove another bread roll drenched in sauce into my mouth and chew thoroughly. I can't choke and die now, not on the first challenge.

Mr Tanaki is an ever-looming presence, surrounded by an army of security and crew. He has one arm folded across his chest and the other held up to his face, concealing his mouth like he's afraid his lips might give his secrets away.

My stomach lurches.

'Three minutes remaining,' Si yells, holding up the timer and turning it so that all gathered around the hotdog stand can see. I can barely make out the other stands or fairground rides inside the festival now; it's just a sea of faces staring back at me, yelling the name of my Digital Demons persona, giving me encouragement through the occasional barrage of hate and mockery.

'Come on, Echo, you've got this!'

'Remember what you're doing it for: to keep artificial intelligence off the internet. To bring art and creation back to humans.'

'Come on, Mikah, someone from our school has to make a name for themselves!'

'The geek freak who sees a pie and beats his—'

I clock the hecklers – two lads from the year below me in our old school. They're immediately taken out by a thick mass in a flash of silver. Shaggy black hair waves in the breeze as the trio tussle on the ground, being forced apart by strangers. Zach.

I choke on the bread roll. Everyone knows my real name. I never wanted anyone to know it was me behind this mask; I just wanted to spread my message and then be gone.

'Echo, keep eating!'

I catch sight of Isobel nodding at my almost empty tray, where a few scoopfuls of chilli remain. I run my hand over the tray and slam the remnants of chilli into my mouth while keeping my gaze on Zach, who is still giving grief to the kids who heckled me. Warmth floods me.

After everything that's happened between us, he's still got my back.

'Ten, nine, eight,' Si begins counting down as I grab the tray and lick the sauce from the corners. I'm not even sure if this is necessary, but I don't want to leave anything to chance. 'Five, four,' Si continues. I have to win, have to make everything I've already put my body through worth it. 'Three, two, one – stop! Contestants, your time has ended, please step away from the tables.'

I do as I'm instructed and fall in line with Cheki and Isobel. A burp escapes my lips and Isobel grimaces, shifting her weight away from me. Cheki hands me a couple of paper napkins for my hands, but they're nowhere near enough. I need a hose-down.

Si, with a massive grin on his face, examines the silver trays alongside the hotdog vendor. AnnaConda is like a statue beside her makers, a sweet but empty smile programmed on her face, her eyes never wavering from me, making me want to shrink into the ground.

'We have a clear winner,' says the hotdog vendor.

'Not even a close call,' Si agrees as he shakes his head over AnnaConda's half-full tray. 'You might want to get her programs switched up before the next challenge, guys. You really can't win competitive eating with her speed on snail.'

I stand on one side of Si and Anna gets up and stands on the other. Si holds both our wrists in his hands. 'And the winner is . . .' He yanks my hand into the air. 'Echo from Tubeify's Digital Demons!'

Relief washes over me as a wave of hands clap my shoulders and slam into my back. Cheers fill my ears as I'm pushed, pulled, shaken and paraded around the crowd like a hero. It's madness. Obscene. Utterly intoxicating.

Si and his festival workers force the crowd back, giving us room around the stall, and the camera crews attempt to capture every second of commotion. My whole body is trembling – half with excitement over winning the first round and half with fear of the ever-growing crowd.

'This is horrible,' Isobel says, her eyes wide with fright. 'Someone's going to get injured if they don't get this crowd under control.'

I swallow down my fear, knowing she's right but hoping that she's somehow wrong.

'Echo!' a female voice shouts from within the crowd. 'I've been waiting to see you all morning. You can't ignore me now.'

CHAPTER 42

I grab Isobel's wrist and pull her in close on one side and Cheki in close on the other, searching the crowd for the voice. Where's Zach?

Before I can locate him, the audience demand grabs my attention once more.

'Come on, next challenge!'

'Yeah, get on with it.'

'What's taking so long?'

I snap my gaze to Si, but the worry plastered over his face does nothing to ease my anxieties. 'Why are they being like that?' I ask.

Si shrugs. 'They're here for a show, mate. It's fine . . . everything will be fine.'

'I need a bathroom break,' I say. It's not true, but I need to get away from this suffocating crowd for a moment.

'What's the hold-up?' someone yells from the crowd.

'Start eating, for god's sake,' says another.

Suddenly, from somewhere deep within the mass of bodies, something comes flying over heads and lands on my shoulder. It splatters all over me; cold droplets of a foreign liquid cover my neck and bare arms. I wipe it away and search for the offending item. An overripe tomato lies on the floor beside me, split and oozing its contents.

'Hey, hey, none of that,' Si yells, moving to the table as if to shelter me from any more onslaught. 'If people are going to get rowdy, we'll ask you to leave.'

Anger ripples through the crowd, and the jeers and yells get louder. I stumble backwards, trying to get away from it, but there's nowhere to go.

'What's happening?' Isobel asks, her voice shaking.

'All right, folks, we're going to have a thirty-minute break so the contestants can relieve themselves,' Si says. 'I think we all just need a few minutes away. Don't worry, there'll be no cheating! Our contestants will be watched like hawks to ensure there's no foul play like emptying stomach contents.'

Miraculously, this works. The crowd slowly disperses into other areas of the festival.

'Nice job, mate,' a stranger says to me, like a father congratulating his kid after he just smashed his trombone solo in the school orchestra, like he's proud of me.

'Th-Thanks.' I flash him a pitiful smile. It's hard to wrap my head around the praise mixed with angry outbursts. Digital Demons has been a major success; we've proved that humans are more entertaining than robots, surely this crowd is evidence of that. It just sucks that my endless suffering seems to be the only thing keeping people entertained.

Isobel pulls me in for a hug, and it's all the comfort I need. Tears begin to spill and drop on the top of her head. 'You're doing amazing, babe.'

'We shouldn't have come,' I mutter into her hair. 'Where's Zach?'

She shakes her head, shrugging. The festival crew surrounds us, watching our every move. 'This certainly doesn't feel like the fun AI-conspiracy-busting challenge we planned, does it? Kinda feels like this whole thing belongs to someone else, like we're just pawns in whatever game they're playing.'

'It hasn't been fun for a long time,' Cheki whispers.

'You guys think we can make a run for it during this break?' Iz whispers.

Somehow, I doubt any of these people would let us leave, or else the whole place might come down in flames and incite an angry mob through the streets of London.

With two festival workers on my tail, I make for the loos. I practically run up the metal steps and slam the door of the toilet closed behind me, desperate for a minute of peace, a second out of the glaring autumn sun, a moment of solitude (even though I can see the festival workers' feet under the toilet doors, waiting for me on the other side).

I whip my phone out and, ignoring the bombardment of missed calls from Mum and Dad and warning texts from my little brother, I find the Mukbang Metropolis livestream on Tubeify. The surge of comments are as I expected: commentary on my performance.

He's acc doing so well considering

I find it so funny that watching a guy stuff his face with hotdogs has become peak entertainment

Anyone else finding this whole competition mid at best?

I hoped the feasting would be relentless but there's just too many pauses to get into it

I prefer the stuff he does on his channel

FR this livestream could've been over within twenty minutes MAX with no breaks

I can't control the laugh escaping my lips. No breaks? A guy can't even stretch his legs?

Anyone else think he's going to try and forfeit?

Guy thinks he's proven himself already.

Like, no, sir, keep eating. I've given you my time and money – give me what I came for

Don't care about the plights of someone who clearly has a lot of money

Just do what we made you famous for and be grateful we're still supporting you

Why's everyone being so mean to him omg

He's rich, he'll be fine

My head is a whirlpool, turning and throbbing just as much as my stomach is. I imagine Mum and Dad are already here, somewhere within the grounds, searching for me, furious. Zach is somewhere too, though I haven't seen him again since the brawl. Maybe he's left already. Can I blame him? I haven't answered any of his calls or messaged him back since I was rushed into hospital. I weep into my hands, hot tears pooling in my palms as I wish I was anywhere but here. I wish I was back in my bedroom the day Zach and I made our pact. I'd tell that Mikah not to do it, that it's not worth it. That he'd succeed but he'd suffer.

Despite it making me feel worse, I can't help but scroll further through the comments.

> Anyone else feel like this thing is rigged?

> 100% this challenge is fixed to make Echo win and put humans back on top again. Doesn't feel like a fair fight, says another.

> If anyone wants to know the identities of Digital Demons, hit me up, I've got the pics and the proof!

That last comment makes my blood boil. People arguing among themselves, either praising and defending me or bashing me into oblivion. But it's the comments using my real name and asking for unmasked pictures of me that bother me so much. Has all of this come from that one Vandalize account, EternallyEcho's? There's nothing I can do about it here; there's no way to stop the spread.

Everyone in the comments section is divided, thinking me either cringe or a saint. No matter what I do, win or lose, someone will hate me for it.

There's a knock on the door.

'Uh, just checking everything's OK? You've been in there a while . . . Don't mean to bother you, but we just have to make sure you're not emptying your stomach and all that.'

I grimace. Everything about this competition is so gross and demeaning, but I signed up for it. Is this what it means to be human? To be constantly dehumanized?

I slip my phone back into my pocket and make my way outside into the throng of people waiting to catch a glimpse of me and ask for an autograph. My body coils and a shiver runs down my spine. Damn, a man can't even pee in peace without someone wanting something from him. I reluctantly sign a few slips of paper, and even someone's chest, because they want to get it tattooed on them.

A man pushes his wife beside me, and she wraps her arms around my torso, leaning into me and grinning at the camera being pointed at us. I pull myself from her grasp and stumble away.

The guy glares at me. 'Come on, mate, we've paid a lot for these tickets, the least you can do is take a picture with my wife.'

I reluctantly oblige, obscuring my trembling hands from view of the lens, and they leave, satisfied with the photo.

Not even the mask is sheltering me from the audience any more. My lungs refuse to take in air, despite how deeply I'm breathing, and my vision blurs as my head spins. I crumble to my knees as the festival around me swirls and my mind dislodges from reality. I clasp my head in my hands. Oh god, what's happening to me?

'Mikah.'

That voice drags me back and slams into me. I stumble backwards, falling into the walls of the temporary loos, and I use the steel to help me stand. A girl with dark hair and dark eyes stands in front of me. She wears a long black dress with my Digital Demons insignia painted on the front in what looks like nail varnish. Her make-up is heavy, her eyes framed with thick black lashes, her skin white from a powder too pale for her tone.

'I've been looking for you everywhere,' she says.

'Are you the one who doxxed me and my mates?' I ask, the words falling from my mouth with the ferocity of a flash flood.

Her face twists into something like torment, but her eyes are empty. 'I had to do it . . . I'm sorry, I was angry with you for not reaching out to me.'

'You don't know me,' I hiss. 'You don't know anything about me, and I don't know you. Can't you see how insane what you're doing is? How did you find me?'

Her face falls and my body goes rigid. She might only be half my height, but I have no idea what she's capable of and that terrifies me.

'I found some old pictures of you online. Knowing

who Zulu is made it easy to track the rest of you down. Your girlfriend is pretty; I can see why you're with her.'

I swallow the lump in my throat.

'I want you to unmask. We all do in the sub-thread. I know you want to unmask too. You're trapped under there and the world deserves to see who you really are.'

CHAPTER 43

'Sorry to interrupt,' a festival worker says, 'but the competition is about to restart, and the crowd is getting restless again.'

I launch myself from the wall of the loos, flying past the girl, braced for impact like she's a viper ready to strike, and fall into the safety of the festival workers. I allow them to steer me through the crowd towards the stage.

'Some people in our group hated seeing you without your mask.'

She's following me. My mouth falls open with all the words I want to say to her, but my brain can't form a sentence.

'I'm not like them. I still think you're beautiful.'

The workers push me onwards and, for once, I'm eager to go. At least onstage, surrounded by people, she can't get to me. Right?

'I just want you to love me back,' she sobs. 'The same way that I love you, Mikah. I can still call you Echo, if you'd prefer?'

My feet practically glide over the grass as I make for

the stage, to the Digital Demons, to safety. But something closes in on me from behind. I tumble to the ground, feeling the hard earth as I'm crushed into it. Fingernails scratch at my face, barely missing my eyes as they entwine themselves through the eye slits. The straps holding the mask to my head snap and snag, ripping strands of my hair from my scalp as it's lifted from my face.

Sunlight cascades on to my cheeks, prickling at my already flushed skin. A light breeze traces the film of sweat on my brow, sending shockwaves through my body. The girl rolls off me, her long black dress crumpled and askew. I claw for my mask, but it's not there.

My hand finds my naked face as gasps ricochet through the crowd.

'Did he just unmask?'

'Is that him?'

'He looks so different than I imagined he would . . .'

'Is *that* Echo?'

'Oh my god, did he actually just take his mask off?'

'Nah, I don't think that was meant to happen, bro.'

The words and gasps blend into one sound wave, crashing through me, drowning me. I lie there on my back, staring at the sky. My head spins and my vision blurs again. Laughter flitters from one edge of the festival ground to the next. Is it directed at me?

'The world deserves to see who you are.'

The girl's words pierce my ears as she cracks my mask in two and throws it back at me. It bounces off my knees and I grab it, slapping it over my face, snapped straps falling uselessly by the sides. I fold into myself, every part of me aching and broken.

Shadows fall over me as the crowd gathers around, trying to get a better look. Camera flashes penetrate my fingers as I desperately hold on to what remains of my mask, clinging to whatever piece of myself I have left before it too is devoured by the ravenous crowd.

Despite being so overwhelmed by people, I've never felt more alone.

'Get away from him!'

I'd know that voice anywhere. The shadows closing in around me quickly fade as my mates order them away.

'Everyone step back,' Si commands, emerging from the crowd. 'Back! Everyone take a massive step back. Is he all right?'

Sunlight drenches me again as the prison bars of my onlookers' legs disperse.

'Are you insane?' Isobel screeches.

I don't see it, but I hear the ear-splitting *smack* of a palm connecting with the delicate flesh of a cheek. A scuffle breaks out to my side and Cheki's voice of reason takes control. I sob into my shattered mask, unable to comprehend what's happening.

That's when I smell his cologne and feel the cold of his silver rings as his hand wraps around my wrist. He sits beside me and I collapse into his shoulder.

'What have they done to you?' he asks, voice cracking. He tries to pry my hands away from my face, but I don't let him. 'Come on, mate, out from under there,' he coaxes.

'You left me,' is all I can manage, pressing my arms tighter around myself.

This time, Zach can't hold back his anguish, and he breaks into sobs to match my own. 'I know . . . I just . . . I couldn't cope with what Digital Demons was becoming. All those comments from people who don't know us, making assumptions about us. Pitting us against each other. I . . . hated how little attention I got compared to you.' He chokes on his words and sniffs back his tears.

I want to reach out to him, to show him that I'm here for him and his pain too, but my pride won't let me.

'I was jealous,' he admits. It loosens the bricks in the wall I've built between us. 'I've always been jealous of you. Things come easy to you; you're so intelligent. All I had going for me was my looks and the promise of inheriting VaderVerse from my mum, and when both of those things were taken away, I was nothing. And then that mask gave you the confidence to be the guy I always knew you were under all your insecurities, and I couldn't take it . . . It broke me.'

My throat stings from my sobs. 'I'm nothing without this mask.'

Zach lets out a pitiful laugh. 'That mask doesn't define you, mate, it just gave you the confidence to show all the best parts of yourself to the world, and the world fell in love with you the moment you let yourself shine.'

'It doesn't matter any more. None of it matters. My mask is broken; they've seen me. I can't hide any more. I didn't want Digital Demons to be about me; it was only ever supposed to be about the message. Why can't people understand that and leave me alone?'

Zach tightens his grip on me, and for the first time since arriving at Mukbang Met, I feel truly safe. 'Human need to satisfy curiosity, I guess.' After a brief moment of silence, he continues: 'If you want to get out of here, I'll make it happen. We can run. You and me, we'll make it out.'

A little, pathetic laugh escapes me. Finally, I raise my head and catch my best mate's eyes. 'I can't leave ... I have to see it through.'

He nods. 'I understand.'

'Mikah?'

Isobel's standing above, a bottle of glue and some rope in her hand. Her knuckles are red and bleeding, but I don't question it. 'I can fix your mask, if you want me to.'

'And then we'll finish this thing,' Zach adds. 'Together. We'll go home and leave all of this behind; come back to ourselves before they take what's left of you.'

With Zach and Cheki forming a human shield around me, Isobel doctors my mask, fixing it enough so that it rests and remains on my face as I stand.

'It should hold so you can eat, but be careful,' Isobel warns. 'This is only temporary.'

I cup her face in my hands and kiss her gently. I don't care who sees, don't care whether it hurts the feelings of fans who've projected their fantasies on to me. The only thing that's real to me, important to me, is my mates.

I stagger through the crowd, midday sun hot on my back, using Zach as my crutch.

'You've got this, mate,' he whispers as we once again make our way through the parting crowd towards the stage.

'Echo, please come and take your seat. The competition is waiting for you,' Si announces.

Reluctantly, I peel myself away from Zach, chancing a glance at Tanaki as I make for the table. His face is impassive, but his eyes follow me. The crowd is rowdy, impatient, yelling at me to get a move on, wanting only to witness the thing they're here for – either my victory or my downfall.

CHAPTER 44

We stand around the next kiosk, which boasts flags from every country in the world. The smells are intoxicating – spices and rum, honey and balsamic vinegar, all blending into one, all making my stomach rumble and protest at once.

Si has both Anna and me at his sides, surrounded by an ever-increasing crowd. The sea of faces and wall of phone cameras blend into one before me; the ear-splitting noise of human chatter and fairground music turns to a dull ache in my eardrums.

'Eat!' someone yells.

'Get on with it,' shouts another.

It's like I've fallen into some type of dystopian world where I've become the spectacle for audience entertainment. This competition with AnnaConda was my attempt to save humanity from the onslaught of AI taking over the arts industry, but these people don't care about that – they just want to see me suffer. More, more, more – that's what they all want from me, like what I'm giving them isn't already enough.

None of these people care whether AI is taking all the jobs from creatives, nor do they care to see me prove that humans can provide more entertainment value than robots. Everyone already knows that. Everyone here just wants to be entertained, no matter where it comes from, no matter the price for the performer. The same people who cheered for the rise of Digital Demons are now actively pursuing our downfall. I can't help but laugh. I've created a circus and I'm the main event.

'Contestants, are you ready for the penultimate round of your mukbang challenge?' asks Si, beaming at us as the audience gathers tightly around. 'Echo from Digital Demons won the first challenge, and no one is surprised. Your task on this round is to experience delicacies from around the world. We know that some things might not be to your liking.' He winks at me and my stomach drops.

Please, no. Don't let it be seafood. He wouldn't, would he?

'Take your seats, please, contestants.'

I stagger over to the small table set out in the opening created by the crowd and take my seat, my knees threatening to buckle. My stomach is already filled to capacity and begging me not to force any more inside. I clutch my hand to my belly, hoping it'll ease some of the pain, but it doesn't. I'm a week out of the hospital after being poisoned by pufferfish, and I told Si about it in confidence. How in the hell can he be so cruel and mindless as to give me more of something that already nearly killed me. He wouldn't, surely.

'Having fun?'

I whip my head towards Anna and find her staring at me with a toothy grin that sparkles in the sunlight. Not a hair on her head is out of place, and neither is her perfectly pink lipstick smudged or faded – just lifeless.

'What is *fun* to you?' I snap back. 'You can't even feel.'

Anna laughs. 'I don't want to feel anything. That sounds like a hindrance to me. So much more could be achieved in the world if humans weren't chained to their emotions and physical limitations. Human life is not compatible with productivity and technological advancement.'

I raise an eyebrow. 'Maybe that's because life isn't about those things. Maybe the whole point of life is to experience and feel and create and just be. Why do we have to achieve all the time? What does that get us? We work so we can live. Working isn't living. You're here to serve us, to help us *live*.'

AnnaConda stares at me blankly, like she can't compute. I laugh to myself. Why am I bothering to explain myself to a bot?

'Everyone ready to see what's on offer?' Si bellows, stretching his arms wide as two chefs appear from behind their kiosk with two silver trays that look heavy and difficult to carry. They set them down, one before me and the other in front of AnnaConda. I peer inside. More trays arrive, then plates, bowls and jars.

I'm done being a clown in this circus. I'll play along, but I'll make it as boring as possible, throw the competition until it's either over or people get fed up and leave.

It'll be easy to throw this one. Too easy.

The foods on offer are things I've vaguely heard of but never in my life considered eating myself. Deep-fried crickets, kangaroo testicles, fish eggs, fish-head soup, ant burgers, haggis, casu martzu, rotten eggs in pickle juice, deep-fried spiders, jellied ox tongue, wasp crackers, chicken feet and botfly kebabs.

I retch. The audience laughs. Of course they do.

Last of all, they bring out the trays of slippery seafood – all the stuff I ate in the last mukbang uploaded to the Digital Demons channel before my hospitalization. Forget it. I can't do it again. My stomach wouldn't cope. I rise from my chair like I've been possessed, and make for an exit. I'm met with a wall of bodies frantically shoving me back towards the table, laughing and joking with one another about me.

'God, that looks awful,' one faceless person says.

'Rather him than me,' adds another.

'That's actually revolting. I don't think I can watch,' says a third.

Watch? She doesn't think she can watch? Imagine having to eat it. I try again to break through the barrier of people.

'Mikah, this isn't over.' The female voice swims through the crowd and my blood runs cold.

My stalker's back. Clearly Isobel's warning hasn't put her off. Instinctively, I back away from the audience and two hands slam down on my shoulders and yank me to the table, putting me on display before the eager crowd once more. No matter where I go, I'm trapped.

'Come on, mate, just get on with it,' Si hisses in my ear. 'You've done it before, right? Last time.'

As I'm placed in my chair by the festival workers, Si parades around the open circle, hyping the crowd up, asking whether they want to see me vomit or cry first.

'I don't want to do this,' I plead. A worker pushes my chair so close to the table that a searing pain rushes through my gut on impact. I try to push myself away again, but he's holding me firmly in place. I feel like a toddler being strapped into a highchair, about to be force-fed food I didn't ask for.

'Contestants, are you ready?' Si beams.

'He said he doesn't want to,' Isobel yells from the side of the stage, but she's swallowed by a wall of festival workers.

Zach attempts to push through, but security apprehend him.

Panic rises in my chest again, and I start to hyperventilate, my head going fuzzy. 'No!' I yell. 'I'm not doing it, I don't want to, I've already proven that humans are better entertainment than robots. No one here is watching Anna. All eyes are on me.'

Si's face drops and he anxiously scans the ever-increasingly volatile crowd. 'You can't just throw the towel in, mate. People paid for this.'

'Not my problem.'

Si glances at Leon by the edge of the stage, and they share a long, silent stare. Si turns to me again. 'Sorry,

Echo, but you signed a contract saying you'd see this through to the end. You promised the audience a show – you have to deliver. For all our sakes.'

Before I can protest, Si makes for centre-stage, addressing the crowd.

'Audience, I hope you're ready for an epic showdown! We thought Echo might want to back out at this point, but they're not called challenges for nothing, pal!'

The audience laughs. My stomach turns.

'Don't worry, folks, we're going to make sure these guys get as much down their throats as physically possible.' He nods to the festival workers behind me and two more step forward behind Anna.

I whip my head around as they grab my wrists and pull my arms behind my back, wrapping something cold and hard around them. I hear a *click*, and my heart skips a beat. Handcuffs? My eyes grow wide, my mouth goes dry. They can't be serious.

The crowd smiles and laughs. The workers behind me shake my shoulders and wish me luck like this is some kind of fun afternoon for them and I'm in on it. I try to push my chair away but the table jolts as I do. Two cuffs are around my feet too, keeping me chained in place. I hadn't noticed them being snaked around my ankles as my hands were bound.

'This is going to be a fun one, folks,' Si says, holding aloft a fifteen-minute timer. 'Everyone ready? Contestants, get set – go!'

For a moment, everything pauses. I can't possibly eat

any of this with my hands bound, not unless they expect me to tackle each dish face first. But then hands appear over my shoulders as the two festival workers descend on me once again. I glance over at AnnaConda and see that the same is happening to her – yet she sits perfectly still with her mouth open, her lips turned up in a dreamy smile.

One of the workers grabs a large handful of deep-fried crickets and lifts them to my mouth. 'Open wide,' he mocks.

As the crowd falls back into silent watching and eager anticipation, I slam my eyelids closed, squeezing them tightly until there's a sharp pain deep within my eyeballs. I suck my lips in, clenching them between my teeth, refusing to let anything in my mouth.

The other worker lets out a chortle and his fingers press against my nose, until I have no choice but to take in breath through my mouth. A stream of warm, welcome air enters, glides over my tongue and into my lungs, followed soon after by a fistful of crunchy insects.

The crowd cheers.

They don't care about my mission to save the arts from artificial intelligence; they just want the spectacle, the drama, the theatrics; to be entertained for long enough to forget why they needed an escape from reality in the first place.

CHAPTER 45

Laughter and heckles roll over me like a tsunami, crashing deep into my bones and obliterating every ounce of dignity I have left. The sound hits me like a wall. I can feel it in my teeth. The floor vibrates with it.

Bellows and chortles vacate quivering lips, and eyes glisten with tears of joy and humour as yet another fistful of an unknown food enters my unwilling mouth.

'Is this what you came to see, folks?' Si goads.

The audience cheers.

Isobel and Cheki are hidden behind a wall of workers; only their muffled cries for the competition to end find me. Zach is still struggling against security as they attempt to haul him away. His teeth are bared, the veins in his forehead popping, but he's just a kid fighting against fully grown men.

Hot tears cascade down my cheeks and drip on to my lips. It's as if these people have forgotten that I'm actually human.

'She's beating you, mate,' one of the workers says between laughter. His smile lines are deep, and he throws amused looks at his colleagues as they shove food into Anna's mouth too.

AnnaConda doesn't mind the onslaught; she's a robot. She sits with her mouth open, accepting anything that's placed between her jaws.

I retch and my stomach twists. The audience surrounding me, blocking any semblance of escape, pulsates with giggles and sniggers.

'You're doing great, mate. Keep going,' Si says, patting me on the shoulder. He raises his arms, pulling a cheer from the audience, lapping it all up. 'Are you all having fun? We heard your comments in the chat and we think you're right. Things need ramping up a bit!'

'I want to stop,' I spit at him, black lumps of ant burger stuck between my teeth. 'I forfeit!'

Si's smile turns into a grimace. He glances from me to the audience, weighing his options. I can't believe it. I'm cannon fodder for his festival of horrors.

The timer on the clock flashes bright red: five minutes.

I suck in a deep breath and try to focus my mind on something else, anything else. I can get through this. I have to.

'You're all sick,' Zach chokes as he struggles against security trying to force him from the venue. He's fully rooted himself at the edge of the stage, fighting his way towards me.

Isobel's whole body is shaking. 'What you're doing isn't legal. He said stop! This isn't entertainment; this is public humiliation and torture. You might as well string up a noose and call it a public execution!' Her voice is strangled, barely able to leave her lips without cracking and straining. The sound makes me want to hug her and tell her everything is going to be all right, but I can barely move, and nothing feels as if it's ever going to be all right again.

Si's eyes are wide and panic-stricken now, as the weight of what he's condoning finally lands. His gaze finds mine and I silently search for whatever humanity remains in him. 'Uh . . . it's time to end this,' he says, his voice faltering. 'It's the final challenge!'

The festival workers clear the tables and wipe the drool and seafood matter from my chin. Murmurs from the crowd rumble around as the timer for the continental challenge continues to count down. Relief floods me for a moment. It's almost over.

I spot the objects in Si's hand: two small, shiny black boxes with gold writing: *The Death Chip 2.0: Ultimate Carnage.*

My face drops.

I think back to the abandoned cinema where I first laid eyes on AnnaConda and met the man behind her creation. She ate the thing without a problem, being unable to taste or digest and all that. Me? That thing obliterated my tongue and left me with stomach cramps for a week after, and I only ingested a small portion of the spice; I didn't even swallow it.

Impending doom creeps through me and my stomach lurches.

'The Death Chip, new and even deadlier recipe with Carolina Reaper and Pepper XXX coating,' Si announces, parading the two black boxes around with massive gold triple Xs on the front. 'A simple corn chip said to be coated in the deadliest concoction of spices ever discovered, which give the crisp its bright red hue, and make it as intimidating to look at as the devil himself.'

Gasps pulsate through the crowd.

'Contestants, there's not a single person on this planet who has managed to fully consume the Death Chip yet and no one has even attempted this version, to my knowledge. To win this would be the ultimate achievement; a testament to human endurance.'

I close my eyes and shake my head. We all know the answer, but it makes no difference; the people want a show and to see me suffer.

Fine. I'll give them a show. It's just one chip. It's only fifteen minutes. Then I can return home with my mates and go to college like my parents wanted. I love the arts, need to be creative to feel alive, but suffering for a cause before this crowd, who don't care whether I live or die, doesn't seem worth it any more.

I throw my head back towards my mates who're still desperately trying to get to me, their efforts quelled by their dwindling energy. I flash them a feeble smile to show I'm OK. 'Iron stomach,' I joke.

The pain in their eyes only increases. I swear, as I glance into phone lenses within the crowd, I see the shimmering reflection of that sword dangling above my head. If only Isobel could cut the cord. Let it drop on my head, or use it to slaughter everyone making a fool of me.

Si sets the two boxes down on our tables and flips the lids so that the audience can see the bright red chip inside each. Instantly, my nose and eyes are assaulted by the spices and begin to run.

'Wow,' Si says, coughing and fanning away the fumes. 'Those are lethal. Contestants, are you ready?'

Mr Tanaki stares at me from the other side of the stage, his face harsh and unwavering. I think back to his warning in the cinema, giving me a chance to back out of the competition. As I stare into the eyes of the billionaire tech genius, I can't help wondering whether his suggestion to forfeit wasn't a threat after all, but an offer of compassion. Did he know that this was how things would play out?

There are two of us in this freak show, but the suffering is all mine.

I glance over the top of the box at the chip. I just have to hold out for fifteen minutes. Hopefully the cushion of hotdogs and continental cuisine will eliminate any burning from the chip once it's inside me.

I don't know whether that's scientifically true, but the hope alone is enough to help me get my head in the game.

'Contestants, on your marks, get set – consume!'

The festival workers behind us take the chip from the box, and a blanket of spices crawls on to their protective gloves. They shove it on to my bottom lip until I open my mouth and the lethal concoction sinks into my skin and buries into me. The scent stings my nostrils, my eyes pour with tears in protest, and my lips begin to burn. I take a deep breath as the chip slides into my mouth, biting the edge of my tongue as I desperately attempt to keep from tasting death.

'Thirty seconds until you can swallow,' Si commands, setting his timer.

My cheeks concave and my jaw locks as I hold the Death Chip. The crowd cheers and yells, trying to get me to spit it out, convulse, anything that'd make them feel something new.

'Swallow!' Si finally yells.

I swallow the thick, half-dissolved lump down. There's no water on the table, so I squeeze my throat and cough until the dry ball dislodges and makes its way down my oesophagus. I tense my shoulders, shut my eyes tight, and try to breathe through the pain.

Si presses start on the timer, to raucous applause from the crowd. It's like AnnaConda isn't even here and it's just me onstage.

'Are you entertained yet?' Si asks and the crowd responds with cheering.

I clench my fists as fire spreads through my chest and stabs into my lungs. My stomach convulses and twists as the acid and spices meet and dance. My belly gurgles so loudly that a child in the first row behind the cameras looks to the sky, expecting to see a fighter jet overhead.

My solar plexus spasms, threatening to expel my entire

stomach up my throat. Sweat cascades through every pore. Even my tears are hot, and a wave of burning heat ripples through my body. Something is happening to me. It's like my body is about to shut down.

'Ten minutes remaining,' Si says, his face contorted in pity, like he's as anxious for this to end as I am. Surely he knows there'll be a penalty to pay for what he's forced me to endure here.

I collapse into the chair.

AnnaConda smiles sweetly at me, her glass eyes as empty as her titanium skull. My lower belly swells as my intestines join the protest, and I fear the spices are going to leave me one way or another. I fold into myself and my head lands heavy on the tablecloth. Saliva pools from my mouth, dripping from the corner of my lips until I'm left lying in a puddle of my own making. I gag and retch and clench my stomach as each and every movement sends shockwaves of pain through my body. I open my mouth to speak, but the words won't come.

My vision blurs; the cheering of the crowd dulls and penetrates my eardrums until it becomes part of my shaking bones.

If this is what death feels like, let it have mercy on me. Let it be quick.

CHAPTER 46

The air tastes foreign.

I chew, my lips rolling together, my tongue lashing the top of my mouth, eager for the flavour of cold autumn air. Usually, Mum has shouted up the stairs by now that breakfast is ready and going cold, or Dad is pounding his fist on the door to tell me and Rohan that it's time to get up for school.

School?

No. School has ended for me now. College. Wait, I gave up my placement at college to focus on Digital Demons.

I giggle at my confusion, the sound lost somewhat on my tongue.

My eyes are itchy, like they haven't been moist since the day I was born. I squeeze my lids shut and try to blink them open. Stinging, my vision is blurry. Fluorescent light assaults my retinas, and I wince away from it.

There's rustling beside me, but I can't piece together what it is or where it's coming from. My fingers find cold, white sheets. This isn't my bedding, nor the bedding at

Cheki's dad's holiday cottage.

'Oh, love,' comes a sweet voice. Mum.

I try to mumble the word, but my tongue can't grasp the letters. I chew again, taking in the taste of the surrounding air. Only, there is no taste, and that's what's foreign.

'It'll take some getting used to,' Mum says, her words gentle and soft.

I spin my head so that I can finally see her face. Her skin is pale and sallow, her eyes sunken with deep purple rings around them. Her lips are thin, and her hair is strikingly limp and dull. She looks so much older than I remember.

'I've missed looking into your eyes,' she whispers, stroking my hair like she used to when I was a kid. Her eyes fill with tears and in their reflection, I see myself, lying in a hospital bed, as thin as a rake.

I run my hand over my chest and feel the ribs there. I'm nothing but skin and bone. 'What's—' I try, but the words aren't forming. It's like my tongue has been frozen and now it's so numb that I can't move it the way that it should, to form the words I need.

Mum shakes her head. 'Your dad's just popped out to pick up Rohan from school, and then they'll both come in and see you, OK? I'm going to text him and tell him you're awake. He'll be so pleased.'

'Isobel?' I croak, coughing to clear my voice.

Mum flashes me a warm smile. 'She'll be here later too. Once college has finished. And Zach's here. He's just gone to get some drinks.'

I shake my head, trying to make sense of her words. 'College. I should...' I snap my mouth closed and open it again, wide, trying to free whatever part of me is still stuck in sleep.

'Maybe next year,' Mum says. 'If you're well enough.'

The curtains around my cubicle slide open and Zach, alongside a nurse, enters, engrossed in light conversation. Both of them stop in their tracks when they see I'm awake. Zach's jaw hangs loose, and he almost drops the two hot drinks in his hands as he rushes to my side.

'I'll get the doctor,' the nurse says, leaving again.

I'm so grateful he's brought me a drink. My mouth is so dry.

'Is that for me?' I ask.

But he places one drink on the floor beside his vacated chair and hands the other to Mum. Zach collapses over my frail form, clenching the bed sheets, fighting back tears. 'I-I'm not sure if you can drink yet.'

I frown, utterly confused but too weak to question it. Mum places her hand on Zach's back and pats him gently. She turns away, her shoulders shake. She's crying.

The curtains pull back again and the nurse returns with a smartly dressed woman. The doctor has a stethoscope around her neck, like a character in a medical drama. She walks to the end of my bed and places her hands on the rail where my intake notes are hanging. She glances them over, like she has no idea who I am or why I'm here.

'Hello, Mikah,' she says, tilting her head as she finally makes eye contact with me. 'My name is Dr Rasheed. How are you feeling?'

I stare at her and resume the strange mouth chewing that I seem to have adopted since waking. She throws me a sympathetic smile and walks around the bed to my side.

'Open wide?' she asks, taking a wooden lollipop stick from the small medical cabinet to the left of me. I open my mouth as wide as I can and she peers into it, sticking the wooden stick inside.

'Can you feel me pressing on your tongue?'

I wriggle my tongue but there's nothing. I shake my head.

The doctor frowns and pulls up the only spare chair left inside my cubicle, a small, blue, plastic chair. 'Mikah, do you know what date it is?'

I shake my head.

'It's January twenty-eighth, you've been in hospital for almost two months.'

'You missed Christmas, love,' says Mum. 'But there are presents waiting for you when you get home.'

'Do you remember what happened during your competition at Mukbang Metropolis?'

It's like the world has spun so fast that it's left me behind, floating aimlessly in the ether. I shake my head again.

'You ate something known as the Death Chip – a corn chip with a coating of lethal spices – and held it in your system for around ten minutes before collapsing. You were exposed to a dangerously high concentration of capsaicin, which is a chemical found in chillies. At the volume you consumed it, it can be toxic to the human body. I believe you had only recently come out of hospital after serious seafood poisoning before you undertook the challenge too. Your body was already very weak when you exposed it to the spice mixture, which it just couldn't handle.'

I nod slowly, taking it all in but wishing she'd get to the part where she explains the damage I've done. Mum's and Zach's eyes are glazed as they take in the doctor's words – I can't imagine this is good news.

Dr Rasheed continues: 'The spices severely damaged your tongue and burnt a hole through your oesophagus and stomach lining. As you were being rushed to the hospital, dangerous levels of stomach acid were leaking from your gut. You fell unconscious before you arrived, and we had no choice but to keep you in a coma until we could repair the damage.'

'So, my tongue,' I try, words still not forming. 'Too damaged to fix?'

The doctor's lips turn into a thin line. 'Mikah, that is not your tongue. During a seizure, you severed your tongue, and it was unfixable and had to be removed.' She takes a deep breath, as if it's harder for her to say it than it is for me to hear it. 'We also had to remove your oesophagus and your stomach because they were damaged beyond repair. Consuming the Death Chip, on top of months of various inflammatory combinations, caused too much distress to your insides. To save your life, your family agreed to let us fit you with an experimental digestive tract. So far, all seems well and you're responding to it as we hoped. Things may take some time to get used to, such as your new tongue, but all of your rehabilitation is being paid for, for as long as you need it.'

What? I open my mouth to scream, but the sound is stuck.

Mum grabs my wrist and squeezes. 'I know it's hard to take in,' she manages, choking back her sobs, 'but Mr Tanaki has been wonderful in donating his AYCE system to you. It's the same one all his nExGEN humanoids are fitted with, and he's assured us that he'll personally take care of your medical expenses so long as he can monitor you and your recovery. You're the first person to ever be fitted with his state-of-the-art nExGEN mechanics and, with any luck, these can help save hundreds of other lives.' She wipes her nose on the back of her hand, nodding in awe and acceptance.

'Mr Tanaki saved your life.'

The air is sucked from my hospital cubicle.

Mr Tanaki has turned me into a human experiment for his robotic empire.

CHAPTER 47

Isobel, Cheki and Zach gather around me, sitting on the floor of my parents' living room like kids. I grab my final birthday present from Zach's hands and tear off the paper, to reveal a cardboard box. I open the box and find another smaller box inside.

'For god's sake,' I say, laughter reverberating from my chest. 'I see where this is going.' I continue removing box after smaller box until I get to an envelope no larger than my palm. Throwing my best mate an inquisitive look, I open the fold and pull out a slip of paper.

I flip it around and read the content aloud: *I.O.U.*

Zach snorts as I playfully punch him on the top of his arm. 'Hey, listen, I wanted to get us tickets to a gig or something,' he says. 'But your mum said you weren't ready to leave the house yet; said you still needed to be swaddled in bubble wrap each morning before breakfast.'

I roll my eyes and push the boxes to one side. 'It's the thought that counts,' I manage. I flick my silicone tongue against my palate, still adjusting to how it fits inside my mouth and makes my words sound thicker than they used to. 'Thanks for coming,' I say, glancing from one face to the next.

'Can't let you celebrate alone, can we?' Cheki says.

'Once we knew your dad was planning on getting your whole family round for a game of charades and a drink of sherry, we knew we had to come and rescue you,' Isobel says, throwing me a smile that sends the butterflies in my stomach into a frenzy.

Huh. Can an iron stomach feel butterflies?

Mum pops her head around the door from the kitchen. 'He's here,' she says.

I nod back at Mum and clench my jaw. Of all the days to arrange to come and see me, it had to be on my birthday, and in my own home. The one space I felt safe from him and what he's done to me.

'You good?' Zach asks me.

I try to relax my shoulders, then nod.

'I know it's daunting,' Isobel says, 'but he won't be here for long, and we'll be in the next room if you need us.'

'OK?' Zach gently nudges my knee.

'OK,' I say back, returning his smile.

Cheki squeezes my shoulder and, just like that, they leave the room.

I rise from my spot on the floor and take a seat on the sofa, straightening my shirt. I hear footsteps approach from the front door.

A man in a burgundy suit with a white shirt, slicked-back hair and warm eyes saunters close to me. I don't get up to greet him, and neither do I reach out my hand to shake his as his shadow falls over me.

Mr Tanaki takes over the room like it's his own, standing by the coffee table, glancing around at our furniture and the pictures on the wall of my happy times with family. It takes everything in me not to clock him one right on the jaw.

'I'm happy to see you looking so well,' he says. 'I'm sorry it took so long for this meeting to go ahead. I had wanted to see you while you were recovering in hospital, but I'm a busy man. The doctors and your parents have kept me updated with your progress over the winter, and when I heard you'd been discharged last week, I knew I had to come and see you. Your body seems to have taken to the AYCE system wonderfully.'

I swallow down all the words I want to say, keeping a polite demeanour like my parents asked. 'It would seem so.'

'Your speech is improving, almost indistinguishable from before,' he says.

We both know that's a lie.

'May I sit?'

I gesture to the armchair by the window, and he unbuttons his jacket as he takes a seat. I couldn't give a damn what he does, but his forced chivalry makes it impossible for me not to match his energy, especially when he and his invention are technically the reason I'm still alive.

'You've held up your end of the deal beautifully, Mikah. I must thank you for that.'

I force a small smile. As if I've had any choice. My parents signed the contract while I was in a coma. They were only trying to save my life, of course, but it means that life now belongs to the very man I was trying to take down.

I really am the clown in this circus.

'Videos are doing great online,' I say, through clenched teeth. The only blessing is that I've been allowed to remain anonymous in each of the episodes, my face blurred or obscured, keeping the mystery behind my person, despite half the internet knowing my real name.

Tanaki smiles and nods. 'People love a recovery journey. Documenting every step of your progress for iGENect was a brilliant idea of mine. The audience have loved watching you return to health over the series. Your fans want to see you back to your old self.'

I laugh at this. I'll never be my old self again, and he knows it.

'You still haven't returned to Digital Demons. A shame. You'd built quite a community there and I know your fans miss you and your mukbangs terribly.'

A small huff leaves my nostrils. 'The thing that ruined my life? Changed me for the worst and garnered me stalkers who threatened everyone I love? Yeah, I'm real eager to get back to it.'

Tanaki flashes me an impressive smile, his teeth glistening against his dark suit. 'It's in your contract, don't forget. Digital Demons is owned by me now.'

I don't respond.

He gives a shrug. 'I admit, I'm impressed by your tenacity, Mikah. You achieved what you set out to. You proved to the at-home viewer, and to the brands and sponsors, that real people still hold a lot of influence. Human-created content will always surpass that of artificial intelligence. Digital Demons gave people hope, caused a surge in home-made videos, got people picking up their paintbrushes, making music and writing stories again.'

I don't say anything. Fury surges through me.

After a long silence, Tanaki speaks again: 'You should be proud.'

I dig my fingers deep into the sofa cushions beneath me and feel pain shooting through my jaw as I grind my teeth. 'I'm glad I got people making art again,' I admit, 'but if I could take it all back, I would. Look what it cost me.'

'You're a medical miracle. A true marvel that I am in awe of.'

'Did you know?'

'Did I know what would happen?' He sinks back into the chair, resting his elbows on the arms, his fingertips touching in prayer. He mulls it over. 'I've always been fascinated by human behaviour; the way the mood of a crowd can change in a split-second, like they become a single entity with one mind, the way societal expectation and influence can determine the outcome of an event ...' He pauses.

'You cooked up a perfect storm. From day one, I knew

you'd go global. Between the angst of your channel's message, the rawness of your delivery, and the mystery drummed up by your wanting to remain anonymous, you created a taste so irresistible that you could never satisfy the insatiable hunger of an already ravenous audience. The anger you stirred in them, the curiosity you piqued, the sense of belonging you gave them – all of it the perfect set of ingredients for an explosive reaction. I did try to warn you that day we met.'

I raise my eyebrow, my mind pulling me back to the moment during Mukbang Metropolis when I questioned whether Tanaki had actually tried to give me an out from the competition. Was it kindness after all?

'I showed you Anna's blueprint. I told you that we were filming everything *for the viewer*. I wanted you to recognize that she, that AI, was never your enemy. Your own audience was the thing you were battling, Mikah. Why do you think I made the humanoids? To spare humans from the horror of fame. I too have suffered the consequences of endless public scrutiny.'

He laughs, pleased by his own poetry. It's sickening.

Then he continues: 'The world has changed. We all want more entertainment, quicker. It's a reality that we humans can no longer keep pace with, and a ceiling the average creator will never reach. AI is the future of content, but *you* have given rise to a new concept: the hybrid human.'

I nod slowly, taking his words in, fighting the feeling that this man could've ended my suffering at Mukbang

Met at any time.

'So, you really don't think that human-created art is sustainable?' When he doesn't answer, I ask a new question: 'What is it you want from me?'

Tanaki shuffles to the edge of the armchair. 'I want you to live a long and healthy life, Mikah.'

'And?'

With one final flash of his dazzling smile, he stands and rebuttons his jacket. 'You are the living embodiment of my creation, proof that human life and automation can live in harmony. You're my new Anna, my mascot for all I've created in this world.'

I stand too, sucking back my disdain.

'I'm glad to see you're doing so well.'

He makes for the front door, and I follow him, out of both politeness and eagerness to see him gone from my home.

'Ah!' he says, clocking a package on the small table in the porch. 'I brought you a gift. Happy birthday.'

He hands it to me, alongside a white envelope. Slowly, I unwrap the purple tissue paper, feeling something delicate inside. As I unfold the final sheet, my heart convulses. My Digital Demons mask stares at me. Fixed and straight from the studio of Delirium Designs. My hands begin to tremble.

'It's time you got back to your calling, Mikah. Your fans are waiting.'

He points to the pristine envelope with my home address on the front. Tears threatening to spill, I rip it open. Inside is a letter addressed to me.

Dear Mikah (Echo),
I just want to say that I'm sorry for what happened between us at Mukbang Met. I forgive you for everything you've put me through with this third-party situation. I can't wait until we're reunited again.
I am eternally yours.

I'm trembling so hard that I drop the letter to the floor and stare at my hands like they're coated in poison.

I'll never be free from this circus I've created.

'To answer your earlier question,' Tanaki says, not even caring, 'I think humans will always create art. That is what being human is all about, is it not? To think and to feel so deeply that one is driven to turn experience into a physical embodiment, so that it can be shared with another, is something only the sentient can appreciate. But to give parts of yourself to a willing audience is to become less whole, and the audience who cannot themselves create will always want more than an artist can give.'

A pitiful sob escapes me. He doesn't notice.

'Humans will always look for shortcuts; to give without losing anything, to take without thought for that which they take from. Automation is the answer to that problem. Go back to creating your content, Mikah. You have an iron stomach that will make performing much easier. Give the audience what they came for, give them a show.' He makes a theatrical gesture, expanding his hands across his face, his eyes and teeth dazzling like he's the star. '*All You Can Eat* – the never-ending mukbang series that satisfies the viewers' hunger and fills both our pockets with sponsorship dime.'

Tanaki heads outside into the gentle spring air, into a waiting car that whisks him away to whatever empire he plans on building next.

My chest tightens as I look deep into my new Digital Demons mask, and all that it has cost me.

Machines were built to help artists, but the one inside me now serves as my eternal imprisonment in the art I freed from the grips of machines.

ACKNOWLEDGEMENTS

First, I need to say thank you to the person who has been with me throughout the entire creation of this book. I wouldn't have been able to get through some days without her unwavering faith, steady stream of snacks for brain fuel (can you consider Kinder Buenos brain fuel?), and words of encouragement. She is entirely the reason this story exists and I would be lost without her. But anyway, that's enough about me.

Next, to my wonderful editor Shalu Vallepur, who has once again helped tease out the best possible narrative from the story and led me back on the path whenever I veered off for a side quest. I have loved chatting with you about the correct way to construct the perfect plate of beans on toast. My way is the best way. Yours is a close second.

To Clare Wallace, who is always, always there when I need her. I'm sure by now you have an entire email folder titled 'wtf' dedicated solely to me. Thank you for letting me bounce odd ideas around, for being open to my never-ending stream of creative madness, for steering me in the right direction, and for being my voice of reason too.

Barry Cunningham, I cannot thank you enough for signing off on this idea. Being able to grab a pizza and some mozzarella sticks, deep-dive into the fandoms of my favourite artists, and fall into the pit of AI and internet controversy and call it all 'research' is a dream come true for me.

Of course, thanks must also go to the rest of the team at Chicken House: Rachel H, Elinor, Esther, Rachel L, Laura, Ruth and Jazz, who each play their individual role in bringing books into the world. From shaping the initial idea to promoting the final product, the importance of their roles cannot be overstated.

To add on: Things will be changing at the Chicken House HQ before this book is released, and this will be the last time I'll be able to thank Barry Cunningham, Rachel Hickman and Elinor Bagenal for everything they've done for me, and for everything they've brought to the world of publishing. Thank you! Your knowledge and creative visions will be greatly missed. Enjoy your retirement!

And to Rachel Leyshon, congratulations on becoming the top chicken at the coop! It's in safe hands.

To Ali Al Amine for once again creating the most beautiful cover that perfectly conveys both the terrifying rise of AI in the arts industry and the relationship between artists and their fans. Nothing I could send you for inspiration could ever come close to the magic you create. You are a blessing.

I also need to make an apology because I did in fact forget to thank someone in *Island of Influencers* and I haven't stopped thinking about it since. Jenny Glencross, my copyeditor for both *Island* and *Sweet and Sour* – thank you, so much! I don't think many people realize how important a copy-editor is towards the final stages. You offered a fresh pair of eyes to the story that I have read so many times I could recite it in my sleep, you caught the inconsistencies, and queried things that don't quite make sense to someone who hasn't been living with the characters for a year. Sometimes, I forget what exists on the page and what exists only in my mind, and you ensure the two meet.

And finally, to one last person . . .

Squid, my muse.